Contents

1. *Preeti*

It was our first visit ever to this small village in the Amazon. Preeti, my wife, and I, visited for a Program between India and Brazil. The day was bright and everything looked great. Upon landing at the Rio Airport, we booked a taxi to the small village where we were supposed to spend the rest of the week. After a two hour drive, we reached our destination and a crowd of tribal men and women greeted us. To our surprise, the people had little clothes to cover their bodies. Women were topless and so were the men. I couldn't help from staring at big voluptuous bosoms.

The sun was setting down and our tribal host showed us the thatched straw hut we were to sleep in. We were presented with straw skirts and were supposed to wear them the next morning. Preeti and I were both tired because of traveling, so we slept without much talking unaware of what's going to proceed the next day. At about 7 AM, I heard people talking outside our hut and I saw a group of village girls waiting to take us to the common breakfast they arranged for us. We had to adapt to their culture and ways of life for the next 2 weeks, meaning to dress like them, eat what they eat and so on. After all, it was about their culture.

I took my shirt and pants off and wore the grass-woven skirt, and so did Preeti. It was a new experience for both of us to be dressed that way, especially for Preeti, and to be topless in public. After some initial shyness and reluctance, we went out of our hut. The girls waiting outside started to smile when they saw us in their traditional costume. One of them had a bowl of paint. She made some colored marks on Preeti's body as per the tribal traditions. Preeti couldn't hide her emotions and I saw her face blush. Just outside the tribal chief's hut, breakfast was arranged for us...wooden tables with fruits and honey. There were about 50-75 people sitting next to each other, and we were seated next to the chief and his wife. The breakfast started. We ate tropical fruits which we have never seen before. Then I noticed something strange. Some of the men were breastfeeding from the women next to them and suckled, while the women continued to eat fruits. Mia, our translator, and the tribal girl from the village realized my curiosity and whispered that it was normal for husbands and relatives to nurse from lactating mothers. Breast milk was consumed as food in the tribe.

We were told that it was considered to be highly prestigious if a guest was offered breast milk. The guest must never say "No" or else it's considered to be an insult towards the hospitality of the host. When the breakfast was over, we started doing the days task as everybody else was doing, like collecting fruit and bringing woods for fuel. I noticed that most women of the village had very developed breasts and long pointy nipples. It was due to extended nursing. It seemed that in the absence of any cattle, women were the only source of milk for the villagers.

The day was moving forward and we started to feel hungry, nevertheless we kept on working like other villagers. Preeti made a scream catching my sudden attention. She was stung by a wasp on her breast and it started to swell. The people around us also came to help and took us to their only doctor, a traditional herbal doc. Our guide told us that the wasp that stung Preeti was common there and the cure is an herbal paste. Sometimes, the point of sting had to be sucked by the herbal doctor to make sure that the sting venom is extracted out. The herbal doctor was on old man in his 70's and had lots of tattoos on his bare chest. Preeti shivered with shock as he took her breast in his hand and applied the herbal paste. While he held her breast firmly applying the medicine, a tiny drop of milk came out from

Preeti's nipple. Preeti had always maintained a supply of milk even after she stopped breastfeeding our son. Drops often came out whenever we had foreplay, but this was obviously an embarrassing moment for her, and she started to look at me with a mix of complain and shyness. I told her that she was going to be okay. I also noticed that the girls who accompanied us to the doctor started chanting " mimo, mimo, mimo," when they saw the drop of milk come out from Preeti's nipple. Our guide told us that "mimo" meant milk in their language.

The next day, four mature tribal women came to us with a bowl containing blue dye. They made some tribal color designs on Preeti's back and on her belly. We had no idea what this coloring was all about, until an hour later when our guide told Preeti, that the design made on her was an indication to others that she was a lactating woman, and lactating women are treated with special favors and respect in their tribe. Then to our complete surprise, I was told that today, I would go alone for fruit picking and collecting woods, and that Preeti would be assigned new tasks. I accompanied Preeti, along with the guide and other women to a hut that looked more like a tribal kindergarten with 10-15 kids, ranging from 6 months to 5 years of age. This was the new environment where Preeti would be working, separated from me.

I departed and started to work with the other men. It was a very bright sunny day and the moisture in the air was too much to endure, but the locals looked quite comfortable with it. Time passed very slowly that day and I missed being with Preeti. That afternoon when I returned to the village from work, I started to search for Preeti and found her in the same hut. "Oh my gosh" I said! Preeti, what are you doing?" She just smiled holding two babies in her lap latched on to her nipples. "This is my new job Preeti replied". I was stunned and confused on our way back to our hut. Preeti told me that its customary for women having milk to nurse village children, and that she did not mind it, as she found it easier than working in the jungle and getting stung by wasps or bees. Finding Preeti happy about it, I didn't complain.

Preeti was getting molded more and more into their tribal culture. In just 4 days, Preeti's breasts transformed and looked heavier and milk laden. Getting continuously suckled by kids was impacting her breast and nipple form. In quite a few days, she started looking the same as other tribal ladies with bare breasts and pointed nipples. Mia, the tribal guide girl, was very frank with both of us. She told Preeti that the tribal ladies were very happy with Preeti for feeding the village babies, and also spoke highly of Preeti's milk. Some of the older kids in age ranges of 4-5 years, told their families that they liked Preeti's milk more than that of other lactating mothers, providing this service to the village. In my opinion, it was because we were of a different ethnic background and obviously that made her milk taste different from others. So perhaps the children of the village find her milk to taste differently. The fame of Preeti's milk spread rapidly and often women and girls came to Preeti with small earthen pots, requesting her to squirt some for them. All that started to make Preeti a little proud about herself and she started to boast about her milk to me.

It was Friday, the last day of our first week there, and as per tribal traditions, Friday was the day of a big feast. At noon, everybody would gather with their fruits and other foods to the central eating place. The tribal people seemed to like us, and we saw many happy and smiling faces. Once again to honor us, we were to sit with the most respected of the tribe. Everything was going normal, and then all of a sudden Preeti pulled my arm to get my attention. I saw the most unbelievable scene. The guy sitting next to Preeti started to suckle from her breast. Preeti held me tight, shivering and shocked but didn't make any sound.

It was a common norm of the tribe and we had to be like them and act like them. After a minute of suckling, he let it go and started to speak to others in their tribal language. It seemed they were discussing something and most were staring at Preeti intermittently. Then they started getting busy with eating food. Our guide told us, that the man told other's that Preeti's milk was as sweet as honey, and is different from milk of their own women. His praise of Preeti's milk created an awkward situation for us. Almost every second person was interested to suckle from her. Preeti just closed her eyes and let them suckle. She was blushing, as this was something very unexpected and new to us. I got jealous, but I controlled my feelings. The following night, I talked to Preeti about it. She kissed me and told me that I should not worry much about it, as this was only a temporary thing, and was not sexual for the tribal culture.

For the next couple of days, the same routine followed. Preeti was getting suckled by men and women, but now Preeti was getting used to it and more confident…no more closed eyes and face blushes. It seemed that her milk casted a spell on the villagers. She was very much respected and everybody bought gifts in form of garlands and fruits for her. In just 12 days, her breasts grew in size, became very pendulous with very developed nipples. She looked very comfortable in her new role as milkmaid. Often she would leak milk, even when she was not breastfeeding. She became a supply house of milk.

During the last day of our stay, the villagers gave a big party in our honor. Preeti was bathed with jungle scents and flower extracts, and was treated like a princess. Her nipples were painted red with a special herbal extract. All sorts of food were served, followed by a traditional tribal dance. Preeti and I joined the dance. It was a very special environment, jolly and cozy. Then all of a sudden, a baby started to cry and caused a let-down effect in Preeti… her milk started to leak as she danced. People started to notice it and came in groups to suckle from her, appreciating her after suckling. The mode of the party had a strange effect on all of us…everybody was lost in merriment and joys. Preeti was out of control, squeezing her milk with her own hands in the mouths of all the people, and looking towards me with pride and honor in her eyes. She was totally transformed and had become one like them.

The time passed quickly and we had to depart from our host. In the evening, an old van came to the village to pick us up. We said good bye to our friends and left for the city. It was all like an unbelievable dream. We flew back to our country the next day with pleasant memories of it

2. The Boss Lady

It was a few days after I'd returned to work from maternity leave. My breasts were swollen and producing a large amount of milk, much more than I actually needed. Every day at lunch, I would retreat to a small storage space just off the break room and use the breast pump while I ate. The employees and temps shared the break room with tenants, and there were often corporate visitors in and out for coffee, so I needed the privacy. Everyone on staff was very gracious about it.

Today, though, the boss lady intercepted me and told me she had arranged a more convenient space for me. We don't call her "The Boss Lady" to her face, of course, but it's an appropriate description. She's a tall, imposing blonde, very no-nonsense. Corporate loves her results, so they give her a free hand when it comes to running the office suites. As intimidating as she can be, we've all learned that she's fair and will stand up for us when we need her. She doesn't let upper management disturb her henhouse.

She has a reputation for professionalism among the tenants, and any visitor can see it in her manner of dress: blouse buttoned to the neck, crisp suit jacket, pencil skirt, low heels. Her hair is kept in a tight bun, never a strand out of place. She wears stylish black-rimmed glasses when she reads. She speaks with clarity and sports a firm handshake. The word "businesswoman" was coined for her.

If she has any personal relationships, we don't know about them.

She led me down the hall to an unrented space that had a desk and chair. I sat down and started unbuttoning my blouse. I was saying something about how considerate everyone was being, when I noticed she hadn't come all the way in. She glanced quickly up and down the hall, then ducked inside and flipped the lock.

Before I could process any of this, she rushed over to me, bent over at the waist, cupped my breasts through my bra and pressed her face into my cleavage. She took a deep breath, in and out, through her nose. I felt the moist heat deep between my breasts.

"Hey... Wha...?" I started to say.

She pressed her left index finger against my lips and whispered, "Shhh. Shhhh."

She quickly jerked my left feeding flap open... AND HER LIPS WERE ON MY LEFT NIPPLE!

OH MY GOD! She was sucking on my left nipple and... and...

AND SHE WAS DRINKING MY MILK!

I was frozen. Every hair was standing up on my neck and arms, and I felt a wave of goose bumps rush over me. My eyes must have been the size of dinner plates. I had NO IDEA what to do!

Her lips were pursed in a light kiss, gently wrapped around only the nipple. But that was enough. She was getting milk! I could feel it!

I breathed in as if to speak, but again her finger pressed to my mouth. "Hmp-mm," she mumbled.

With her left hand still gently warning me silent, her right hand cradled my left breast and lifted slightly. Her puckered lips parted just a bit, bringing the entire areola into her mouth. I felt the nipple move inward.

I gasped.

I was still paralyzed, but my impressions were vivid. She was standing to my right, bending across my body. I could smell her cologne, and I had a close-up view of her left ear and neck. She was making no sound, but I could FEEL every rhythmic suck. My heart was racing so fast and hard I could feel it in my ears. I felt like I would fall over. I hadn't experienced that kind of total body fear since I was a child, and I remember thinking back then, "This is what a frightened rabbit must feel like."

I was shaking uncontrollably, but I managed to whisper, "B-boss lady, please..."

Oh, WHY did I say that??

She momentarily stopped sucking and I saw her left eye look up at me.

She responded by pushing my knees apart and kneeling in front of me. She wrapped her arms around my waist, pressed her face to my breast and opened her mouth wide, sucking in as much flesh as would fit. She sucked HARD. I felt my nipple yanked into the back of her mouth, where it was squeezed tight by a muscular tongue. A great surge of milk spilled out.

My shaking voice quavered, "Uuuuuuuuhhhhhhhh...."

There was no sound in the room. I could hear her breath rushing in and out of her nose, and I could hear her throat swallow with each suck. Oh my god! She was sucking SO HARD! It made my nipple sting. And there was SO MUCH MILK!

She didn't move. She just sucked and sucked and sucked. My poor, swollen nipple surged in and out of her throat like a piston, pouring out its secrets.

I was breathing heavily, and starting to come down from my adrenalin rush, but I was still in a total panic. I felt weak.

Then I noticed my right nipple was standing up hard. It wanted some attention, and it was leaking milk on its own.

The boss noticed, too.

She pulled open the right flap, and her mouth latched on hard, leaving my reddened, squirting left nipple to point into the cool air.

She squeezed and pulled the poor thing as she greedily devoured my right breast. Milk sprayed with each pinch.

Again, the boss sucked hard, in silence. Suck. Suck. Suck. She was FEEDING on me.

She switched back and forth a few times, sucking earnestly, making a POP or SMACK when she pulled loose, pinching and pulling the other. My chest and belly were covered with milk.

I came to a sudden realization: This felt AMAZING.

I made a decision... to just... let it happen.

I lay my head back.

She sucked.

And sucked.

And SUCKED.

And SUCKED MORE.

It seemed to go on for hours.

But of course, it didn't. Lunch break ended, and we went back to work. I stumbled through the rest of the day, and at home that night, my husband couldn't figure out why I was so sleepy.

The next day, it happened again. We didn't say a word. I just opened my blouse and she fed.

We meet every day for lunch now. We've switched to an unused reception room on another floor. It has a couch, so I can cradle her head while she feeds contentedly. We never speak.

We are going to try meeting on a weekend soon.

I don't know what to call my new relationship with the boss. I mean, it's not a lesbian affair. I admit to having the occasional orgasm while I feed her, but I don't want to have sex with her. That's not what it's about.

I certainly haven't told my husband about it. I wouldn't know how. It's been going on so long now, where would I even start?

It's not as if it's made problems for us. In fact, it's totally revived our sex lives. I get home from work before he does, and every evening when he arrives, I pull off his pants and DEVOUR his cock. I can't get enough! I suck him as if my life depends on it. I swallow his cum, then I keep sucking till he's hard again, then I swallow more cum.

I didn't enjoy oral sex before. I saw it as a chore, just to make him happy. But now, I'm FEEDING. Just that little change of perspective makes all the difference. I suckle at his cock every chance I get. Some days, I get 3 or 4 loads of cum at a session. We don't go out, he doesn't watch TV, I don't call my friends... all because I'm on my knees with his cock in my mouth.

I'm content at work, and I'm content at home.

3. *Bhakti*

My mom Bhakti, age 30, sleek figure, 36 bust, silky black long hair had applied for a model hunt for some advertisement. The Ad was supposed to be that of a Long Hair Video. She filled up her form last week. It was Saturday afternoon, I was back from collge and Bhakti (my mom) was watching soaps on TV. I was studying in college. My papa and sister were not in town as they were to attend some marriage that weekend at some remote town.

Bhakti was 5'8" tall lady. She had a sleek figure. Her attractive long hair was one of her best asset. She used to get aroused if someone played with her hair or opened her hair bun w/o her knowing it. She had black long waist length hair. Every single hair on her head was straight. People staying around us used to get attracted towards her hair and every time they see her hair used to praise her hair and beauty. Every uncle or say male relative of mine tried to touch her hair or play with her hair but she never allowed them to do it and so their desire to play with her hair was not fulfilled. That afternoon, door bell ranged. I opened the door, a stranger guy asked me to call "Bhakti Madam". I asked mom to come on door. That guy asked mom to attend an audition / screen test at a local studio same day around 8pm. Mom was happy to know that she was selected by "Long Hair Video" people for audition. That guy left, I closed the door and we both went to her bedroom which had a huge mirror. She was very happy and was literally dancing. She asked me to go to my room as she wanted to take her own time in getting ready for the audition. She had 3-4 hours with her to do so.

By this age of mine, my incest feelings towards my mom were

already matured. I had spent hours and hours playing with her hair at night when she used to sleep beside me. Her milky melons or say breasts were second best attraction for me. I used to slowly touch her breasts and squeeze them at night when papa used to be away and I got chance to sleep next to her. Her beauty was like that of Indian actress "Bhakti Kapadia". I had made a special opening or say a hole in her bathroom for capturing her wet hair + nude scenes.

Just as she went inside the bathroom, I followed her. She took off her suit first. She stood complete nude in front of my eye hole. She turned her back towards me thus giving me the complete view of her nice ass and her hair bun. My eyes were running over her nude back and got stuck in her lustrous hair bun. She slowly removed her hair stick with one hand and shook her head to let all her silky hair cascade over her bare back. Her back slowly covered her entire back till her waist. Her hair reached almost her hips. This view was marvelous. My dick was completely erect. She turned on the shower and was done with her bath in another 15mins. I ran to my room just as she turned off her shower. She came out of bathroom in her bathrobe. She came to my room with her hair dryer as electric plug/ socket was not working in her bedroom. I pretended to read my book. She opened her wet hair bun and my entire bedroom was covered with her fragrance. By 7pm, we were ready to leave our house for studio. At studio, a guy opened the door and asked our names. He took us to another big room with lots of lights and a camera placed in it. Mom introduced herself to the coordinator and he made both of us sit in another room attached to the same room. There was a huge TV. in our room from where we could see the things in front of camera. There were very few people next to camera and lights. I was seeing some shoot for the first time in my life. Even mom was excited but nervous. After 10-15 mins, a guy came and asked my mom to follow him. He asked me to sit in same room and see shooting through huge glass opening on the wall. Mom returned after 10mins, she was briefed on what kind of role / dialog it is. I asked mom, what will you be doing in front of camera?

she replied "I will be brushing my hair, combing it and at the most washing it , may be a guy will do all these "I was shocked "A guy" She said "Don't worry, I won't do anything wrong. But I knew that papa was away and so she might go naughty." I smiled. I was getting butterflies in stomach on hearing the script. I was madly awaiting the shooting of such wonderful scene. I wished I was that guy. Mom was again called in another room. She came back to me after 15 long minutes. She was happy, she told me that director turned out to be his college friend and has selected her for the actual shooting which is supposed to happen in an another hour.

I was happy too to know this. We both then went to make-up room where a hair-dresser cum make-up artist was assigned to beautify mom's looks as per requirement of the Ad. But he didn't seem to be a good guy. He made me and mom sit on chairs in front of the mirror. He asked my mom to wrap a towel and come back. She did so. He opened all her hair while standing behind her. He started running his fingers through her hair. He then started applying make-up on mom's face and neck. He then asked mom to reveal her cleavage a little by sliding her towel a little downwards. Mom disagreed. He went and called the director to convince Mom. I was seeing all this. Director took my mom in a corner and convinced her. She was Ok with it now. I was happy as something good was coming next. Mom came back and sat on same chair next to me in front of mirror. I could see soft bulges above her towel. I felt like squeezing them. I was sitting next to her on a chair and makeup guy was standing behind her. He slowly opened her hair bun. He combed her hair with a comb for few mins. He then came in front of her and sat on a stool of similar height. He asked my mom to look above towards the ceiling as he wanted to do some makeup on her neck towards her breasts. She did so. Makeup guy looked at me, winked and then kept his hands on her breasts over her towel. He started unfolding her towel thus started slowly revealing her boobs. He revealed her breasts a little and did some makeup from lower neck till partition in-between her boobs. Bhakti's huge melons were looking very tempting. The makeup guy was again and again seen adjusting his pants. I knew he too must be getting jerks in his penis as Bhakti was so beautiful. He then requested my Mom to be patient as he would further reveal her cleavage for makeup as it is must as per requirement. Mom seemed to be very comfortable till now. Makeup guy got a pair of brushes with him. He then sat on floor next to Bhakti's legs. He started applying some foundation on her open thighs. She was getting tickling there and couldn't control. She started moaning a little. Makeup guy slowly and gradually rubbed her soft brushes on her thighs thus arousing her for the coming scenes. Mom was aroused by now but was controlling her feelings.

Mom was given a white dress and asked to wear it. She immediately changed her clothes in another room. She was looking gorgeous in that dress. The dress was great too as it started from her breast till her upper thighs. Her cleavage can be seen though boobs were under the dress. She had to give up her bra as the dress was backless. I asked mom about her open back, she said "Krish, it is for my long hair to be seen in its full glory". I smiled. I was more happy. Curiosity in me to see my mom's hair flow over her bare back was increasing. I was asked to take my seat in previous room from where I can see the shoot from a huge TV. screen. I was given soft drink and accompanied by two guys in the same room to see the shoot. They were talking among themselves. After sometime, Bhakti came in the view. Those guys started passing dirty comments on her figure. One guy said "what a babe, man. Look at her boobs, I feel like massaging her." Another replied "Yaar, I feel like licking her entire body". I couldn't tolerate this but being new to the place and too younger than them, quietly sat there. Mom came and stood in front of the camera. All light men/ spot boys etc left the set. Only camera man, Director and Bhakti were in my view. I was surprised on this. Mom's hair was tied in a huge bun over her head. Her skin was glowing. I could hardly hear what director was asking her to do. She seemed to be very happy and smiling all the time.

Shooting started. Everybody was quite. Camera started. Mom was standing in front of camera alone for few seconds. A smart looking guy came and stood next to her. They both faced each other. That guy smiled at mom. He kept his palms on her cheek. Took his face closer to hers and planted his lips on hers. I was shocked to see this. Scene was turning interesting and hot. Mom turned her back towards the camera. The smooch was deepening. Back of my mom was facing the camera and so was her thick huge bun. The guy kept his hand on her bun and shook it. Her silky long hair cascaded over her back. The smooch was still continuing. He used both of his hands to completely open all her hair. He started running his fingers through her hair. I was erect. I wanted to join them. But couldn't. This continued for few more minutes and suddenly it was all dark. Camera started after few minutes of darkness. I was anxious to see what has happened in this time. Camera started. Wowwww !!!! Mom was sleeping completely nude on floor with all her hair covering her breasts and vagina. She was smiling in front of camera. She seemed to be consumed some liquor and was not under control. I stood up at my seat. Guys around me threatened me and made me sit and watch the screen. Mom was lying on a mattress. All her long silk was shinning over her body. Same guy came and stood beside her. He got a bucket of water and poured it all over her body slowly. All her hair turned wet thus revealing her huge melons. She started rubbing her palms over her breasts. That guy sat on floor beside her and started revealing her boobs out of her hair. He rubbed her titties and mom started moaning. He then stood beside her. He bent on her and took her hair in his hand from back of her neck. He then slowly pulled her hair making her stand nude next to him. He covered both of her boobs with her wet hair. He took a comb and started combing her wet hair. Making sleek streaks on her silk. One more guy came in to the picture. He sat on floor between her legs and immediately started licking her clit. She started moaning. She tried kicking off that guy twice but she didn't seem to have power to do so and then submitted her to the pleasure she was getting.

I was shocked and ran out of the door and went to the room where this all was happening. A guy with a big knife in his hand made me sit in the corner and watch. Both guys started rubbing her boobs and nipples. All her wet hair was over her body partially covering her private parts. Both guys took out their 9inch long cocks and started inserting from both sides of my mom's holes. She was moaning loudly. After 10mins of fucking her hardly, the guy with knife threw me on nude body of mom. I was erect. The guy with knife asked me to comb my nude mom's hair. He made me sit in her lap and suck milk from her nipples. He made me smooch her and play with her hair. He made me insert my 5" cock in to her vagina and jerk. He made me smell her hair and dig my face in to hers. After all this, I and mom were left alone. We both came back home after few hours.

Those movie people kept her calling on weekly basis for similar shoots. She enjoyed it too. She hid this from my dad. By the time I started working. We used to spend long hours in bed together. I start with playing with her hair and end up fucking her holes.

4. Sunita

My name is Reddy Kotari. I am 19 years old and I live with my parents my dad's name is Rajesh and he works in an Indian company and my mom's name is Sunita and is a housewife. We stay at Pune. One day during my summer vacation I was watching TV when mom called me and said to accompany her to the market. Mom was wearing a red color saree and a matching blouse. Now to describe mom looks, mom was 38 years old at that time and her figure was 34-30-36, she is 5.5 ft tall, she has fair complexion and has a cute face. She is slightly on heavier side. Mom always wears saree above her naval. She is conservative in nature but she also bit submissive.

After going to market with my mom and doing the shopping, mom said to me that she has given a new blouse for stitching to a new tailor. So both of us went to tailor's shop. Tailor's shop was on at the far end of the market. It was a small shop. Tailor looking at my mom smiled and said hello to her. His name was Ansari. He was around 45 years old, 5.9" tall, medium built, clean-shaven. He gave my mom her new blouse and when my mom opened her purse to pay him. He said, "why don't to try the blouse first and see if it fits?" Mom replied, "ok, but where will I change?" Ansari opened the door behind the counter and welcomed us in. The room was not well lit just little light coming from the door we had entered he told my mom to go behind the partition and change. The partition was nothing but a curtain hung on the wall. There was zero watt bulb on the wall behind the curtain, which was off. Ansari switched on the light and mom went behind the curtain. What mom did not realize that because of the light we could see her silhouette? Mom first removed the pallu of her saree and let it fall on the ground and then started unbuttoning her blouse. I looked at Ansari and he was rubbing himself over his pant. There was a weird smile on his face. When I again looked at my mom's silhouette she was wearing her new blouse and it looked like she was having a difficulty in buttoning her blouse. Mom spoke from behind the curtain to Ansari, " the blouse is very tight and cannot button a single hook", Ansari said, " really, that's not possible I have stitched the blouse according to your old blouse's measurement, why don't you come out and show me how it is not fitting? Mom replied "out there" somewhat shocked at Ansari's comment to parade her in front of others. Ansari said, "yes, that's ok no one out here except for your son and myself and I will also close the door so that no one passing looks in". Mom said, "Ok, close the door first". Ansari quickly closed the door and mom came out from behind the curtain. I was shocked looking at my mom. She was holding the pallu of the saree in her hands and the pink blouse was open and her big white bra could be seen from the gap I could also see her little cleavage. She came in the middle of the room. Ansari was also looking at mom breast area. He went closer to mom and said "you are wearing a large bra, you should were the small bra with this blouse and it will fit perfectly". Ansari went to the steel cupboard in the corner and after searching for sometime removed a very small bra. It was a pink color bra and had just two small triangle piece of cloth and the straps were more like thick strings. It was not brand bra but a stitched one. He handed the bra to mom and told her to try blouse again.

Mom went behind the curtain and dropped her pallu and removed her blouse and unhooked bra. I could see mom breast silhouette clearly. I looked at Ansari and again he was rubbing himself and also licking his lips. He looked at me and winked. I felt disgusted looking at him but at the same time I was getting an erection. I looked at the curtain again and mom finished putting her blouse. Mom spoke from the behind to Ansari, "the blouse is not fitting properly I am not comfortable in it and also the neck is too wide". Ansari replied, "can you come out and show me the blouse again". Mom said "ok". Mom came out from behind the curtain. I was again shocked looking at mom she was wearing the pink blouse and it was showing too much of her cleavage. The blouse had only three buttons. Mom looked flushed. Ansari was leering at mom. He went close to mom and said, "You are not wearing the bra properly". Mom said, "How do you know that?" Ansari said, "I can show you that." And he went closer to mom and started to undo the blouse hooks. Mom was taken by surprise by this but before she could say anything the blouse wide open. I too just kept looking at mom breast that were just covered by the small bra and it seems like they are going to spill out any moment. The bra was bit transparent and I could see mom's nipples slightly. Ansari meanwhile was taking a good look at mom's breast. Mom was clearly embarrassed by this but she was just not saying anything to him yet. Mom was about to open her open mouth to say something but Ansari cut her off in middle and said, "I told you, you are not wearing the bra properly", he continued pointing at mom's breast, " you see this small bums on the bra?" Mom after looking down said, "yes" tailor continued, "your nipples should be in these bums for better hold of your breast". I could clearly see mom's nipples were at different angles. Mom was about to turn and go back behind the curtain when Ansari caught her arm said, " let me show you" Mom was about to object but Ansari caught hold of mom's right breast with his left hand and pressed it. He then with his right hand adjusted the nipple; he repeated the same procedure with her left breast. Mom was clearly shaken by this act. Ansari then hooked her blouse. I was completely aroused by this whole act and so was Ansari. I could see a bump in front of his pant. It took Mom some time to come out of the shock.

Mom put her pallu back on her shoulder and acted as if nothing big as happen. Mom told Ansari, "but still the blouse is showing too much". Ansari replied, "you wanted me to stitched the blouse according to latest fashion and you look great in it" Mom blushed slightly. Ansari took my mom towards the steel cupboard, which had a large mirror on its door. He made Mom stand before the mirror and he himself stood behind her very closely almost touching her body. He then removed the pallu from her shoulder, circled his arms around her a kept his just below her breast slightly lifting them and said, "look at yourself, you can turn any man on" Mom blushed at his comment. He continued, "you should also wear your saree below your naval". And before mom could say something he moved both his hands that were resting below the breast to her belly and then slipped his fingers inside her saree and pulled it down till her naval was clearly visible. This was the first time I had seen mom naval. It was big round and deep. Mom was now just breathing heavily. I could hear her clearly. Ansari after pulling mom saree below her naval started fingering her naval with his right hand and placed his left hand on her left thigh very closed to her vagina. Mom told him, " I will take the blouse and bra" now mom wanting to get away from him before things get out of hand. Mom asked him, "how much for the blouse and bra?" Ansari still holding mom at the same position said, "For you it's free". Ansari was now pulled mom towards him closely and was grinding his bulge into Mom's butt. Mom wanted to free herself. Ansari said, "You also want this". He was now kissing my neck. Mom said, "no". Ansari replied, "you are just feeling shy because of son's presence but it seems like you have turned him on too". Both of them looked at my crotch area and I was posing a tent in front of my pant. I was wearing a track pant and loose cotton under wear therefore the bulge was more visible.

Ansari now had his both hands near the area where the saree was tucked in. Mom was looking at my crotch shocked that she had turned me on. She did not realizing that Ansari had pulled the saree out of her petticoat and was now undoing her petticoat knot which holds the saree. Mom suddenly realizes what was happening and caught her saree and petticoat with her both hands. Ansari left my mom from and quickly came stood in front of her. He then placed both his hand on mom's neck and below ear and gave a long smooch. Mom stood stiff and did nothing; I was too shocked with this turn of events. Ansari then using his right started undoing mom blouse and when it was open he started pressing her boobs over her bra. Mom was still stood motionless. Ansari left my mom's lips and brought his mouth on mom's breast and started sucking her boobs over her bra. At the same he pushed mom's hand that were holding the saree and petticoat. Mom eyes were now closed and she let her hand go. Somehow the saree and petticoat were still clinging on her body. Ansari still kissing and sucking mom's boobs pushed the saree and petticoat to the ground. Now mom was standing in her open blouse and bra on the top and big white panty. Ansari was now kissing and sucking mom's boobs and was cuddling mom's ass. Then he looked at me and pointing his index finger called me to join him. I followed his instructions and went stood behind my mom. Mom's eyes were still closed. I placed my both hands on mom's shoulder and slowly removed her blouse and unhooked her bra but could not remove it completely because Ansari was still on mom's boobs. I looked down on mom and Ansari had removed her panty and was now cuddling mom's white naked ass with one hand and with other hand rubbing her vagina. I could not see her vagina as I was standing behind her. Ansari now moved below towards mom's naval and started licking it. I looking at mom thought I should also participate in the act. Mom looked bit tried because she was standing for long time, so I brought the chair kept on one side of the room and made mom to sit on it. Mom opened her eyes and looked up to me. I could not control myself anymore and kissed mom on her lips. I was kissing her and with my right hand removed her small bra that was just hanging on her breast. I looked down on mom's breast for the first time. They were round, slightly sagging down but had nice black nipples that were erect. I moved towards mom's boobs and took her left boob in my mouth and started pressing her other boob. After some time with both her breast I went down and started kissing her naval. I was kissing and licking her naval and at the same time pressing her boobs with my left hand and my right hand was fingering her hairy vagina. Her vagina was already wet. Ansari meanwhile started undressing himself. After I was satisfied with kissing and touching, I looked at Ansari who was naked and was sporting an erection. He had circumcised dick and it was 6 inch long. He then rolled a condom on his dick. I stood up and he took mom to the mattress made her to lie down on it. Mom was just obeying him. He made mom to spread her legs and then directed his dick in her vagina and slowly started fucking her. Mom was moaning and Ansari was picking the speed. I started undressing and when I was naked I took a look around and on the table Ansari had kept the condom box. I took one condom and rolled it on my dick. Ansari meanwhile was fucking Mom harder and I could hear his balls slapping against her ass. Mom was moaning a bit louder. Ansari at the same time was pressing her boobs and kissing her lips. Ansari suddenly announced that he was going to cum but mom spoke for the first time to delay it. But it was too late and he was already cumming. Ansari got up and I kneeled down between mom's legs. Mom all of a sudden caught my hips and pulled me towards her. Mom spread her legs wider and i slipped my 5 inch dick in her and started fucking her. I too like ansari started pressing her boobs and kissing her lips. Mom was again moaning and then mom wrapped her legs around my waist and locked her arms around my shoulder. After sometime Mom had intense orgasm even I could not hold on and started cumming. I got up after some time. Mom was breathing heavily. Ansari was already sporting one more erection. Ansari then told mom to get on all fours. After mom got on all fours, he kneeled behind mom and caught her hips and entered her. Ansari kept moving in and out of mom. I discarded the used condom from my dick. I then went in front of mom and started kissing her lips and pressing her boobs. Ansari told me to put my dick in her mouth. I kneeled down so that my dick was levelled to mom's mouth. Mom did not take it in her mouth. Ansari saw this and slapped her thigh and shouted her to take it her mouth. I pushed my dick towards mom's mouth and she wrapped her lips around my dick. Now Ansari stop moving in and out of mom but he pushed and pulled mom. All I had to do was kneeled and Mom's mouth was going back and forth on my dick. Ansari came after sometime and pulled himself out. Mom stopped sucking me and I was not happy with this. Mom lay down on her back and told me fuck her. I quickly got on my feet and took a condom, rolled it and went near mom and entered her. I started again fucking her and came after sometime. Mom had not cummed yet and after I pulled out, she started fingering herself. I knew what mom wanted and I went near my mom and started licking her vagina. I found her clitoris and concentrated all my attention to it. She came after 5 minutes.

Ansari was looking at us and smiling. We all got dressed up. Ansari kissed my mom for the last time and said us to visit him again. Mom and I did not speak the entire journey back to home. After mom and I reached home, Mom turned towards me and said, " you should not mention this incident to anyone and whatever happened today will not happen again" I was sad hearing this. Mom saw the look on my face and said, "You wanted to do it again" I replied, "yes mom I love you". Mom said. " I love you too and I really enjoyed your licking me," she continued, " what I meant by not repeating the incident again is we will not involve Ansari again". We went towards her room and started undressing and had bath and sex together in the bathroom.

Our relationship still continues till today. We have sex whenever we are alone.

5. *Vandana*

I always had a fantasy of seeing my wife make love to another person. I never thought that it would become a reality. But it became a reality .When I first mentioned it to her, she became very angry .In fact for two days she did not even properly talk to me. She was born and brought up in a very conservative and religious atmosphere. Even the word sex was dirty to her. Later I started to mention it whenever we made love. Soon she also started to like it .But she did not admit it.

But whenever we mad love, I used to tell her about my fantasy. She told me that it would always remain a fantasy. Anyway the fantasy became a reality and coming to my story.......

I am Sudheer Kumar happily married to my wife Vandana Jeetasree. I am 33 and she is 28. we have a daughter anu who is in the KG class aged four. We are an average middle class family from Kerala. I work in a government firm. Vandana is a house wife. When we were married I was working in a private firm. It was only after one year of getting married I got my current job. My first posting was a bit far from my native place.(to protect secrecy I am not mentioning it). Anyway coming to my story, at that time Vandana was six months pregnant. I went to the new place. Though a distant cousin I was able to get a suitable place for accommodation in the new place. It was only after our child was born that I took my family to the new house. It was a rented house which had a cheap rent. The house belonged to one Vishwanathan. He stayed a little further from our house. He was about 40 years of age married and had two children. Right from the time we met we became very friendly. He taught in a nearby +2 school. He was well built and robust. It was hard to believe that he was a teacher. After I brought my wife and child to the new place we became more friendly. People used to call him Vishwa. My wife who is very reserved also became very friendly with him .At times we used to go to his home. His wife Geetha also was very friendly with us. Vishwa used to come at least twice to our house. He used to enquire us whether we have any difficulties or needed some sort of help. He had arranged a servant to help my wife in the kitchen. Within the three years that we had stayed there we had become good family friends with Vishwa and his wife. We admitted Anu to the KG classes in the school were Vishwa was teaching. I used to take her in the morning and Vandana would bring her back. Vandana had seemed very happy over the period of time. Once when I returned home from office I noticed Vishwa's bike in the front porch of the house. As I entered the house I heard some laughter. It was my wife .There was Vishwa telling some jokes and she was laughing at it. She told me that Vishwa was telling about some of the students and their behavior in the school. Vishwa told me that the school day program was approaching and invited us to be present for it. He left then.

It was after supper in the night that certain thoughts had come into my mind. Vandana would at times be telling about Vishwa. When we were married Vandana was very shy in bed. It took me some time to persuade her to tell of some thoughts on sex. We had a fairly active sex life and we loved each other very much. Most of our sex was limited to missionary position. I had once tried anal but it was painful for her and she did not like it. There was an employee's meeting in our department which was in Trivandrum . It was a two day program. I had to leave. I told Vishwa that I won't be there for two days .He told me not to worry about my family and that he would arrange the maid servant to stay in my house and that he would see to it. I left for the two day program and returned.

It was on Saturday and Sunday and I returned by Monday morning. I had already applied for leave on Monday. Vandana greeted me at the door. She had taken the child to the school and just returned. I saw that she was not in the usual mood. I asked her whether anything was wrong. She told me that she wanted to tell me something. I told her that I would take a quick wash and would come soon. When I came she was sitting in the dining room with my tea. After I had my tea I asked her about what she had to say. She told me not to get angry and to gently listen to her. I shall give you the details what she said to me. "Vishwa came in the morning since it was Saturday and classes were only upto 12. He asked me whether I needed any help or something to buy. I told him that I did not want anything. He told me to get him a glass of water. When I had gone to the kitchen he had followed me. He told me that I was very beautiful and Sudheer was very lucky to have me. After drinking the water he took my hands and kissed it . I was very shocked at his behavior. I pulled away my hand from him. He then told me that he had admired my beauty and had a special love for me. I told him not to say such things. Suddenly he came closer and embraced me. I had never expected something like that. he was so strong for me. He kissed on my lips. He pressed me against the wall and gave me a kiss. Then he rained kisses in my face and breasts .I couldn't stop him and all I could do was to obey him. Then he kissed gently on my lips and said that he loved me very much. He then let me go and said that he was sorry .He told me that he wanted to make love to me. I told him that it was wrong and it would ruin our family reputation. He then left."

Hearing all this first thought that had come to my mind was to go and bash him. But there was some thoughts going on in my mind. I had a fantasy of seeing my wife with another man this was a thought that had come during the last one year ever since Vishwa and Vandana had become good friends. I asked Vandana whether she likes Vishwa. She was shocked at what I had asked. She told me that she loves me more than anything in the world. I told about my fantasy and she was more shocked. I told her that since he had made a pass at her it would be easy to fulfill my fantasy. She did not reply to it. That night when Anu was asleep I called Vandana and asked her about it. I told her to be frank and asked her whether she likes Vishwa. She told me that she had liked him and that she loves me only. I kissed her and that night we made a very passionate love. The next day I took Anu to school and met Vishwa there. He was as usual. He asked me about my trip. I told him that everything was ok. In the evening I asked Vandana about my fantasy. She asked me whether I was serious. I told her that I want to make it happen. She told me that it would ruin our relationship. I told her that I loved her very much and nothing would happen. The next few days I kept on telling her about my fantasy and asked her to make it a reality.

It was Vandana who used to bring our daughter from school. At times she would be able to see Vishwa in the school. Ever since the incident in my house Vishwa's visit to our house had reduced. I told Vandana to be friendly with him. All these days I kept telling Vandana to make my fantasy a reality. And finally Vandana told me on a Saturday that she had talked with Vishwa at the school. He told her that he was sorry for his behavior and to forget it. I knew that some more effort and she would fulfill my fantasy. I knew that she had a special liking for Vishwa. And finally the summer vacations were starting. The exams were over and Vishwas's wife and children had gone to their native place .I knew that this was a perfect time. I kept on repeating my fantasy to Vandana and finally she asked me" Sudhee are sure you want me to do this ?" I told her that I was longing to see this and it's only a fantasy. And then she gave me the big YES. She also made a condition that it would be once only. That was a very happy day for me .That night we made a very passionate love.

The next day Vishwa came to our house. His visits were less. I was about to leave for my office. I told him to talk to Vandana. I left for my office. My thoughts were centred around how she would behave to him. In the office I was thinking of what would have happened at home. When I returned home Vandana gave me the details. Vandana had prepared tea for Vishwa. He again apologized for his behavior. She said that it was over and she had forgotten.. Then they started to talk. He told her that lately his sex life was not good and his wife had not much interest. She went to the kitchen and they continued the talk .As he was about to leave Vandana called him towards him and gave him a very passionate kiss. She said that Vishwa was very thrilled and surprised. The kiss was longer than anticipated Vishwa kissed hungrily. His hands started to roam in her breast area. Soon she pushed him free. She told him that she wanted to make love to him. Vishwa had a surprised look on his face. She told him that she would tell him of the day when they could make love. Vishwa left the home as a happy person . When I heard this I was totally shocked and thrilled and wondered whether this was my same wife Vandana. She asked me whether I was happy with all that happened. I finally made plans for the big day and my fantasy was going to become a reality. I decided the day and made some arrangements in our bed room so that I could watch the entire happenings. Vishwa came in the morning as I was leaving home. As usual I told him to talk to Vandana. Vandana was about to take our child to the nearby playschool. Since it was summer vacation we had admitted Anu to a nearby play-school. After I left Vandana, Anu and Vishwa went out to the play school. I had already told a plan and she did what I told her. And the day of my fantasy arrived….

Vishwa came at 9.30 and Vandana was at home after taking Anu to the play school. She greeted Vishwa. As soon as he entered she closed the door. All this while I was hiding in a special portion of the storeroom next to our bedroom. Certain brick portions were loose and I had made it in a special way to see all that would happen in our bed room. Vandana took him straight to the bed room (all instructions as I had given to her). As soon as they entered she locked the room. Slowly she went towards him and Vishwa kissed her lips. As soon as I saw this I got an erection. The kiss was slow at first and then it became very passionate .her hands were on his neck and Vishwa had his hands on her waist. Slowly the front portion of the sari was pulled down and his hands were roaming in her waist area (.my wife has a little belly and she is awfully sexy.)She started to have her hands on his hair .those same things that she does when we make love. Vishwa's hands were now roaming in her bum area. My wife has shapely bums. At first she seemed hesitant with this but soon his kisses made her hot. Slowly Vishwa started to remove her sari. She seemed to co-operate in a very good way . Once the sari was removed she helped him to remove the blouse and bra. I could not believe at what I was seeing. There was my wife exposing to Vishwa .Once the bra was removed Vishwa watched her some time.Ever since our daughter anu was born she had her breasts little sagged. But they were still hot. She stood in her petticoat. Vishwa reached for her breasts. Slowly he lowered his face on her breasts and started to fondle and kiss them. Vandana moaned with pleasure. He began to suck her tasty tits. He then lifted his face and kissed her lips. Then he reached for her petticoat. She helped him to set it free. She had not worn anything underneath. There was that bushy pubic hair sticking out of her snatch. There stood my wife completely naked in front of Vishwa. He reached for her pubic area .He slowly had his hand caressing her pelvic area. He lowered himself down and then buried his head in her pelvic area. Vandana let out a loud moan. I could see that he was kissing and eating her vagina. As he was doing this his hands were roaming along her thighs and bums. At times I could see that he was squeezing her bums.

After a few minutes he turned her aside and started to kiss her bums. I was very much turned on by seeing the happenings. I had never done such things. Here my wife was enjoying all this. He squeezed her bums, kissed it and even licked her anus. I never thought a school teacher such as Vishwa would do such things. After some time Vishwa got up and started to remove his dress. He removed his shirt and pants quickly then his underwear. He was robust and well build .He should have been a sportsperson not a school teacher. As imagined his penis was big in size about 8 inches long and very thick (mine is six). There were dark strips of pubic hair. It was erect and seemed like it was about to explode. He again reached for Vandana and kissed her passionately. He took her hand and placed it on his penis. He then whispered something in her ear which I could not hear. She smiled gently and started to fondle his penis- a scene that aroused me much. He then sat on the bed and pulled her on his lap. The kissing continued in a very intimate and hot way. Was she fulfilling my fantasy or hers? He started to suck her juicy breasts like a he was very hungry. Slowly he laid her on the bed. Then he got from the bed and reached for his pants. I wondered whether he had stopped. He pulled something from his pants' pocket. Soon I found out what it was condoms. He took one and started to put it on his penis. As soon as he had put he reached for Vandana. Slowly he reached for her and kissed her lips. As he kissed her, she slowly started to open her thighs inviting him. She reached for his penis and guided it into her pussy.

As soon as he entered her she let a loud moan. She had her thighs wrapped on his hips. The first few strokes were strong and he was wild on her. Then it was gentle and he pumped slowly and kept on kissing her. After they had climaxed he got up from her. He removed his condoms and started to wipe his penis. Vandana seemed totally relaxed. She got up from the bed and headed for the bathroom. After some time she returned. Vishwa went near her and kissed her. He told her that it was nice sex and he had enjoyed it very much. He started to kiss her again. He turned her and started to rub his penis on my wife's bum she started to moan again,. At the same time he kept on kissing her neck. The rubbing became very intense and finally he had his penis in her bum. Slowly at first and then he started to fuck her bum in a very intense way. It seemed that she had some pain and then I could see that she was enjoying it. Vishwa really tormented her butt and finally he had his semen dripping from my wife's bum. He turned her towards him and they started to kiss again .he laid her on the bed and started to kiss her again. I never thought Vishwa had such vigor.

He pulled Vandana on top of him and they started to kiss and feel each other. They rested for some time and Vishwa took Vandana to the adjoining bathroom. I could not make out or see what took place in the bathroom.(Vandana told me later that Vishwa had cleaned her and that they had taken a bath together).They returned after a few minutes and then both of them got dressed. Vishwa kissed her and thanked her for the love and affection.. He then left. The entire proceedings had taken place within a span of 70 minutes.(I had masturbated twice during this time)

I came from my hiding place. Vandana seemed totally exhausted. She smiled at me and asked me whether I had enjoyed the show. I went straight to her and kissed her passionately in her mouth. I asked her whether she has enjoyed it and she said that she did enjoy. I thanked her for fulfilling my fantasy. She told me that since the fantasy is over, not to mention about it again. That night we made a very passionate love. But what had happened was the beginning of a new series of affair that my wife was to have with Vishwa.

6. *Swati*

My name is Raja and I am from India. This story goes back to eighteen years. I was only eighteen years old then. My mom Swati was thirty seven years old and I had a sister who was married and was just twenty. My father ran away from the house may be to become a Sadhu. I was just fifteen years old then. We have never heard of him till today.

My mom was just sixteen when she was married. My sister Anu was born one year after the marriage. I was born two years after that. My father was a very high profile man working as a civil servant. We lived in a small town in Nasik near Mumbai. My mom continued to study even after her marriage because of my father's encouragement. I don't know being a civil servant how he managed to marry my under aged mom. After completing her college my mom took up a job in a local bank.

We lived in a beautiful duplex bungalow. It had a large living room and two bedrooms in the ground floor and two bedrooms on the first floor. We also had a little garden in the front yard as well as in the back yard. In the front side we had planted flowering plants and in the backyard we had some fruit plants. We also used to grow some seasonal vegetables like bringal(Eggplant), bhindi(lady finger), tomato, spinach etc.

My father's job was a very stressful job and he had a nervous breakdown. It was then he suddenly left the house one day, leaving us to fend for ourselves. Fortunately my mom had a job so she took over all the responsibilities.

But absence of a father figure had some other effects. My sister was already seventeen and she had a boy friend. She would often come late at night and ignored my mother's warnings. I always used to be in awe of her as she was elder to me and often used to bully me she was always stronger than me. There was no question of me telling her anything. I knew her reaction would be violent and may even get physical.

Just after a month of her eighteenth birthday she eloped with her boyfriend and married him. Her boyfriend was a twenty five year old young man then. He was an accountant in a nationalized bank. Fortunately their marriage survived and they are now settled in Mumbai as a very happy family. My sister is also now changed after giving birth to her two kids. Her motherhood has changed her completely. She is now quite affectionate towards me and my mom now.

My sister came to our house when she was almost nine months pregnant. It is usual in India for women to go to their mother's house for their first delivery. My mom welcomed her daughter with open arms. She was an unruly child but for my mom she was her own flesh and blood. I did not like her home coming but after all she was my sister too. My dislike towards her crumbled down. She was very humble then as the maternal instinct had taken over. So we all were waiting with excitement for the baby to arrive.

After two weeks she gave birth to a beautiful baby girl. She looked more like my sister. We were all overjoyed to see our family tree growing. This bundle of joy was a god send gift for us. After two years we were all together and now we were closer to each other than never before. It is amazing how a baby can change the lives of the people surrounding it.

But there was a small problem. My sister was producing very little milk so my mom was giving the baby cow's milk. The baby was not able to digest it properly and would cry endlessly for hours. So my mom asked my sister if a wet nurse can be employed. But my sister strongly refused to do so. She did not like the idea of an unknown lady breastfeeding her baby. My mom came with an incredible solution. She offered to feed the baby. My sister did not have any problem with that. But my mom had last fed me sixteen years back and she was now totally dry. So she consulted our family doctor. The doctor advised some medication and asked my mom to start trying to feed the baby from the same day. The doctor told her that more than the medicine the stimulation by the baby will promote milk production. Within a week my mom started producing enough milk to satisfy the baby's need. We were all relieved. The baby now only cried when she needed milk. My sister stayed with us for about six months during this period my mom had taken leave from her job. My sister left for Mumbai leaving behind sweet memories of the baby. My mom and I both cried when she left.

That day was very uneasy for us. The house looked empty without the baby. I and my mom were very sad. The day went by without the usual fun. After dinner I went to my bedroom for doing some homework. I was in the first year of engineering collage. It was about 1 am past midnight and I heard some sobbing noise from my mother's bedroom. I quickly kept aside my home work and rushed towards my mom's bedroom.

"Mom what is it mom why are you crying?" I asked standing outside her door. There was no response. I pushed the door but it was locked from inside.

"Mom open the door" I said knocking at the door.

A few minutes after Mom opened the door. She looked very uneasy and was sweating. Her eyes were wet and she looked exhausted.

"What happened Mom?"

"No nothing I am ok." She said

"Mom c'mon I am also missing the baby but she can't stay with us forever." I said.

"I know honey I am sad for that but I have a different problem." She said.

"What happened mom?" I asked in a worried voice.

"Raja I am not able to get the milk out and it is paining now, I am feeling as if they will explode" she said in a painful voice looking at her own breasts.

"Let us go to a doctor mom." I said

"At 1 am which doctor you can take me to?" she asked me in a painful voice.

She was right and the situation was grim for her.

"I tried to squeeze it out but it doesn't come out that way" she said.

I had some knowledge in this matter. I knew that if a woman is stressful she would not lactate. She has to be relaxed to lactate. My Mom was tense and was not able to release the milk the more she tried the more she would have been tensed and unable to release the milk. Suddenly my mom sat on the floor. She was sweating and breathing fast.

"Raja bring me some water I am not able to breathe" she said in a low voice.

I was terrified I ran to the kitchen to fetch a glass of water for her. She could hardly take a few sips.

"Oh god I will die" she cried.

"Don't cry mom I will help you, I will suck your milk mom" I said unable to think of anything else.

"Please Raja do it before I die." She almost begged me.

"Ok mom be relaxed and don't worry." I assured her.

I sat beside her on the floor. She bent my head on her lap and removed the end of her sari. Her blouse was almost at the brink of tearing off. She somehow unhooked the bottom three hooks and forced out one of her huge breast. It was swollen with milk and was quite huge. Her nipple was dark brown and was projecting out. She moved my mouth towards it. I took it gently in my mouth and started sucking it very slowly. But the milk was just dribbling and after about a minute when it received stimulation from my lips it started to flow a little. As my mom felt a little relief she became more relaxed and the milk started to spurt in my mouth. Even her other breast started to release the milk spontaneously. I was surprised by the gush of her warm milk. It was thin, a little salty and more sweet I really liked her milk. At first I only had her nipple in my mouth then as I sucked her she moved my head closer towards her breasts and lightly squeezed her breast. I then took her entire areola in my mouth and even some part of her breast. She reacted to this with a sudden deep breathe and closed her eyes. I increased my speed and emptied her breast in a few minutes. When I felt that there was no more milk left I removed my mouth from it and looked at her.

"I think it is finished." I said.

"What about the other one" she smiled and asked me, she was more at ease now because even though I did not suck her other breast, it had already released some of the milk spontaneously. Actually it was still releasing the milk and her blouse and belly were wet with it.

"Yeah I know" I said.

"Look my blouse has already become wet so please don't mind" she smiled and unhooked the remaining hooks and removed her blouse exposing her both breast. She then wiped her belly and breast with the end of her sari. Even though she dried her breast it was still releasing the milk. For the first time I saw her half naked. But there was no shame in her eyes. She was looking very lovingly towards me.

"Come honey it's this one now." She said and pulled me towards her other breast.

I took her breast in my mouth and she took a very deep breathe. I started to suck the sweet nectar from her breast. Her other breast was lying on my chest. She was moving her fingers through my hair and was looking at me very very affectionately, just as a new mom would look at her baby. Sometimes she closed her eyes enjoying the feeding. In between she was squeezing her breast gently. After a few minutes I emptied her that breast too. She knew that but continued to hold me against her breast moving her fingers through my hair. After sometime I released her breast from my mouth. I looked at her; she was smiling and was looking very satisfied. Her wet nipple was just touching my lips she made no attempt to move it away. She gently bent down and kissed my cheek. I don't remember when she had last kissed me.

"Thank you honey I am feeling much better now, you have saved me." She said.

"It's my duty mom" I said and smiled and got up. Her blouse was already wet and sticky so she did not put it back. Instead she also got up and looked in the full size mirror which was just in front of her attached to the wall. Her one end of the sari was lying on the floor.

"You are a good boy." She said looking at her reflection.

My eyes were now glued to her breasts. I did not realize their size when I was sucking them because I was to close too them. But now I was looking at them from a distance and I realized how huge, round and firm they were besides her upper body was totally naked. I was watching her mesmerized. My dick was erect and I was excited to see her like that. My mother realized I was watching her. She then turned towards me facing me half naked.

"You are watching me Raja." She said as she smiled.

"Mom they are so big." I said while keeping my eyes glued to her breasts.

"I know and all my blouses are out of size for them. Already I cannot wear any of my bras with ease, they all hurt me." She said without making any attempt to cover them. My mom was talking with me about her blouses and bras this was turning me on.

"Ok honey I need a sleep now." She finally said pulling the end of her sari and wrapping it around her to cover herself.

"I am also feeling very drowsy mom. Good night." I said and walk towards my room. My dick was paining now. So I went to toilet and quickly released my tension all the time fantasizing about her. Masturbation had never given me such an intense orgasm before. I fell asleep as soon as I lay on my bed. The milk had made me drowsy.

Next Day

Next day morning I got up did all my morning routines and walked in to the living room. I saw my mom arranging my breakfast on the table. She was wearing only blouse and petticoat. I had seen her only in blouse and petticoat countless of times before. She used to come out of her bathroom after showers like that. This she was doing since I was a child and I never felt anything about it. But today it was different. Now I was seeing her in a different perspective. Suddenly I felt a rush of blood in my dick. Her exposed breasts were still dancing in my memory. I was now turned on by her condition.

"Oh honey I am late today actually I got up late because yesterday you know I could not sleep on regular time." She said.

"I know mom. But how are you now?" I asked.

"I am ok now but before you go to college please help me out like yesterday because you will be back only in the afternoon. I don't know if I can hold on for that long" she said.

"Ok I will" I said gladly.

So after finishing my breakfast I took a quick shower and went to my mom's bedroom. She was not there so I went into the living room. She was sitting on the sofa watching morning news. She was now properly dressed and combed. I went and sat besides her. I was only wearing my shorts.

"Ahhh the baby is not here now and my leave is also exhausted I must return to work from next week." She said.

"Yes we should now move on with our lives." I said.

"But I don't know if I could get into shape till next week. My milk production should stop or at least reduce so that I can be in the office properly." She said.

"Don't worry mom I think you will be ok by then" I tried to assure her.

"Let's hope so." She said.

"Ok mom I will leave for collage in half an hour." I said.

"Oh honey come here and help me before you go." She said and pulled me towards her. I went into her lap and placed my mouth right in front of her breast. She then unbuttoned a few buttons of her blouse and offered me her breast filled with milk to the brink. I latched on to her breast and started sucking her breast. She was relaxed so this time the milk immediately started to flow in my mouth. Just a few seconds afterwards the milk started to spurt in my mouth, the stimulation provided by my lips and tongue had helped her release it freely. Milk also started to flow from her other breast wetting her blouse and belly just like yesterday.

I was excited and had closed my eyes and would open them periodically to take a look at my mom and her other breast. My mom was totally relaxed and looked very happy. She was lovingly moving her fingers through my hair and occasionally squeezing her breast to increase the flow of her milk. Her sweet milk was now gushing in my mouth I enjoyed that taste and sucked her breast dry. I wanted to continue but she pulled out her breast from my mouth and pulled me towards her other breast. She unbuttoned the rest of the buttons and removed her blouse exposing herself to me.

Her other breast was now in front of my mouth. I quickly took her nipple between my lips and started to suck. I kept on sucking even after there was no milk left in it. She knew it but this time instead of pulling out she let me to continue. She was also enjoying the sensation of my lips and tongue sucking her nipple. My dick was rock hard and the bulge was quite obvious to notice. I don't know if my mom looked at it or not but she was continuously watching me sucking her with delight. A few minutes later I released her nipple from my mouth. Her nipple was still on my lips and she was not making any attempt to move it in fact just after a few seconds she lunged forwards and moved her nipple in my mouth and pulled me towards it.

This time I took her whole areola and part of her breast in my mouth and started sucking it. I was also moving my tongue over her nipple. She had now closed her eyes with excitement and her breathing had increased. My dick was paining and it needed a release but my mom was now holding my head with her both hands and was pressing it towards her breast. I increased my speed and grabbed her breast with my both hands. She moaned and continued to moan she was excited and her initial small moans turned into much louder one and suddenly she clasped my hair tightly I opened my eyes to see her. She had shut her eyes tightly and had raised her chin she had her lower lip between her teeth.

"Shhhhhhh aaaaahhhhhhhhh Rajaaaaaaaaa" she moaned loudly.

I think she had experienced her orgasm. She held me like that for a few seconds. Then slowly her grip on my hair loosened and she released her lip from her teeth and lowered her chin. She slowly loosened her tightly shut eyes but still kept them close. I released her breast and looked at her. But she was in a state of ecstasy and kept her eyes closed enjoying her orgasm. A few seconds later she opened her eyes to see me staring at her.

"What happened mom?" I asked her but I knew what had happened.

"It's nothing honey I just felt a little pain when you sucked me in the end." She was obviously lying how she could have admitted that she just had an orgasm?

"Are you ok mom?" I asked.

"Ohhh Yessss" and she took a sigh of relief. She was looking satisfied and happy after the session. She covered herself with her sari and went to her bedroom to change in a new blouse. I ran towards my bathroom which was attached to my bedroom and quickly released myself I was so excited that I came just after shaking my dick three or four times. I then quickly changed in to my regular clothes to go to office.

"Bye mom I must run I am late today." I said as I rushed out of the door.

"Bye honey but don't rush, watch out for the traffic" she said. I did not pay attention to her as I had to run towards the bus stop to catch the bus.

That Night

That day in the collage was never ending for me. My mind

was revolving around my mom. I wonder if she too was going through the same condition. Usually while coming back from collage we guys would stay back near the bus stand to hang around the girls. Girls would also leave two or three busses chatting with us. A few boys had girlfriends and I was in a process of finding one. Her name was Anuradha. As I was waiting for the bus she came near me.

"Hi Raja." She said

"Oh hi Anu, You look beautiful today." I complimented her.

"Thanks and you are also looking handsome where did you get that smart hair cut?"

"Oh c'mon you can get this done from anywhere." I said.

"Can we go for a movie today?" She asked me. If she had asked me this question two days ago I would have become crazy. I had a huge crush on her. But I wanted to be with my beautiful mom as early as possible at the same time I did not want to hurt this beautiful girl.

"Thanks Anu but my mom is sick and there is nobody to look after her and do the household work. I must go home today." I said.

"Ok then can we go tomorrow or someday after that?" She was persisting.

"Ok I will tell you tomorrow." I said. Just then the bus came we both got in to it. Anuradha sat by my side. She was sitting very close to me brushing her body against mine. Obviously she wanted to seduce me. But my mind was filled with thoughts of my mom. Anuradha was talking with me all the time but I was not paying any attention to her. I was only occasionally saying a 'humm' 'oh I see' etc. Finally my bus stop arrived and I said bye to Anuradha and got down and ran towards my home.

My mom opened the door for me and greeted me with a smile.

I removed my shoes and went to my room to change into my shorts and t-shirt. I came back in to the living room where my mom sitting on the sofa watching TV. I sat beside her. She enquired about my collage, my friends and my girlfriends. I told her I did not have any girlfriend. Then she talked with me about her days in school and college. She told me many incidences which she had never told to anybody before. We were really talking like friends that day. Although she was my mom she was only thirty seven and nobody would have said that she was my mom. People often mistook her as my elder sister. For the first time she was talking so freely with me. I really felt very close to her that day. She told me her tightly held childhood "little secretes". She told me about the boy on whom she had a crush when she was in fourth grade. Then she told me about her conservative parents and her forced marriage with my dad when she was just sixteen. Some of her incidence were funny some were sad. In fact she had revealed her life to me.

Our talk continued till late in the evening when she realized it was time to prepare dinner. So she went in to the kitchen. I followed her.

"Ok Raja now you go out let me prepare our dinner." She said.

"Mom I want to learn cooking, I want to help you." I said

"No thanks I don't need any help in my kitchen. But if you want to learn then today you just stand near me and watch. Watch everyday what I do and you will know everything. Then you can try making some easy dishes." She said.

"Ok mom" I said and stood at a distance from her watching her prepare our dinner.

I was also watching her beautiful curves. She was not a typical Indian woman. She was quite beautiful with a fair complexion and big dark eyes. Her nose was straight and sharp and lips were full. She always sported a red bindi making her look more feminine.

She was quite tall with broad shoulders for a woman. When in home she most of the time would tie her sari quite deep below her naval She had a full figure with very little flab on her belly. Her waist was quite narrow and hips were wide. She had a nice round bottom and it swayed beautifully when she walked. Most of the time she would keep her hair tied. But on weekends when she shampooed her hair she would let them loose. Her hair reached just below her bottom. She was a perfect woman.

I was watching everything curiously and for the first time I noticed how her breasts and bottom moved up and down when she cut vegetables and made chapattis. I also noticed how her bangles made clinking sound. Everything she did was getting me aroused. When she was working I was asking her questions why she did this and that. She would briefly explain me the reasons. Anyway I enjoyed everything.

"That's all" she said keeping a lid on the vessel.

"Good it was great." I said.

"We will have to wait for sometime till this becomes a little cool" she said.

Then after sometime we had our dinner. My mom always cooked nice food. Actually it was simple dal rice chapatti and a vegetable but I always liked whatever she made. May be everybody likes what their mothers prepares for them. I think it's her love for her children that makes the food taste good.

After we had our dinner we watched a Hindi movie on TV. By the time that movie was over it was 11 pm and was time to go to bed. But I was anticipating with excitement for my mom to call me. So I decided to go to my bed room. I wanted her to call me.

Meanwhile my mom went to the kitchen and cleaned the dishes and kept the leftovers in the fridge as usual. In the bed room I had switched off the lights and was pretending to be asleep.

After about an hour my mom walked in my room. Although the lights were off the room was still illuminated by the moonlight falling on the window. My mom walked towards my bed and sat on the edge for a while. She then slowly placed her hand on my back and started to shake me very gently to wake me up. I pretended to woke up rubbing my eyes.

"Wake up Raja and please help me." She said in a very soft voice.

"Oh yes mom I forgot and slept." I lied. I was about to get up and sit when she stopped me doing that.

"It's ok. Just move away a little so that I can lay here. My lap hurts with your weight I think it will be better if I lay while you help me.

"Ok" I said, but in my mind I said "Wow this is unbelievable."

So I moved right up to the other edge of the bed near the wall giving her ample space to lie comfortably. She lay and turned on to her side facing me and moved closer to me. I was excited with anticipation, my dick was already up and now it was stiff like a rock. She was not wearing her sari. She came to me just in her blouse and petticoat. She then began to unhook her blouse. This blouse had hooks in the back and not in the front so she unhooked the blouse with some difficulty. She removed her blouse completely exposing her breasts to me. Her huge breasts were looking absolutely glorious in the moonlight.

I was at the edge of the bed so she reached my head with her head and pulled me towards her breasts. Her lower breast was already spurting milk and it was falling on my face. I moved my mouth towards it and latched on to it. I took her entire areola in my mouth. A gush of warm and sweet milk began to flow in my mouth. Her other breast was resting over my cheek it was also releasing milk spontaneously. My mom began to wipe it with a small towel which she brought with her. Then she placed it in between her breast and my cheek. This she was doing so that the milk won't wet me, but I would have never minded that.

She started to move her fingers through my hair gently. Soon she was moving her hand on my back very slowly. Her touch was so assuring and motherly that I can't forget it even today. I clearly remember how it felt. There was pin drop silence in the room I could even hear her every breath. I still remember the sweet clinking sound made by her bangles as she moved her hand over my back. It was such a heavenly feeling being with my mom like that. Soon I had emptied her breast. I then switched on to her other breast. She removed the towel as it won't be required any more. I emptied her breast in a few minutes and continued to suck her. She did not make any attempt to stop me. I knew she enjoyed this.

Her breast were already empty she no longer was feeling any stress because of them. So it was the time for her to enjoy now. As in the morning she grabbed my head with her hands and pressed it towards her breast. I also took her breast as much as possible in my mouth and started sucking it hard and moving my tongue all over it. I could hear her increased breathing. She then moved closer to me by grabbing my back with one hand and my head with the other. First time now our bodies were pressing against each other. She then put her thigh on my thigh and began to moan as I sucked her frantically. Her breathing and moaning increased as she was nearing the peak but she was trying to keep her voice as low as possible trying to control her excitement. But eventually she could no more hold on and peaked. She clasped my hair and pressed her thigh tightly against my thigh. I was also excited enough. And when she pressed her thigh against my thigh she had also pressed herself against me I was sandwiched between her and the wall. I could no longer hold my excitement and I too came shooting inside my shorts.

I had one of the most intense orgasms that night. I think mom too had a wonderful orgasm. She did not seem to move. She was just enjoying the feelings. She wanted to dwell on her orgasm. I was exhausted and ecstatic. Slowly my mom's grip around me loosened but she still kept her thigh on my thigh my face was in between her breasts. She then began to pat lightly on my back as if she was putting her baby to sleep. But believe me I was so drowsy because of her milk that I quickly fell asleep in her arms.

I woke up in the morning I was alone in the bed. I thought about the night it felt like a dream to me. Then I went to my bathroom to piss and found out my penis was glued to the underwear because of my dried semen. I poured some water over it to loosen it up. After doing all the routines I returned to my bed thinking about my mom. I wanted to make love with her, but how? I knew she enjoyed my sucking and thought that maybe she can give up herself to me. I was trying to find a way to reach under her waist. But then I also thought that maybe she is enjoying just because of the situation which was not in her control. And if I try to seduce her she will be offended by me. I did not want to hurt her emotions as I loved her so dearly. So I brushed aside my thoughts and headed towards the living room.

My mom had already served my breakfast on the table. My mom had made delicious upma that day. I ate my heart out I helped myself three times. I thanked my mom for such a lovely breakfast.

"Honey I hope you remember your duty before going to college." She said

"Yes I know mom. I will be back in a few minutes" I said and went in my bathroom for a shower. I returned in the living room. My mom was waiting for me on the sofa.

"Mom you will get hurt with my weight" I reminded her.

"It's ok. It hurts but not much. Now come to me." She said.

I obediently followed what she said and finished my job as usual. This time she did not climax she just wanted to be relived off the burden from her breasts. It was 9 am and it was time for me to leave. This continued for a week and within a week her milk production was already reduced. She could go to her office without any problem. She needed to be relived only in the night. She also asked me to sleep with her in her bed room. She said that her bed was a double bed much bigger than my bed so it was comfortable for both. I was delighted by her offer and enjoyed sleeping in her arms every day.

After One Month

It was a month now since I started sleeping with her. Her milk production was much less now and even if I stopped sucking it there would have been no problem. But she wanted me with her every night and offered me her breasts. I used to suck her for long periods even after emptying her. When she needed an orgasm she would pull me towards her and would press her body against mine. I would then suck her frantically till she climaxed. Other times she would just like to mother me and would pat me like her baby while I sucked her. On such occasions I did not cross the line by trying to move towards her or by sucking her frantically. I was adjusting myself as per her needs.

But now this was frustrating for me. I wanted to move below her waist now. I wanted to kiss her lips. I wanted to suck her tongue. I wanted to get connected to her. I wanted to see how my mom looks without any clothes on her beautiful body. I wanted to feel how it is to be inside a woman. I wanted to feel how it feels to be inside my own mother's body. I wanted to make love to her.

I remember on a Friday night I was very horny and I had made up my mind to do something with my mom. That night when she opened up for me I started slowly but quickly emptied her as there was not enough milk in her breast now. I continued to suck her; she pulled me towards her and pressed herself firmly against me. I took this chance and put my hand on her back and pressed her further towards me. To this she reacted with surprise and suddenly loosed her grip on me and pushed me away from her. She quickly switched on the table lamp.

"Raja what are you doing?" She was upset.

"Mom I love you" I said and pushed her on her back and I got on top her.

"Raja leave me you can't do this just get away." She was angry now.

But I was on fire, she was already naked waist up and I was on top of her. Her voluptuous breasts were pressed against my chest. I pressed her further and tried to kiss her lips. But she turned her face away. Then she tried to push me away by placing her hands on my shoulders but she just could not push me. I wasn't her baby as she treated me; I was almost an adult with a very good built and way too strong for her to even push me away. I then hold her hands and placed them just over her head one above another. I held the wrists of her both hands with my left hand. Her wrists were thin and I could easily hold both of them with my huge palm. She was not able to move her hands any more. Her Body was trapped below my body but she was trying to move her waist, thighs and legs. She wanted to get out of my stranglehold. I arrested her legs movement with my legs making her almost immobilized. My both legs and one hand was tied to make her immobilize but my one hand was free while she was totally captivated. Realizing that it was not possible for her to get herself free she stopped struggling and started to plead.

"Please Raja don't do this. I am your mother this is sin." She pleaded.

"If this is sin then why do you enjoy my sucking" I said.

"No I don't" she lied.

"Don't lie mom, I know you enjoy it." I said.

"No Raja I only feel a relief from pain when you suck my milk." She lied again.

"Lie again. There isn't enough milk to cause you any pain. Mom I am not a baby I can read your expressions when you climax" I said.

"No. That's not true." She was not accepting.

"You enjoy your climax and leave me high and dry don't you think it's unfair?" I asked

"No Raja I don't," She still was not accepting.

"I don't want to argue with you mom. I want to love you. I promise you will love it" I said in a seductive voice.

"No Raja please." She pleaded again.

I ignored her and moved my hand towards the strings of her petticoat and with some struggle managed to untie them. She was trying to twist but could not prevent me doing my job. Then I pulled her petticoat with all my force and removed it from her body. I removed her panty in a similar way. She was now totally naked trapped under me. I did not want to force myself inside her. So I started to seduce her. I wanted to arouse her so that she would herself cooperate.

I started to kiss her neck and exhale my warm breath over her ears slowly. I had still her hands under my control. I then slowly moved my face in between her breasts and started to rub my face with them while placing small kisses frequently. I now moved my mouth over one of her nipple and started to exhale my breath over it teasing her. I kissed her nipple very slowly. I had sucked them so many times but I have never kissed them. The moment I kissed it, it became erect. She took a deep breath and raised her back and her chin with a slight moan. This was a first sign of success. I then kissed her nipple very gently again and again. With every kiss she moaned and arched her back. I moved my mouth over her other breast and repeated everything, her reaction was the same. She was now feeling the heat.

Now I moved tip of my tongue over her nipple very gently teasing her. I began with a circular motion and then switched over to form a shape of "8". The moment I created "8" she started to arch her back lifting her breast towards me. Her breathing was increased and her moans were louder. She had stopped struggling long ago so at this point I released her hands and moved my face over her belly and started kissing her belly slowly. She was moaning and she had placed her one hand on my head grabbing my hairs. I then started to kiss her belly frantically. She started to moan with pleasure and held my head with both her hands. She was now lusting for sex. Her resistance was now turned into a violent ocean of lust. Her 'no' had turned into a passionate 'yesss yesss yesss'

I moved further down and started to kiss inside of her thighs just above her knees. She could no longer reach my head so she clasped the bed sheet with her palms tightly. She began to twist and moan with pleasure as I moved upward continuously kissing her thighs. Her moans turned into screams as I reached near her pussy. The musky aroma of her pussy was driving me mad. I placed my mouth over her pussy and started to kiss it gently but when I started to kiss it violently she began to scream and started to raise her waist.

"Sssssshhhhhh aaaaahhhhhhhh Ohhhhh my goooooood Rajaaaa-aaa."

She grabbed my hairs tightly and pulled my head towards her. She then pulled my t-shirt over my head. Her hands were trembling her body was shaking and her breathing was erratic. She then placed her trembling hands behind my waist and pulled my shorts down up to my knees. She had closed her eyes and breathing heavily. I removed my underwear and my thick dick sprang out of it. I placed myself between her legs. She then opened her eyes to have a look at me.

"Oh my god Raja that's way too thick."

Her eyes were glued to my dick with excitement. She was excited with anticipation of my thick dick penetrating her. I had never seen such excitement in anybody's eyes. I never imagined a woman would look at my penis with such excitement. I always thought penis to be an ugly organ of our body. But here was the truth lying between my legs and staring at my dick. She was so excited with anticipation that unknowingly she parted her legs. She was all the time looking at my dick with awe.

"Mom are you sure? There is no going back after this" I said

"Raja don't talk. I want that thing inside me." She almost screamed.

"Ok dear as you wish" I said and lowered myself over her.

As I was trying to find the right spot she grabbed my dick and placed it on the entrance of her pussy by parting her pussy lips with her two fingers.

"Go go go go now push it in" she said with excitement.

I pushed myself but could not go in beyond an inch then I pulled out and again pushed it inside her. This time I pushed with more force and managed to go a little further.

"Aaaahhhhhhhh aaaaiighaaa" she screamed with pain

"Mom did it hurt" I pulled out and asked her. Surprisingly her reaction was that of anger.

"Raja don't pull out just push it all the way don't stop" she screamed with anger.

"It will hurt you mom" I said.

"Don't bother about my pain just do what I told you. I want that thing inside me all the way immediately" She said in a hoarse voice. She was on fire and needed my dick to douse it.

"Ok here you go" I said

I started to push my dick inside her but the resistance was not allowing me to slide it easily. She wasn't wet enough. I was fearful of any injury to her. So I was pushing me inside her but still not with a substantial force.

"Rip my hole apart just rip it apart tear it like a paper." She realized I was not trying hard enough and grabbed my buttocks, raised her pussy towards my dick and pulled me with all her might. My dick went all the way inside her semi wet pussy.

"Aaaaahhhhhhhh aaaaaiiiiiighhhhaaaaaa ssssssshhh aaaahhhh ssssshhhh aaahhhh"

She was in real pain she had closed her eyes and clenched her lips under her teeth trying to overcome her pain. I moved my dick out a little and slid it back again. I did this for a few times until my dick was coated with her love juices and it became slippery. I continued to do this gently. Now the pain from her face was gone instead she was now moaning with pleasure. My dick was clasped tightly in her slippery pussy. I could feel this tightness near her entrance. Her pussy lips were getting dragged in and out as I moved my dick in and out.

"Ohhh my god Raja it's feeling so good ummmmm ahhhhh"

"You are so tight mom ssssssshhh aaaahhh"

Then my mom opened her eyes and lifted her head to have a look at my dick.

"My god I can't believe this" she was watching my dick move in and out of her body with excitement.

"Wow Raja I have never felt so good" She was still watching with excitement.

"I love watching this, my god you are so thick." She said her eyes still glued to my dick.

"Mom I won't be able to hold on for long." I said desperately.

"No honey. Hold on for me." She said and lowered her head on the pillow and closed her eyes.

I increased my speed at the same time I began to control myself holding my breath.

"Faster Raja faster tear me apart" and she spread her legs wide apart.

I began to move frantically between her legs. Her pussy was overflowing with our combined love juices and was slippery but still it had clasped my dick firmly. Her breasts were swaying up and down and she was moaning "sshh aahh sshh aahh" with my every thrust. My dick was hard like a rock, it has drawn blood from all parts of my body and it was now paining I was ramming and slamming my dick inside her hole ravishing her like an animal. She then started to arch her back and raise her pussy. I began to feel some more tightness around my dick.

"Aaaaah Rajaaaaaa this is so gooood sssshhhh aaaahhhh."

"Aaaaiighhh I can't hold now moooomm."

"Don't hold I am coming Rajaaaaaaaaaaaaaa sssssshhhh aaaaahhhh" and she pulled me towards her and buried her nails in my back, arched her back and raised her pussy forcing it with all her strength towards my dick.

"Sssssssshhhhhh Aghhhhhhhhhhhhhhhhhh" I screamed as I came shooting my hot semen inside her pussy.

"Aaaaaiiiiighhhaaaaaa aaaaaaaaaaaahhhhhhhhhh" she too came violently as she sensed my warm semen strike over her cervix. I shot threads after threads of semen inside her filling her pussy with it. Waves of ecstasy ran through our bodies. Suddenly the tension was released my pubic muscles were automatically contracting and relaxing ejecting semen inside her. My dick was pulsating. My mom's pussy was also pulsating with my dick.

I was no more a virgin and I had just experienced the most intense orgasm of my life. My mom was also ecstatic. She had closed her eyes and gripped me tightly. We lay in that position for a few minutes. Then her grip loosened by this time my dick had also become soft so I pulled out. My dick was drenched with our love juices.

My mom was still lying still. Her eyes were closed and she looked relaxed and calm. Her breathing had returned to normal. She did not move an inch of her any body part. She looked very very satisfied.

I went to the bathroom and wiped off my dick and returned to the bed. To my surprise my mom had fallen asleep. I felt proud about myself. I had satisfied her to the extent that she fell asleep. This was her mute acknowledgement of my manhood, her appreciation of my lovemaking. Although this was my first sexual intercourse I lasted enough to give her climax.

I stood beside the bed watching her naked body for the first time. She looked like a sculpture. She was quite fair with dark hair and beautiful dark eyes which were now closed. Her lips were full, juicy, red and inviting. Shoulders were broad and breasts as you know voluptuous but firm. She was sleeping with her slender arms above her head. She had not shaven her under arms and they had ample dark hairs. Her waist was narrow and her hip was quite wide giving her a nice curve. There was a huge gap between her thighs where they joined her pubic area. It is because of this that her hips were quite wide.

Her pubic area was covered with thick curly black hair. The pussy lips were barely visible because of this. But I could clearly see some of my semen had rolled out of her pussy and trickled down towards her buttocks. Her thighs were fair than rest of her body and unlike a typical Indian woman her legs were quite long compared to her upper body.

I was watching this beauty mesmerized. She was a very good mother and now I realized that she was a wild and passionate lover in the bed. I wonder why my dad left the house when he had such a beautiful, passionate and faithful wife. I picked up my clothes and put them on. Then I pulled a thin cover over her. She was still asleep and was not disturbed by this. She was sleeping blissfully. Then I switched off the lamp and slept beside her.

Saturday Morning

The next day was a Saturday. Normally we would sleep longer than usual on weekends. But my mom always used to get up before me. But that day I got up before her. My mom was still sleeping blissfully. It must have been 5.30 am in the morning. The sun was not out but the sky had begun to brighten. I turned on my side and began to watch my beautiful mom. The cover had slid down to her waist exposing her upper body. I was watching that visual feast.

Just then an ambulance passed by our house with its siren on. This broke my mom's sleep. She opened her eyes to see me watching her. She quickly realized that she was still naked and I was watching her. She quickly pulled the cover to cover herself and looked at me. I smiled and she blushed and kept her hands over her face. A few minutes later she suddenly moved towards me and hugged me tight.

"Oh Raja It was so good yesterday. Thanks you did it. Actually I needed it desperately but how could I acknowledge it so flatly? After all I am your mother. Please don't say I am a liar" She said in a very soft voice.

"I am sorry mom; I understand how difficult it is for a mother." I said

"Good. Anyway I really enjoyed yesterdays encounter." She said

Yes mom I was in cloud nine" I said.

"Me too" and she rubbed her nose on my chest.

"Mom you are so good at this (love making)" I said.

"You too but how did you learn? Was it not your first time?" she asked.

"It was my first time mom." I said.

She then kissed me for the first time on my lips and put her arms around my neck.

"Raja I had never been pulled in and out like yesterday." She said blushingly.

I did not know what to say so I kept quite caressing her back.

"Wow you made me so full there, you are way too thick." She complimented me.

"I thought you are tight mom." I said

"No. Your dad was not that thick. I always had a baggy feeling with him. I always wished if he had a thicker penis" she said.

"Was he so small?" I asked.

"No. The length may be the same as yours but not that thick" she said

"Does it make so much difference?" I asked.

"Yes. I always wanted to spread my legs wide apart but could not do it because it made the baggy feeling more prominent. Yesterday I could do it as much as I could. I was feeling so free to part my legs without any worries and you were pulling me in and out, oh my god what a feeling it was."

"Thanks mom I did not know anything about this." I said.

"You will learn lot of things with me. I promise." She said.

"Ok. Then can you tell me how you feel when you experience your orgasm?"

"Oh it's difficult to explain honey." She said.

"Please mom, try to tell." I insisted.

"It starts with a feeling of ants are crawling inside, a kind of tickling sensation. Then my vagina starts contracting and relaxing and I feel to suck the penis inside it. I feel a sweet depression between my naval and the chest bone. Waves of pleasure run through my body starting from my vagina and striking my heart. I start shaking and want to dig my nails deep inside your back and after that I become limp unable to do anything. Still it is quite difficult to explain but yesterday it was mind blowing. I had never experienced such an intense and satisfying orgasm ever in my life. More than the intensity it provided me deep deep satisfaction." She said with a very big smile.

"I see that's why you fell asleep." I said.

"Yes for the first time I fell asleep after having sex."

Then she inserted her face against my chest rub her nose against it and closed her eyes. I started to caress her back. She was enjoying being loved and cuddled. We were in this position for sometime. Then she woke up and sat on the bed. I was laying and watching her. She started to tie a knot in her beautiful long hairs. Her voluptuous breasts were swaying and bouncing as she moved her hands to tie the knot. My eyes were glued to her breasts. She was giggling and watching me as she tied the knot.

"Ok honey I will make some breakfast now." She said.

"I am not hungry mom." I said.

"But I am. You have drained my energy completely." She said with a smile.

"Ok" I said. I was in no mood to get up.

She got off the bed and started to walk towards her bathroom, just then.

"Oh my God" She said and rushed towards the bathroom and emerged after a few minutes. This time she was wearing her night gown which she had kept in her bathroom. I knew she was wearing nothing inside it as all her under garments were lying on the floor.

"What happened mom?" I asked her.

"Nothing honey it's just your semen which started to roll out on my thighs" she said.

"Is it?" I asked.

"Yes, never in my life I was filled to this extent." She blushed.

I was proud of myself. I also then got up and used her bathroom to relieve myself. Later I went to my bathroom brushed my teeth took a quick shower and presented myself at the dining table. Mom was busy preparing something in the kitchen. I was reading the news paper but my mind was occupied with her thoughts. I could not sit there so I walked into the kitchen. My beautiful mom was preparing pohay. I walked behind her and put my arms around her belly and placed my dick between her ass chicks. She just closed her eyes for a moment raised her chin and then open her eyes again. She felt good as I was moving my hands just under her breast teasing them softly. I then slowly kissed her cheeks; she had closed her eyes and enjoying the sensation. But then suddenly she pushed me away.

"Ok Raja please let me finish this. We have the whole day and the night for this. But right now I am hungry." She said.

"Ok" and I eased my grip allowing her to carry on and I returned to the dining table waiting for my beautiful mom. I was not at all interested in food; I was only interested in her now. After some time she came out of the kitchen and served the breakfast. I hastily finished it. She took her own time. All the time I was looking at my beautiful mom's face. She was now embarrassed.

"Raja. Stop it now don't look at me like this, it is embarrassing." She complained.

"Oh sorry Mom." I said and I put on the TV and started watching it. My mom finished her dish after some time and picked up my dish and went to the kitchen for washing.

I sat on the sofa watching TV. She came back with two cups of tea. She offered me one and sat beside me sipping her. She was sitting very close to me brushing her body with mine. My dick had already sprung into life. After she had finished her tea I pulled her towards me. This time she did not resist but gladly came into my arms. We immediately locked our lips and started to probe each other's tongue. After a lot of kissing and cuddling we separated.

Then we talked about some unimportant topics. My mom told me my lot of childhood mischiefs. Then she told me about her childhood, the school where she went, about her classmates. She was talking with me like a long lost friend suddenly found. It was good to know that my mom was a sensual woman. She too had her childhood heartthrobs she was just like any other girl at her age. We think of our moms as an asexual being. After their marriage women devote themselves to their family their children and their self identity is lost in this process. They dress modestly speak modestly and they are just moms.

That night the sex was divine. There was no force and no rush. We made a very passionate love on my mom's bed. Our bodies just melted into each others arms. Last night was a wild night filled with lust but that night was full of passion and desire. We made love very gently and slowly taking our time. Exploring each other's bodies kissing and cuddling. Actual intercourse was just an extension of the whole love making process. For the first time in my life I realized that sex is not just penis and vagina. It is a much more than that. Our whole body, mind, and soul are interacting to achieve one goal, the ultimate joy of life "Nirvana". This is a state of bliss where we lose ourselves and a deep sense of peace prevails in our minds. There is no ego, no desire to win and no fear to lose.

After that divine love making my mom started to mother me. She started to kiss me like her baby and lovingly gathered me towards her and offered her breasts to me. There was hardly any milk in it but I started sucking her like a baby she was caressing my back and planting kisses over my head. Her maternal instincts had taken over now and I soon fell asleep in her loving arms. But every time we did not make love like this. Sometimes it was wild and on other occasions it was passionate.

Break For One Month

We were now living like a couple deeply in love. We used to have sex almost every day excluding the days when she would experience her periods. During her periods I used to massage her feet, legs, buttocks, waist, back and shoulders to relieve her of her pain. This way I won her heart. She was already mine but my love and care made her more devoted towards me. I also used to do all the cooking and cleaning so that she would get complete rest. She was also working in a bank. She used to come home after 5pm. I used to come home before her. Many times I used to cook and keep everything ready for her. She used to feel so proud of me.

I was going to college and as a part of the course we also had to go on a yearly tour. Unfortunately just after six months we had to go on a one month tour. I was very disappointed. I did not want to miss even a single day without her. But I had to go.

During that period I kept in touch with her over the phone. As the days went by we were both eager to see each other. That month was the longest month of my life. It seemed to never end. But finally the wait was over as we all picked up our bags for the journey return home. It was Friday night when I reached home. I rang the door bell.

My mom opened the door with a big smile on her face. I went inside and kept my bags on the floor and spread my arms. My mom rushed into my arms and hugged me tightly. Soon our lips locked and we began to probe each other's tongue. We separated after a while. We were both happy to see each other again.

"Oh honey why don't you take a quick shower? You will feel better after a long journey" she said.

"Yes mom I was about to say that"

"Ok, then I will serve the dinner" she said.

"Yes I will be back in a few minutes" I said.

I went to my bathroom and shaved myself and took a quick shower. When I came out I saw mom had kept my shorts and a t-shirt on the bed. I quickly got into them and went into the living room. My mom had already served the dinner. The dinner was delicious. Mom had prepared my favorite mutton biryani and raita. After the dinner she served me falooda but she did not take it. The food was really excellent and moreover after a gap of one month I was eating home made food prepared by my loving mom. After eating everything I kissed my mom's hands.

"Mom you are a great cook. Nobody can match you." I said.

"All children like food prepared by their mom." She said.

"No mom really you are the best." I said.

"Ok honey It's time for action, I am starving for a month now."

"Me too mom" I said and I hugged her and kissed her lips gently.

"Ok then you wait here watch some movie while I clean up everything" she said.

"I will help you mom" I said.

"No you must be tired. Just do what I say. I will call you when I am ready." She said.

"Ok" I said and walked towards the sofa. My mom picked up the dishes and went into the kitchen. I was waiting impatiently for her to call me. After a few anxious minutes she yelled from her bedroom.

"Raja come in"

I switched off the TV and rushed towards her room. Just when I was about to enter the door I saw her standing in front of the mirror. I was struck by a bolt of lightning when I saw her and stopped right there. She was wearing a beautiful red sari and a red blouse. She had let her beautiful dark hair loose, which were hanging just below her buttocks. She was wearing beautiful gold bangles. She was also wearing beautiful flowers in her hair. Her sari was tightly hugging her body showing her beautiful curves. The sari was tied way below her naval and a thin line of her pubic hair was just visible to me.

"Raja come near me." She said.

I came out of the trance I locked the door and walked towards her slowly. I slowly put my arms around her back and pulled her towards me.

"Shhh Ahhhh Raja. I missed you so badly" she said

"Me too, Mom." I said and started to move my hands over her

back. She was just hugging me tightly and trying to feel me as much as possible. I lifted her chin and placed a small kiss on her lips. She moaned with joy. I then lifted her in my arms and placed her on the bed. I was on top of her and she was under me. Her voluptuous breasts were trapped under my chest. She was pulling me tightly towards her and I could easily see the lust in her eyes. I knew today she wanted a wild sex.

My condition was no different. I was moving my face between her breasts and she was moaning with pleasure. Today there was no point in kissing and cuddling. I removed her sari's end over her breasts and I put my hands around her back to unhook her blouse. She lifted her back slightly to provide access for my hands. I quickly unhooked her blouse and threw it on the floor. Suddenly I could smell musky aroma of her armpits. It was too intense. I had noticed that whenever she was horny that aroma would increase. That day it was so intense that I could smell it from a distance. I always liked her aroma. So I grabbed her both hands and placed them over her head giving me a full view of her underarms with thick black hair. Then I slowly lowered myself into one of her armpit and smelled it. My God that smell was so arousing that my already hard dick started paining.

"Mom you smell so wild today" I said in a hoarse voice.

"Raja my whole body is waiting for you. Just tear me apart today. I want you to rip my hole today, don't show any mercy just spread me wide open and pound it and fill it with you semen till it floods." She said in an excited voice.

I was occupied with the musky aroma of her underarms I was sniffing them in turns. My dick was paining with each sniff. I was on fire and my mom's aroma was adding fuel to it. My mom's hands were over her head and I was holding them down to smell her armpits. But suddenly my mom started to twist and turn and raise her waist. This meant that she wanted my dick inside her juicy pussy. She was aching for that. I released her hands and she quickly raised her back and unhooked her bra releasing her voluptuous breasts. I quickly removed her sari which was half unwrapped.

Then as usual I was struggling to untie the strings of her petticoat. She was irritated and pushed my hands away and in a swift move untied the strings and slid her petticoat along with her panty up to her knees. I helped her by removing them off completely from her body. She was now totally naked and on fire. It was now my turn to undress, I quickly removed all my clothes and placed myself between her legs. My mom was watching my dick with the same excitement as the day when we first had sex. Her eyes were widened and glued to my dick. The excitement of getting penetrated by it was clearly visible on her face. She had already spread her legs wide open in anticipation.

"Raja hurry up I just can't wait anymore" her voice was shaking.

"Neither can I wait mom" I said.

But I did not want to penetrate her directly. I wanted to tease her and drive her mad. I wanted her to beg me for inserting my dick inside her. So I slowly lowered my head and started kissing inside of her thighs. She was moaning with pleasure and twisting her legs. She was eager for penetration. But I continued to kiss her thighs and slowly moved towards her pussy. As I got near her pussy the aroma of her pubic region was driving me mad. This was totally different from her armpits and was much stronger as I got nearer. Her moaning and twisting was increased. I was not giving her what she was anticipating instead I was firing her up.

"Oh Raja what are you doing honey just come inside me I want to feel you there I want you to rip that hole apart between my legs. Ahhhh Rajaaaaaa get inside honey just get inside your mom's choot(pussy)" she was now aching to be loved.

I ignored her and moved my mouth over her pussy lips and

planted a soft kiss over them. Suddenly her body trembled and she grabbed my hair and started to pull me towards her. But I did not move instead I started to kiss her pussy lips frantically. She was out of control and was twisting violently in the bed. Next I slipped my tongue over her pussy lips and started licking and kissing them.

"Oh my God Rajaaaaaaa Sssss Ahhhhhh" she moaned loudly.

I ignored her and continued to lick her. Then I pushed my tongue inside her vagina to the extent I could and started to move it in a circular motion licking the vaginal walls. The taste of her juices and the aroma was driving me mad. It was like a slightly salty solution. My mom was now twisting frantically in the bed. Her breathing had increased and her voluptuous breasts were swaying as she twisted.

"Pleaaaaasee Rajaaaaa get inside me nowwwwww" She screamed.

I had driven her mad. But for me this was not enough. I wanted her to beg. So I lifted my head and glanced at her.

"Yes my good boy now get in don't make me wait any longer mom needs your penis desperately" she said in a hoarse voice.

"Ok mom" I said.

"Yesssss" She said and placed her hands over her thighs and tried to part her legs which were already parted to the limit. I placed my rock hard dick over her pussy lips and instead of inserting it I began to rub them with it. I pressed my dick hard on her pussy lips and began to slide it over her pussy lips and her clitoris. I was rubbing the lips very hard but as I reached her clitoris I slowed down taking care just to rub it gently or just tap it teasingly. My mom's body was exploding with anticipation but I was not letting my dick go inside her. She was driven to the point where she could no longer hold. She was now beyond any control all she wanted was my dick inside her body and nothing else.

"Rajaaaaaaaa please push it in I can't hold any longer, you will kill me" her voice was shaking terribly.

I continued to do what I was doing ignoring her plea.

"Oh my God Rajaaaaaa Pleaaassssee . Please Raja get inside me." She pleaded.

I still ignored her.

"Aaaaighhh Rajaaaaaa I beg you please Raja please" This time she literally folded her hands in a begging gesture. She was on fire and about to explode and needed my dick very badly. I was also on fire by now and my dick was paining as it has gathered blood from all parts of my body. So I gently pushed by dick inside her pussy for the first time.

"Ssssshhhhhh Aaaahhhh Wow Raja Aaahhhh you almost made mama cry" she moaned with pleasure.

I started to move in and out in her slippery pussy. Although slippery it was still clasping my dick and her pussy lips were getting pulled in and out as I moved in and out of it. As I continued to move in and out of her pussy it started to leak with her juices wetting my balls and her buttocks and eventually wetting the bed sheet. There was no time to stop and stare I increased my speed a little.

"Sssshhh Aaaah Rajaaaa you are pulling me in and out wow Sssshhhh Ahhhhhh"

"Mom you are so tight mom" I said

"Aggghhhhh Rajaaaaa tear my hole apart I want to be ravished by you today"

I increased my speed further.

"Yesss like this Ssssshhh Agghhhh"

Her beautiful voluptuous breasts were swaying as I moved in and out of her pussy.

"Faster Raajaa tear me apaaaaaart" She screamed.

I began to move my dick inside her hole frantically.

"Ohhhh mom I can't hold any longer" I screamed.

My mom was also nearing her climax. She was arching her back and raising her waist to offer her pussy to me. She did this when she was nearing her climax.

"Do it Rajaaaa filll me filll my choot just flood it with your seeds" she screamed.

"Ssssshhhhh Aggghhhhhhhhh"

I came inside her pussy shooting warm semen over her cervix and walls of her vagina.

She arched her back and almost screamed.

"Sssssssshhhhh Aaaaiiiiiiighhhhaaaaaaaaaaaaa"

She too came violently. She pulled me over her body and clamped by buttocks with her legs and dug her nails in my back. She wanted every millimeter of my penis inside her pulsating pussy I could not feel her pulsations but I knew they were there. Her body was shivering and she had closed her eyes tightly. Waves of ecstasy were running through our bodies as we were melting in to each other's arms. Time stood still, we were drowned in an ocean of pleasure and joy. I don't know how long we were in that position. But ultimately my mom loosened her grip and we separated. My mom fell asleep. I knew this must have been a very satisfying orgasm for her. I had seen this happen only twice. I watched my mom's beautiful naked body. Her hands were over her head exposing her beautiful unshaved underarms and her legs were slightly parted with my semen dripping out of her pussy. She was in a state of bliss. I slowly covered her and went into the bathroom to cleanup myself. When I returned my mom had not moved an inch she was sleeping blissfully. I put on my shorts and slept beside her.

The next day morning when she woke up she looked at me and blushed and came into my arms. She rested her head against my chest and said.

"You almost killed me with pleasure yesterday"

"You liked it na mom?" I asked.

She did not say anything but nodded her head and blushed and then hugged me tight.

We still live in the same house. The outside world doesn't have a clue what goes inside our house. I am 36 and she is 55 but we have a great sex life. At one stage my mom wanted a baby (when she was 45 I think) but I thought it was too risky at her age beside she had to undergo a surgery to correct her tied tubes. She still rues the fact that she could not become pregnant from me.

Meanwhile I married Anuradha the beauty on whom I had a crush. I am a father of two beautiful kids one boy and one girl. Sex is great between me and my wife. But I and my mom always find a way to see each other. My mom lives downstairs while me and my family lives upstairs in the same house. Anyway life is great for us and I wish this goes on forever.

7. Anu

Anu was standing in the kitchen looking out of the window. She is working as a maid in the house of a rich landlord. She is on this job for past few months and apparently facing problem as she is having a six month old kid, which feeds on her breast which drains almost every time. She is a dark complexioned woman who has taken up this job due to dire necessities. The child of her is born due to an illegitimate relationship with a drunkard who rapes her one night when she was alone in her home. She got the job due the sympathetic corner of her story and the kind nature of the landlord made it very easy. While she was busy finding a life she wish looking out of the window, suddenly her baby lying on the sofa of the dining room started crying aloud.

"Oh again it got hungry. Need to feed it."

She unbuttons her tight blouse slowly and then gently circles her chocolate brown areolas. She then gently presses her protruded nipples and white milk oozes down her breast to her flat slim belly.

"Yes it's full now. Good time to feed the baby."

She walks out from the kitchen with her left breast open, dangling and oozing droplets of milk. She picks up the baby and carries her to the nearby room designated by the landlord for her. She makes herself comfortable in the bed and hugging the baby close to her breast she just carelessly thrusts the nipple on the baby's mouth as if she doesn't like nurturing the baby at all. The baby that was crying since long eventually stopped crying while started suckling on the huge breast. After a while Anu finds her baby asleep.

"The baby has almost suckled one of my breasts dry. If Aniket returns and finds no milk while suckling he will be mad at me. I better drink some milk and have some food to replenish my breasts before he is back from his school." She gets up from the bed and walks off to the kitchen to check out some food from the refrigerator. She drinks a bottle of cold milk and comes back to the dining hall sofa and lies down unhooking her blouse, leaving her two sexy breasts open for Aniket. Aniket is son of the landlord who is 20 years old and studying in high school. He fascinates Anu's breast and so do Anu loves him suckling and biting on her massive soft boobs. She would rather keep the baby unfed and feed Aniket. She likes the way Aniket teases her nipples which makes her pussy wet. More than nurturing she takes it as a way to enjoy sexual ecstasy. While lying there she falls asleep until she feels sudden warmth on her areolas and a tremor of snug pain around her left breast. She opens her eyes and finds Aniket devouring on her breast wildly, biting her nipples hard.

"Ah! It pains." Anu moans. "How many times I said you not to bite my nipples hard. It pains a lot. I know you are mad with hunger but be a bit polite suckling on my tits."

Aniket stops for a moment and then starts off with a complaining face "Aunty your breast milk is getting declined in taste day by day and today you even forgot to smudge your nipples in honey. It's really tasteless for which I am forced to suck on them harder to draw more milk to feel the test."

Anu was searching for an issue to get this handsome young stud to give her a good fuck. She uses this issue to tempt the young boy to give her a good fuck in order to enjoy her lovely breast milk. She apparently pulls her breast out of Aniket's mouth.

"What happened?" exclaimed Aniket.

"My little sweet heart I am not a milking cow that I will provide you creamy milky tits throughout the year. I need to get fucked in order to produce sweet milk. Even a cow needs to get fucked for producing milk. So if you aren't ready for fucking me then forget to suck those chocolaty nipples."

"No no I will do whatever you say. Please don't stop feeding me breast milk. But I wonder that if I fuck you and you become pregnant, then things will turn over me real bad."

"Don't worry for that I have emergency contraceptive pills with me that would help to avoid any unwanted pregnancies. You just do your job. From now onwards you will fuck me at least three times a day for a month or else forget about my milk."

Aniket nodded and agreed at the deal. Both then headed towards Anu's bedroom. Anu undressed herself and helped Aniket in undressing his clothes too. Then Anu went down for Aniket's dick. She only started rubbing it and the whole four inch slug thickened into a rod of six inch. Anu tried to swallow it but it was so huge in size that she could only lick its big head. Aniket who was getting really heated grabbed her hairs and thrusts his tool onto her throat and starts stroking.

"Uh, suck it bitch. Taste my meat you huge breasted whore." In the mean while Aniket reaches orgasm and cums out a thick load of sperms down her throat. Anu engulfs the whole load with much difficulty almost chocking her to breath. After that she resorts to bed exhausted and panting. Aniket who was still hard now climbs up to bed and lies on top of Anu caressing her black nipples.

"Aniket I am tired and exhausted, so please don't fuck me now. If you want to suck my milk then go for it but no sex further" says Anu with a sullen tone.

But Aniket was much worried about getting qualitative creamy breast milk. Therefore instead of stopping he removes Anu's panty and makes her completely nude. After that he starts fingering her puffy pussy. Anu was already exhausted but soon got into excitement and started moaning and shivering with pleasure. The eternal bliss that she was enjoying was coming out with the momentarily spurting milk that was leaking from her swollen breast. Aniket notices that and slowly suckles up the milk.

"See aunty, if teasing your pussy makes you produce sweet milk then what will happen if I fuck you regularly. Then there will be enough milk for your baby and even for me and I can enjoy on those huge chocolaty nipples anytime I feel like."

"Ok fine but I am tired and I can't take more. Please I beg you stop this for today from tomorrow I promise that I will undress myself and become your whore anytime you want me to do," pleads Anu.

Her pleadings didn't make any difference. Aniket divided her legs and positioned his cock in front of Anu's love hole. The moment he tried to thrust it, he felt it became really tight due to excitement. Suddenly he felt pity on Anu so he reached for a moisturizing cream and smeared his cock with it. Then he clasped Anu's hand and dodged his entire six inch tool into her soft hole with a single powerful stroke. Anu cried aloud due to pain. She couldn't bear the penetration of the huge shaft and became unconscious instantly. She lied in the bed like a helpless prey in hands of a predator. Tears rolled down her reddened chicks. Her pain created more excitement for Aniket and he then started stroking violently. Anu's tight love hole was bleeding due to violent strokes. The tight muscles of her vagina kept on tightening so hard that within few minutes Aniket climaxed. He lied exhausted on top of her for a while then got up to check up her milk.

Anu was still lying unconscious and was moaning "My pussy is burning. Bastard, stop it now and have mercy on me."

"Yes aunty, I will leave you alone but let me test your sweet milk that you have produces in your chocolaty breast."

Aniket engraves his teeth on one of Anu's creamy soft breast and started sucking it. While sucking the left breast he started squeezing her right breast and a stream of milk started flowing from it. Aniket quickly shifted to her right breast and as he pressed his teeth a flow of fresh warm milk flooded his mouth. He gradually had his third erection in the process and wanted to cum again on her love hole. Anyways his cock was inside her pussy which was now pressing against the wall of Anu's vagina. Anu in the mean while gained some strength and consciousness could feel the twitching of his cock inside. Anu made some deliberate noises to get Aniket excited and bring the session to a fast end. The pain was getting more intense every moment. Aniket and Anu started working on together this time. Aniket's each and every stroke rocked her hips, resulting in tremulous shuddering of Anu's body. At last Aniket filled her Inner walls of her pussy with his love juices. Just then the baby cries and Anu pushes Aniket aside and wipes out the love juices smearing his cock with her blouse and walks off to the bathroom to get fresh. When she came back refreshed she picked up the baby from the cradle and came to her bed. Aniket was still lying exhausted probably asleep. She looked at Aniket's face and saw the exhaustion in his face and she felt pity on him. She adjusted Aniket and her kid side by side and then opened her blouse. Then she gave the right breast to the baby for suckling and thrusts the left breast into Aniket's mouth.

"Hey, come on suckle the milk" said Anu as she apparently felt that Aniket has fallen asleep. She squeezes her breast and milks out into Aniket's mouth and once again he started to suckle and started biting her nipples softly. "Oh, stop biting bastard," says Anu biting her lips and enjoying the ecstasy.

8. Mansi

"The boss and his wife want to take us out to dinner." Bharat announced when he got home.

"When?" I asked, knowing that this time I really didn't have a thing to wear. With a four-month old baby, Bharat's lousy salary and me not working, we couldn't afford a new dress anyway. Well, not anything that would compare with the creations Mrs. Walia wore. Perhaps I should wear an old one I wore to the Christmas party then perhaps Mr. Walia would take pity on us and give Bharat a raise.

"Next Friday." Bharat answered, "and don't say you haven't got a thing to wear. There's always your black and white dress."

"My black and white dress?" I echoed. I knew Bharat loved it. Very low at the front and no back at all. The skirt was separate panels that showed my legs (and sometimes more) when I moved. Before the baby it really pushed my 36B's out. Now, with milk laden 36DD's I would practically fall out of it. Precisely what Bharat had in mind! Perhaps Mr. Walia would also be impressed and give Bharat a raise!

On Friday I skipped lunch. Luxuriating in a bubble bath instead, I gave myself a mini-makeover. I shaved my legs, under my arms and attacked the stubble on my mons. My pussy hair had been shaved when the baby was born and now was at an uncomfortable length, neither long nor short. I knew Bharat would prefer me shaved, but I just hadn't had time to deal with things like that. I spent a long time doing my hair and makeup and then slipped on the little black and white dress. I tucked my boobs inside it as best I could, but decided that there really was a little too much showing. Although that would be alright in the confines of the restaurant, in the street I needed to be more covered up. I took out my favorite little black jacket and tried that on. I liked the effect and took it off again. Lifting the front panel of the skirt, I admired my shaved pussy in the full-length mirror. I could feel how juicy I was getting and put my foot on the dresser next to the mirror to get a better look. Dipping two fingers deep inside my juicy pussy, I smeared the moisture on the sides of my neck and under my chin

The doorbell rang. It was the babysitter. I hadn't realized what time it was, I had been enjoying myself too much.

Giving the babysitter final instructions and the phone number of the restaurant, I jumped in the car, jacket over my arm and drove downtown to the restaurant. I knew Bharat and Mr. Walia would already be there.

Sure enough, they were sitting opposite each other in a booth. Bharat got up and kissed me.

"You look wonderful, darling." he said, allowing me to slip passed him into the booth.

"Nice to see you again, Mansi," said Mr. Walia, shaking hands with me across the table. "Bharat has been telling me all about the new addition." We continued to talk about babies until Mrs. Walia arrived. She sat opposite me and while she and I continued to talk babies, the men talked business.

We were on our third round of drinks when I began to feel a slight dampness in the boob area. I knew what was happening, my boobs were leaking milk. I excused myself, covering the wet patches on my dress as best I could with my arms. Mrs. Walia said, "I'll come with you my dear."

Once in the Ladies Room, she took a firm hold of my arm and pulled me into one of the stalls, kicking the door closed behind her.

"I know what the problem is, she said, "And I know how to solve it." She took a wad of toilet paper and as she extracted my left breast from my dress, which was easy to do, applied the toilet paper to the damp spot. She did the same with the other breast so I was left standing there, both boobs exposed and two large wads of TP stuck on my dress. Bending down, she took one swollen nipple in her mouth and began to suck. I could feel the relief of pressure almost immediately.

"Your milk is delicious." she announced as she came up for air "It's been a long time since I tasted anything quite so wonderful." Then she went to work on the other one, suckling for all she was worth. It was tremendously erotic watching this older lady sucking on my boobs, and although Bharat had done it many times, it seemed more erotic with her. Here I was, standing in the Ladies Room of a restaurant with a woman whom I didn't know very well, suckling the life-giving sustenance from my full breasts. I could feel my pussy begin to juice up.

Mrs. Walia was obviously aware of the effect she was having on me. Her hand found its way between the panels of my skirt and touched my freshly shaven mons. A low moan of appreciation came from her lips as she stroked around my pussy, eventually finding my clitoris. She continued to suck hard on my distended nipples as now she also worked on my erect clitoris. I could feel my knees weaken as the orgasm welled up deep inside me. She continued with insistent strokes on my clit, occasionally dipping her fingers deep inside my sopping pussy. She took my nipple between her teeth and pulled away from me, stretching it out. My knees buckled as I came, and I practically fell on the floor, but Mrs. Walia saved me. She sat me on the john to catch my breath. Lovingly she caressed my boobs as she adjusted them inside my dress and asked if I was ready to go.

"As ready as I'll ever be." I replied.

Mrs. Walia picked up both our purses and taking five crisp $100 bills from hers, slid them into my purse.

"This is for you." she said. "I know what a cheapskate my husband is, and I know you could use the money. Use some of it to buy a new dress for the next time we do this."

Did she mean the next time we all had dinner together or the next time she attacked me in the Ladies Room? In the four years Bharat had worked for Mr. Walia we had only met socially four or five times. Did she mean we were going out to dinner more frequently from now on? Just in case, I resolved to buy something I could get my boobs out of as easily as this little black and white dress.

9. Jeet

I have been having a sexual relationship with my mother for the last 4 years now. My mother is slim, with firm 38DD breasts and an ass you just cannot take your hands off. She wears only sarees with silk sleeveless blouses which show a lot of creamy cleavage, and through which, if you see closely, you can see her nipples protruding.

It all started when I caught my mother getting fucked by my uncle. He was around 35 yrs old, a family friend and I used to call him uncle because he was like a brother to my mother, or so I thought. I used to call him Jeet Uncle.

One day, I had come from school early, and since I had my own key, entered the house. I was about to enter the kitchen when I heard some voices, one pleading and the other authorities. The pleading voice belonged to my mother and the other voice belonged to Jeet uncle. Something was fishy about the way they were talking so I hid in the bathroom and waited out there where I could hear and see both of them clearly. My mother was saying, "Jeet, I really need some money as I lost rs.10,000 in a bet with my friend, and it is imperative that my family doesn't find out."

"How much do you need?" asked Jeet Uncle. "Around rs.15,000," said my mom. "But I will not be able to repay you for a year."

On hearing this , Jeet uncle replied, "See, I can lend you the money, but if you want me to keep my mouth shut, you shall have to pay me."

"Pay you with what? I don't have any money. If I had, I wouldn't be asking you for a loan." replied my mother.

"Oh, I don't want money" said Jeet Uncle.

"Then what do you want?" asked my mother.

On hearing this, he put his hand on my mother's face, slid it down to her shoulders and then suddenly slipped it down to her blouse and gave her left breast a firm squeeze. "I want this." said Jeet.

On hearing this, my mother got angry and asked him to get out. To which he replied, "Think about it, there is no one who will lend you money and keep his mouth shut. You don't have any other choice, Unless of course, you want your husband to find out."

Tears came to my mother's eyes as she realized that she really did not have any other choice. "All right, what do you want?" asked my mother. "I want to own your body for the next one year" he said. "Okay, but my husband and my son should never find out." He gave her the money, and waited till she kept the money in the safe and came back.

When she came close to him, he caught hold of her hand and pulled her close to him. "Sit on my lap and face me." said Jeet uncle. My penis started twitching as I saw my mother's perfect buttocks being placed on his lap. He held her face with both hands and kissed her mouth. Then he slid her pallu down to her waist to reveal her firm melons in her blouse. He ran a hand over my mother's breasts and thoroughly squeezed her boobs. He then started kissing her neck and went down to her cleavage licking at her creamy and delicious cleavage.

Then he started unbuttoning her blouse. he removed my mom's blouse and finally revealed to me her firm breasts in her lacy half-cut brassiere. He removed her bra and exposed her full, firm milky breasts with dark brown nipples. He started sucking on them vigorously. Then he took her hand and led her to the bedroom. I followed them to the bedroom hoping to see more action, but unfortunately, the door was closed and I couldn't get through without them knowing it.

The next day, my mother was wearing a green silk sari with a low cut silk sleeveless blouse, a blouse in which I had jacked off hundreds of times. I was sitting at the dining table and she was serving me. That time, my dad had gone for a trip and was not expected for around 3 months. From across the table, she bent to serve me, giving me an excellent view of her creamy cleavage. Seeing that, I got really hard. After dinner, me and my mom were sitting on the sofa watching T.V., when we got talking.

While we were talking, I casually put my hands on her melons and squeezed them. On seeing this, she slapped me and said, "You little bastard, what the fuck do you think you were doing?"

I slapped her back and said, "Shut up you slut, I know all about you and Jeet uncle."

On hearing this she was shocked and then slowly started crying. I said, "I want your body mom, and if you don't want me to tell dad, you will have to bear with anything I do to you."

Saying this, I put my hands on her breasts again and fondled them. She said, "Okay, we'll do anything you say, but we cannot have sex. I'm your mother, for god's sake!" Getting what I wanted, I quickly agreed.

I removed the pallu of her blouse and made her sit next to me. I started fondling her breasts through her blouse and then started unbuttoning it. I removed her blouse totally. Then I saw my mother in her bra, with her breasts straining to get out. I then removed her bra and then started sucking on my mother's nipples. After sucking her breasts for what seemed like ages, I took hold of her head and pressed her mouth to my hard dick. I made her remove my jeans and rammed my dick into her deliciously soft mouth. After a few strokes, I was so horny that I came in her mouth and forced her to swallow my cum.

After that incident, I was very free with my mother's breasts. Everyday after school, I used to go home, remove my mother's blouse and suck and squeeze her breasts. Even while serving food, I used to just reach over under my mother's pallu and lift up her blouse and start sucking on her breasts.

10. Sarita

I got the guts to narrate a incident that happened in my life 2 yrs ago. I am Nakkhul from Chennai working for an MNC and I m 22 yrs old. We are a family of 4, my dad, my mom, my younger sister and me. My dad owns a small scale industries and he keeps roaming half the time in search of new clients. My mom Sarita, is about 44 yrs old and she is a housewife. We are a quite well of family. Now let me describe about my mom, she is fair, slim, about 58 kgs and she is very very hot. Her structure must be like 34-30-34. Seems she was a babe during her college days and my dad was lucky enough to get her during that time. There have been times when i have noticed that people keep staring at my mom's assets even when i am with her.

Now let me start narrating the story, this happened during my final year of engineering. I was enjoying my study holidays for my final semester at home, and one evening my mom asked me if i could accompany her for shopping. Since i was feeling bored i agreed to join her and we started off to T nagar in our car. After shopping for quite bit, my mom wanted to give her cloth for stitching her blouse. Generally she bring a sample cloth to give it to the tailor for measurement. This time i was aware that she didn't get one with her. Since it was very crowded at T nagar that day, i asked my mom to go and give the blouse for stitching and told her that i will wait in the car. The tailor shop is at the first floor. My mom went up to the shop to give the cloth to the tailor.

After waiting for about 10 mins, I luckily found a place to park my car and since i was getting bored, decided to go upstairs to join my mom and also was wondering why it was taking time.

Generally my mom just gives the cloth to the tailor and return back within 5 mins. When i reached upstairs i noticed that there is were no helper boys working. The entire shop was empty. When i was about to enter, i was hearing my mom and the tailor speaking (his name is Sahil).

I didn't go inside immediately and was waiting outside and tried to peep inside, i heard the tailor saying that he doesn't have any measurements with him and was asking my mom to bring a spare blouse. My mom didn't know what to do and was keeping quite. By this time i got the chance to peep in and noticed that they both were in another room inside, i went to the window from the main room and started peeping inside. After a lot of confusion, the tailor asked my mom if he can take the measurement there itself. After a bit of hesitation my mom agreed and the tailor came out with a tape from his drawn and came close to my mom.

He first asked my mom to turn around and started taking the measurement. I first thought that he was a decent man, but suddenly i noticed that he was staring at my moms back. After taking the measurement on the backside, he asked my mom to turn toward him, my mom didn't remove her pallu and was waiting for the tailor to take the measurements like that itself, but the tailor didn't move at all and was asking my mom how he can take the measurement without my mom removing her pallu, my mom was very hesitant and dint know how to react, while speaking itself the tailor came close to my mom and removed her pallu from her shoulder without her permission and my mom was just taken aback in a shock. The tailor then started taking the measurement from her shoulder to her belly, at this time his hands were brushing my moms boobs in the front and this aroused my mom to a great extent.

And next the tailor took the measurement in the side ways and the tape was over her boobs this time. My mom without knowing what to tell, was just waiting for this one to get over.

Next the tailor kept the starting of the tape from the nipple and was taking the measurement, my mom was completely aroused now and she closed her eyes in ecstasy, the tailor looking at my mom, started pressing her nipple from the blouse itself. Suddenly my mom asked the tailor "what are u doing?". He responded that he wanted to take the measurements properly and he started to unbutton my mom's blouse. My mom without protesting kept quite and she was definitely horny by now. By now, the tailor removed my mom's blouse and my mom was in was just in her bra and i could clearly see my mom's cleavage and this caused a huge tent in my pant.

Now the tailor started taking the measurements again and now he was pressing my mom's boobs harder. My mom was completely out of her senses and she was enjoying the entire scene. I was shocked by her reaction to his pressing. The tailor looking at my mom, got to understand that she needed some attention and he went behind her and started unbuttoning her bra, my mom suddenly realized this and asked the tailor, "what are u doing".

The tailor said, "Nothing Sarita just trying to take the exact measurements". My mom was shocked hearing that the tailor was calling her by the name, but by this time she has already submitted herself to his seduction. Guess she wasn't fucked by my dad for a long time. Within a flash, the tailor removed the bra and he started taking the measurements again, my mom by now has started breathing heavily and she was letting out light moans. The tailor taking advantage of the situation decided to take the initiative and started pressing my moms left boobs from behind, and my mom was now completely in his control and she was resting her head in his shoulders. The tailor now threw her bra away and he now started pressing both the boobs madly. I was completely shocked that my mom didnt even show the slightest of resistance to his entire act.

By now, my mom turned around and the tailor planted a deep

kiss in her mouth. They kissed for a while before the tailor started to remove my moms dress one by one. And in the mean time, my mom was busy unbuttoning his pant and she pulled out what could be called as a monster cock, it was about 10 inches in size and my mom was just taken aback.

The tailor now, held my moms head and guided it to his cock and she took his tool in her hand, her hand was not covering it full. She started stroking his cock as the tailor sat on sofa in that room, smiling and mom too giving him naughty smile, "how you feeling Sahil?" she asked. Sahil smiling and said, "aaaahhhh gooodd take it mouth then I will know how good you are." At his order, mom immediately his tool in her mouth. She was not able to take it full it was so huge. Sahil pressed her head on his dick, mom was taking it inch by inch and in few strokes it entered her mouth completely. She was sucking it faster now.

Sahil was moaning loud, "yyessss mam take it all yyessss aaaaahhh hhhhmm mam you are a great cock suckerrrrr" He was pressing her head to go deeper in her, it was touching her throat, mom was sucking it faster and as he was going to cum, he held his cock tight, "mam I am gonna cum" mom looked at him, held his cock tight in her mouth and he shoot cum in her mouth. She drank all the cum and sat on sofa, kissed him. They sucked each other's tongue and enjoying the cum. This time my mom was very wild in her kissing and she was behaving like an actual slut.

After that my mom asked him to fuck her pussy, he obeyed the order and tore her panty, her hairy pussy was exposed, he then starting licking her pussy, she cummed all over his face. Finally he put his shaft around her pussy and starting pressing, It was desperate scene of my mom getting fucked by a the tailor, he started hammering her pussy faster and faster, she asked him to slow down, but he didn't not hear to that and he was just ramming it deep into her with strong and hard strokes. It was able to hear sounds like chup chup chup. mom with pleasure and pain was moaning like "aaaahhh aaaaaaahh hhmmmmmmm oooohhhhh yyyessssssss fuckkk me harder-rrrrrr yyessss fasterrrrrrrrr deeeppeeerrrrrrrrr ooooohhhh aaaaahhh yyesssssss."

He slowed down for a moment, while mom raising her hips to get him more inside, he then again increased his speed, he was touching her g-point again and again and mom was experiencing the real pleasure, it was clearly visible on her face, her expression, her action, holding him tight and she climaxed. But he was not yet complete, she looked at him, "mam, I can delay my orgasm to longer period to give you immense pleasure."

I also attributed, after that when I went to see what is happening next, I was amazed to see the scene, my mom made the tailor to lay down on the sofa and she started licking his dick he cummed on her face the final part was more interesting, he asked him to give her a ride she then sits on the tailors dick and starting riding his dick. He was under enormous pressure and he started cumming in her pussy. She initially scolded him for cumming in her pussy and told him that she might get pregnant.

But she said that she will manage by sleeping with my dad who'll be back by next weekend. She said that it was time for her to get ready and that i would be waiting down. I sensed that she was getting ready and went down into the car; the mom came after about 5 mins and apologized to me saying that it was over crowded in the tailor shop. But I only knew the actual reason why it took such a long time.

11. Sita

My older brother Rohan had everything in life, so it seemed. He had been blessed with extraordinary good looks and intelligence. Although he did have a rather quirky side, for the most part you could call him the American-Indian male, at least in public.

Rohan graduated from Pitt law school and then joined my father's firm. A couple years later he married his college sweetheart, Laurie. They often talked about having children, many children. Laurie and I became very close. She even confided in me about their wonderful sex life. Although Laurie admitted, with a wink, that Rohan liked to get kinky on occasion. And she said she readily indulged his fetish because she loved him so much.

Kinky? Well, I did know Rohan liked to wear lingerie. I first discovered that fact one day when I came home from school early because I didn't feel well and I found Rohan in my bedroom... Naked. Going through my dresser drawers. I watched him pick out a bra and admire it. Then he turned and saw me. He didn't seem startled.

I didn't know what to say, so I said, "Uh ... uh ... Rohan ... so you like my push-up racerback bra?" I didn't think it would be wise to comment on his huge boner. At that point in my life I wasn't too sure what I might be expected do with such a thing.

"Yes, it's lovely. What color is this?" he asked as he licked the insides of the cups.

"Periwinkle," I replied.

I hurried out then, saying I had to get back to school. So I went back and suffered with the cramps. Better than watching my brother act like a pervert I thought. I never said anything about that incident but every time Rohan came home from college I knew he had been into my intimate apparel. And his fraternity became infamous for clandestine panty raids. The coeds complained vociferously that the thieves not only took panties, but bras as well. They bitched incessantly about having nothing to wear under their tight sweaters. But nobody else complained. University police thought the matter rather humorous and gave the main culprits names like Bra-man and Thong-dong.

Once when Rohan came home on break I got into his laptop computer when he went out with his buddies. I wouldn't exactly call it porn. Breasts. He had thousands of pictures of breasts, every size and shape imaginable. And then I opened his briefcase. Victoria's Secret catalogues. He had circled some of the bras with a magic marker. He didn't circle the girl in the bra, just the breasts in the bra.

I also found a notebook in his briefcase. He doodled. Not that he could draw but I knew what they were supposed to be when he put one or two word captions under the pictures like bahama mamas, balloons, bawagos, bazongoes, bazookas, beamers, bee stings, big brown eyes, blinkers, bodacious tatas, bombs, bosom, boulders, Bristols (English--if you've never been hit on by an English dude and seen the "Aaah, Bistol" advertisements you won't get this one. Bristols is rhyming slang, short for Bristol cities, meaning titties), brown suckies, bust, Cadillac bumper bullets, and on and on and on through the rest of the alphabet.

But time passed and I mostly forgot about Rohan's little idiosyncrasies.

* * *

Laurie died just hours after giving birth after she developed a massive pulmonary embolism. The sheer joy of the new baby became lost in the despair of a mother's death.

"Sita, you must help your brother through this difficult time," my mother softly to me after the funeral.

"Yes, Mother, so I must."

* * *

I didn't take me long to begin producing milk. A friend of mine with no neck hooked me up with his drug dealer, an unscrupulous Scottish pharmaceutical executive who was in the States to peddle "Stiffy" in the black market (that's the subject of my next story, "Size Matters, But A Stiffy Matters More"). But no steroids for me. I took massive dosages of Domperidone.

Rohan named the baby Laurence. "Just don't call him Laurie," I cautioned. "It's Larry."

I moved into Rohan's house to take care of the baby. Rohan took a few days bereavement leave and then went back to the office. My father thought it best that Rohan immerse himself in work and Dad immediately gave him a big case.

Larry slept a lot and hardly fussed, except when he was hungry. But when Rohan would try to feed the baby the bottle, Larry wouldn't drink it and my brother wondered why. I didn't tell him what Larry liked to suck on. My mother watched the baby during the day while I worked. But only being a few blocks away, I shook loose several times a day to feed Larry. Or Mother brought him there and I gave him a drink in her car in the parking lot.

My parents and I hounded Rohan to go out with his friends some time and have a little fun. He just seemed so depressed. Finally, Rohan agreed.

Rohan's friend Bharat came over to pick him up. He came in for awhile and had a beer.

"Where are you guys going?" I asked Bharat as Rohan finished in the shower.

"Hooters at Station Square is having a big bash. Free wings with every pitcher of beer. But I don't like wings."

"Oh, you don't?" I inquired, just making conversation.

"No, I like the breast."

"Just like Rohan," I muttered knowingly.

"What, Sita? I didn't hear you."

"Why is it that the male of the species is so fascinated with breasts?" I snapped irritably, partly because he had been trying diligently to look down the front of my brand new AIX Armani Exchange white silk open-back halter dress. I hadn't worn a bra. The boss had told me to get all dolled up for work that day to impress some important clients. So I did. But I couldn't party with them that night I had insisted because I had to care for my infant nephew. The dudes looked so disappointed.

"Huh?" Bharat blurted.

"You know--boobs--tits."

"Well . . . I . . . uh . . . it . . . uh . . . they . . ."

Just then Rohan walked in the living room and saved his friend from further embarrassment. They, at Bharat's urging, left in a hurry.

I looked through Rohan's collection of old movies and decided on The Pawnbroker with Rod Steiger. I had seen it before and really liked it.

Soon I slipped off my dress and lounged around in nothing but my panties. I crashed on the couch and fell asleep watching the movie. Hours later I heard Larry fussing and went and got him. Immediately he latched onto my nipple and went at it greedily. I took him to the living room, started the movie over, and fed him on the couch.

And then Rohan walked in.

"What the . . . Sita . . . what . . . what are you doing?"

"Watching The Pawnbroker. Rod Steiger was nominated for an Oscar for this flick. Do you remember that 'blood on my hands!' final scene?"

"I kind of . . . uh . . . well . . . after I saw . . . uh . . . the rack on that black chick . . . I can't remember what happened after that."

"True, the movie did set a new industry standard for frontal nudity," I expounded. "Rohan, is that all you think about-- boobs?"

"Uh . . . well . . . I must . . . uh . . . say that yours are rather impres-sive, my dear sister. But why are you lying on the couch with Larry in nothing but your panties?"

"I'm teaching him how to please a woman, Rohan," I joked. "It's best a dude gets started learning early because many men don't seem to be able to grasp the fundamentals." I snickered, think-ing of my last lover. He had never performed cunnilingus until he met me, and once I "taught" him he never wanted to stop. Which was fine most of the time but people do have to sleep. Unfortunately he got transferred to San Francisco and phone sex just didn't seem an adequate substitute for what we had to-gether in person. So I got a dog instead.

Larry had lost my nipple when he fell asleep. Now he opened his eyes and looked at his father with what I swear seemed like a twinkle in his eyes. "He's the one who looks pleased," Rohan remarked.

"Rohan, you remember that picture of you and Mother when you were a baby and she was breastfeeding you? The one I always laugh at every time I look at it. Mother says she didn't wean you until you could talk. According to her, the first sentence you ever said was, 'I want the breasty!' Like father, like son."

"Why yes, of course I remember, Sita." He stared at me even more intently, focusing his eyes on the area between my neck and navel.

Just then Larry latched onto my nipple again and began to gobble hungrily.

"Yes, that's right, Rohan, I'm breastfeeding your son."

"But . . . how . . . what . . . how . . ."

"Oh, don't be so naïve, Rohan. Many adoptive mothers are able to breastfeed. Why, even some men breastfeed. Don't you listen to Rush Limbaugh?"

"You know, I do recall him talking about it. I don't think he likes the idea."

Rohan sat beside me on the couch as I nursed Larry. He looked at me so . . . so . . .

"What is it, Rohan? You are looking at me quite oddly."

"Not oddly, my dear sister--lustfully. I want the other one."

"Huh?"

"I want to suck your other nipple. Please, Sis? Laurie told me she would let me breastfeed."

"She did?"

"Yes. She knew how much it would mean to me. Won't you let me breastfeed, Sita?"

"I just don't don't know . . ."

"Sita, did you know that your breasts are lopsided? Larry prefers the right one, doesn't he?" I nodded in affirmation. "You're going to end up with boobs that don't match and you'll either need an implant for the smaller one or breast reduction surgery on the bigger one."

"Oh my God!" I wailed. I shrugged in resignation. He was my dear brother, and he had been through so much with the death of his beloved wife. "Don't drool on my puppies. They don't like slobber."

Larry had fallen asleep again. Rohan picked him up and put him in his crib. My brother returned to me and began to tease and tweak my nipples with his hands. The tips soon stood at attention. "Nipples are packed with supersensitive nerve endings and there is a direct connection between the nerves in your nipples and your clitoris," Rohan said rather scientifically.

"You need to use your mouth, Rohan," I advised matter-of-factly. "That's the only way you're going to get much milk."

He did, gently biting and playfully pulling on my nipples with his lips. Then he slowly licked my areolas with the flat of his tongue as he would an ice cream cone. And then he latched onto one of my nipples with his mouth and got more into it than even his infant son had done. Rohan got milk. He sure did.

I leaned back, closed my eyes, and let him drink from my left breast. But this felt different than Larry doing it. Really different.

"Rohan, you're so smart. I know you know this. What does breast milk contain? You know, stuff that's good for you?"

He didn't act like he wanted to answer so I pulled him off my nipple.

"Okay, okay." Rohan proceeded to tell me that breast milk contains casein, a fancy word for the special protein that helps to prevent gastroenteritis, respiratory infections, otitis media, some cancers, juvenile diabetes, and allergic reactions. And of course iron, lactose, and Vitamin C. Not to mention DHA--Docosahexaenoic Acid--which encourages brain development and stimulates vision. Oh, and lipase, lactace, and amylase.

"Well, I am worried about your health, Rohan, because you don't eat right. I mean, you bring Taco Bell home every night. Seriously, take a good look at the people who work there. You are what you eat. Now, you go right back to what you were doing." He latched on a nipple again, this time the right one.

"I'm trying to make them look like twins," he paused to comment contentedly.

"Oh my God, I can't believe this is actually turning me on," I moaned softly after about five minutes as I slipped my hand down my panties.

But then I heard Larry fussing again and I lost the mood. I pulled Rohan's face away from my nipple and went to his son. He protested vehemently, "I want the breasty!"

I came back in to the living room with Larry in a few minutes and said, "I shouldn't have let you, Rohan. This isn't right. No more boob juice for you."

* * *

Two days later I got a lecture from my mother as she watched me nurse Larry.

"Sita, breastfeeding is such a natural and beautiful experience, isn't it?"

"Yes Mother, it sure is."

"Rohan spoke to me yesterday, dear. He is so upset. About you not permitting him to ... you know."

I frowned. "Mother, I shouldn't have let him do it that once. A moment of weakness on my part. Do my breasts look lopsided?"

"No, not really. Sita, your brother is still in a state of shock over Laurie's death. We need to humor him."

"You mean you want me to ...?"

"Yes honey, I do."

After contemplating this for several minutes, I finally nodded. "So you think I should be a surrogate wife to Rohan? Until his period of mourning is over and he finds someone new?" Mother nodded solemnly. "Well, I'll tell you this, Mother, I'll breastfeed his son and I'll breastfeed him, but I am not fucking my brother!"

Mother smiled and purred, "Do you recall what my favorite president once said? Oral isn't sex."

"Mother! You want me to suck my brother's cock? I'm ... I'm ..."

"Well, that or let him have sex with your breasts. I just can't stand the thought of Rohan jerking off all the time. It's so juvenile. Once he has sufficiently mourned the death of a wife whom we all loved, he'll find a new someone special. Your familial duty as his only sister is to get him over the hump."

"I am not humping him, Mother!"

"Sita, let me give you some motherly advice."

Mother informed me patiently me that if I digested enough semen I wouldn't have to take vitamins because it contains aboutonia, ascorbic acid, blood-group antigens, calcium, chlorine, choline, citric acid, creatine, deoxyribonucleic acid, fructose, glutathione, hyaluronidase, inositol, lactic acid, magnesium, nitrogen, phosphorous, potassium, purine, pyramiding pyretic acid, sodium, sorbitol, spermadine, spermine, urea, uric acid, Vitamin B-12, and zinc.

"But Mother . . ." I protested.

"One 'typical' serving is only 15 calories! And if you get it in your hair it's much better than any conditioner on the market."

"Mother, I don't worry about calories, I'm not fat!"

"You won't get fat if you suck it instead of fuck it. Not only will you avoid an unwanted pregnancy, women who perform the act of fellatio and swallow semen on a regular basis at least several times a week may reduce their risk of breast cancer by up to 40%!"

"Really?"

"Oh, yes indeed. They did the study at North Carolina State University on over 15,000 women. Why, I have the report right here. Listen to this from Dr. A.J. Kramer of John Hopkins School of Medicine: 'I think this study removes the last shade of doubt that fellatio is actually a healthy act. I am surprised by these findings, but am also excited that the researchers may have discovered a relatively easy way to lower the occurrence of breast cancer in women.' Oh, and Dr. Helena Shifteer, one of the researchers at the university says, 'Only with regular occurrence will your chances be reduced, so I encourage all women out there to make fellatio an important part of their daily routine. Since the emergence of the research, I try to fellate at least once every other night to reduce my chances.' Do you believe me now, Sita?" * * *

That night Rohan came home from work looking rather haggard. I sat on the couch nursing Larry.

"Wow, you look beat, Rohan. Tough case?"

"The jury has been out for twelve hours now. We thought it would be quick. They keep asking to review testimony and exhibits."

"I think you need a drink."

"Yeah, I think I'll make a Long Island Ice Tea. Do you want one?"

"That's not what I meant, Rohan. You can have a drink from my breasts."

"Really?"

"Yes, my dear brother, you can. Now put Larry in his crib. He's asleep."

Rohan returned and sat beside me. He latched onto my left nipple enthusiastically.

Ten minutes passed in which all I heard was hungry suckling. Rohan lifted his head, and belched.

"You sure got milk, honey!" he complimented.

"And what are you going to give me in return, bro?"

"I dunno, what did you have in mind?"

"Well, I need my nourishment too."

"Can I make you dinner?"

I snuggled up to Rohan and gave him kisses all over his face and neck. I licked his lips as if I was lapping an ice-cream cone, sucked on the tip of his tongue, and grazed my lips against his. Then a full-blown lip-lock. He began to get fired up and went for my tits again.

"No Rohan! You had your drink. Now I want mine."

"Drink of what? Hey, I have some Irish Crème."

"Yeah, we are part Irish, bro. I'll take some Irish crème. Make mine with aboutonia, ascorbic acid, blood-group antigens, calcium, chorine, choline, citric acid, creatine, deoxyribonucleic acid, fructose, glutathione, hyaluronidase, inositol, lactic acid, magnesium, nitrogen, phosphorous, potassium, purine, pyramiding pyretic acid, sodium, sorbitol, spermadine, spermine, urea, uric acid, Vitamin B-12, and zinc."

"Huh?"

I had begin to play in his crotch. I unzipped him. He seemed to be getting the idea although he still looked a little puzzled. "Yes, Rohan, I want to drink your cum." I pulled his cock out and began to fondle it. But I couldn't get it to grow. "What's the matter, honey? Don't you want a blow job?"

"Oh Sita, I just feel so guilty about letting my sister giving me head."

"Really? You'll suck my tits but you won't let me suck your dick?"

"It's ... just ... I ... uh ... well ... it ..."

"Did Laurie do fellatio?"

"All the time. She loved to do it."

"So pretend I'm Laurie. I know, we'll put a blindfold on you. Do you have any blindfolds?"

"Uh ... no. But I know what we could use."

"What's that?"

"Your bra."

I glanced at my nursing bra hanging over a chair along with my blouse. "The cups are probably a little milky." "Awesome!" he cried as he fetched the bra and covered his eyes with it. He managed to also cover his nose and mouth with one of the cups. He got an immediate erection. Talk about rising from the dead.

"I want you to cum in my mouth, Rohan." I knelt in front of him and stared at the big throbbing cock about ready to burst inches from my face. "I want your cock in my hungry mouth." I breathed on it gently and then rubbed the tip all over my face. "How bad do you want a blow job, bro?"

"Real bad, my pretty little sister, real bad," he moaned. "I feel like I'm going to explode."

"You are going to explode, Rohan. Right down my throat."

"Do you think I have a big dick, Sita? Laurie is the only one I ever had sex with. She said it was big. But she never had any other dicks, so she also said."

"You sure do have a big dick, Rohan. Really big. Just the way I like it. But not too big. Otherwise I couldn't get it all in my mouth."

"You can get it all in your mouth? Oh my God! Laurie couldn't do that."

"Stayed tuned and I'll show you. You know, I think your dick is too big. I'm going to do you a favor and make it smaller."

"Huh?"

"I'm going to suck it until it gets smaller. Would you like that?"

"Yes, I think I would like that. Very much. You are so beautiful and I'm so glad you're my sister."

"Yeah, your cock-sucking sister. I think you're horny, Rohan, real horny." I stroked his cock with one hand, held his balls in the other hand, as I flicked the head with my tongue. "I think you want to cum in my mouth real bad. I think you want to shoot a big load all over my face and tits, don't you honey?"

"Uh . . . yes . . . I . . . that would be nice."

"Not to worry, baby. I'm going to gobble and guzzle you like you wouldn't believe."

And then I did. I closed my mouth over the head of his cock and slid one hand up and down on the shaft as I gently tugged on his balls with my other hand.

12. Ravi

I am Ravi from Mumbai. I am 25 yrs old and the story I m going to tell is of around two years back. We have a very big family. Whenever there is any function or any issue we come together to get a solution. In this case my grandfather was very serious and my house was full of people. I have a cousin sister who is married and is having a 3 yrs old child. I always had a crush on her. She was 5.4 inch and had a sexy ass. She was fair and smooth skin. She was suppose to come that night. That day slept on the hall with everyone. Around 3 am I felt that there was someone's leg on my stomach. I just kept hand on that leg and what I felt is such a silky skin.. and I took my hand till thighs and there was no cloth till there...

Oh man I opened my eyes and I saw my cousin's leg but her child was sleeping between us. I could see that her sari went totally to her waist and her legs were naked. I just rubbed my hand on them..Oh.... I could not stop myself and I started kissing them slowly... She was sleeping and did not know that I m kissing her legs and licking them...

I moved her child little aside and slept beside her took the blanket on both of us..kept my face in front of her breast and to my surprise her blouse hooks where already removed with only one remaining...I kissed her navel like anything and licked them....with My other hand I slowly pulled up her sari a little and put my hand into her panty.... and I could feel hairy pussy.....my rod stood up.

I unhooked her last button of the blouse looking at her face... what if she gets up. Now she was in boobs were visible to me with bra....I just hugged her and kissed her boobs....and I was rubbing my rod on her panty... Oh shit she opened her eyes...I pretended to sleep hugging her......but she came to know what I was doing...she just pushed me back,

hooked her blouse, pulled her sari down and turned her back and slept...But I was not done till now... I again put my hand on her waist making sum sound as if I m putting my hand while sleeping..She pushed my hand back.. With a lot of courage I just again hugged her tightly from behind and this time my rod was touching her ass..She did not do anything....

I slowly kept rubbing my rod behind her.... I also started running my hand on her stomach.....After 5 mins I stopped them to check whether she slept or not...but to my surprise...she took my hand towards her breast.....I was so hot by the time......I just press her breasts with my hands.. she also responded...

Then with my other hand I unhooked her bra from behind and released her boobs..I was kissing her on her back and then neck..Slowly I came down and pulled her sari up... and could see her sexy ass with black panty on it...i kissed her on her ass checks....i was doing this inside the blanket..Slowly I moved her wet panty a little and started rubbing her pussy with my hand... She moaned slowly..then I inserted the middle finger inside her love hole and I was fucking her with my finger...she started moving her ass in fucking position....after that I went a little closer and kept my tongue near her hole licked it with my tongue...her sweet pussy was having such a great taste..Her volume raised...

I got a little afraid as there was my mom sleeping beside her child and also other people. After fucking her with my tongue....she got really horny...When I came kissing her ass to her back and neck....she told me in a low voice....give me your dick...I opened my shorts and my six inch handsome came out....I took her hands to my dick...

she took it in her hands and started feeling it....i was enjoying her boobs by that time...then she slowly whispered in my ears....RAVI I WANT TO FEEL YOUR DICK IN MY PUSSY....I WANT THAT FEEL....I told her...WE DON'T HAVE ANY PROTECTION......she was really horny and had nothing to hear....she just said..

IT DOESN'T MATTER ANYTHING TO ME FUCK ME WITH UR DICK....RIGHT NOW....as she said....i did not even wait for a second....just lifted her ass a little up placed my dick between her ass checks......she guided my dick to her love hole with her hands then I just inserted my dick without a condom.... OooooOH...it pained a little but when my dick got totally inside..

got little wet....she opened her mouth wide.....i just kept my hand on her mouth so that she could not make any sound.....i could feel her pussy....it felt like heaven inside it.....she was just enjoying the fuck. I just hugged her tightly from behind and kept on fucking her from behind...after 5 mins...she layed her boobs down and I went on her fucking her ass...

bye sleeping on her...... after a long fuck.... I was to cum......she said......put it on my asshole........i want it there,...i just removed my dick and cummed everything on her asshole....which also went down to her pussy....she started rubbing her pussy with her hand enjoying my cum on it....

I told her I am going to wash my dick in washroom....she stood up and came with me...she pushed me inside and locked the door from inside. She bent down took my rod in her hand and gave me a fantastic blowjob...my dick was touching her innerthroat...Oh. It was totally inside her mouth....I got charged....she was still in the saree around her waist...

I just sat on the English Toilet pulled her towards me and she readily came and sat on my dick.....I just removed her blouse and bra....and was madly kissing her boobs....she said do not leave and love bite.....as her husband may come to know...i was sucking them and licking her armpits.....it smelled so great......

I fucked her for around 20 mins......after a hardcore fuck she pulled up her sari....put her bra and blouse....got ready to go out.....i pulled her to me and gave her a lip lock.....for around 5 mins.....hugging each other tightly.......At last she said... U R SO VERY HOT.....WILL MEET U SOON IN THIS SITUATION...I said...I WILL BE WAITING FOR IT SEXY...

then she went out and saw if all are sleeping then she waved hand to me so I went out.... she slept in her place and pulled her child towards her... and I slept at my place... within 1 hour we had to wake up.....My grandpa got perfectly alright... and all had to leave... it was the last night she was sleeping in our house...she was wearing a nighty...

13. Ritu

So I m a well built unmarried guy working in a Multi National Comapany in Delhi & a kind of freak trying to experiment everything in my life including giving ultimate freedom to myself. Anyways the sweet experience I am going to narrate here which changed me altogether is a very recent 2 yrs back. I have been in Delhi for quite some long 6-7 years living in apartments & hostels.

Untill recently in 2007 I changed to a new locality in Delhi with my 2 friends who are very reserved & kind of still not matured enough when it comes to dealing with women. We were searching for a flat & found a decent Ground Floor Flat at a nice locality the very next day of shifting when I returned home from office as usual.

I found somebody walking down the stairs, We have a common entry / exit for all the floors & door of which is unfortunately right in front of our Apartment. I got my key, unlocked the door & opened it. Immediately I found a female voice "Aaccha to aapne liya hai Ground Floor"(Alright so you have taken the Ground floor) "Haan ji"(yes) I responded.

This Lady was Ritu living with her husband and a 4 yrs Girl 3 month's baby on 1st Floor & 2nd floor was not given on rent by Landlord. "Sab kuch theek se re-arragne ho gaya"(So have you rearranged everything) she asked "Haan Bhabhiji"(Yes Sister in law). This Bhabhiji(Sister in law) word I don't know how came out of my mouth but later we ended up in Bhabhi Devar (Sister in law and brother in alw) kind of scene.

Ritu was from Rajasthan. A Lady with Milky white skin, Face without any marks, Long Strong Black Hair, Dark Eyes who can speak their own language. On top of this she was having figure which every female wishes / dreams to possess. Boobs like sweet ripe mangoes hanging from trees. And Ass which would make every man go ride.

Now every day I would return from office she would come down and stand on my door to talk with me with her baby in hands. Our talks gradually started with personal details & as day by day passed we kind of started talking emotions & you know once you talk emotions with somebody u eventually become close to that person. Until now I didn't had any desire for this lady.

After few days she started bringing something to eat for me like sweets, dishes cooked in day or something like which I taste & praise a lot for her cooking. Day by day I found Ritu feeling friendly with me & talking / expressing emotions very comfortably & there was no barrier among us.

Inside myself I praise her for this boldness to take initiative to talk with me and I like such type of ladies who like to live life keeping all social & so called taboos aside. I found that Ritu isn't happy with Jeetu (his husband) as he isn't kinda guy to deal rightly with women as he frequently abused her & her parents & used to shout a loud so that entire locality can listen.

She used to discuss this & other issues with me & also used to praise me that I speak to her in very polite manner & the girl I would marry would be very happy and all that. Also she liked my attitude & energy to handle house hold chores with equal participation like Cooking skills, Washing, Cleaning etc.

She used to come down to talk to me in her nightie & I never used to notice anything. One day she as she came down I found that she is wearing something new sort of nightie. This one was having a deep neck & her cleavage was apparently visible in this. To my shock I found that today she isn't wearing any Bra at all. I was stunned!!! By this amazing change in her.

I tried to keep my eyes away but couldn't. Other days she used to go to upstairs when the baby used to cry but today she came inside my room. I was like eyes opened without a blink. Anyways I didn't show that I have taken notice of this. I was behaving very normally. Ritu came inside slowly sat on the bed. I went inside the kitchen to have a glass of water.

Our Kitchen has a window opened to the room wherein on Bed Ritu was sitting with baby. The door of room was very slightly opened. While I picked up the glass from the Kitchen Almirah(cupboard) I tried to peek inside the room wherein Ritu was sitting. She sat comfortably on the bed & now was trying things so that baby can calm down. But bay wasn't at all.

I was standing inside kitchen watching all this. The nightie today she was wearing was having a button on Cleavage area so that the deep cut between both sides doesn't falls aside to apparently bare her fruits. She took her hands towards this button & unbuttoned her nightie. Oh my God!!! Such a milky fruit inside.

Amazing size & with kind of appeal that it instantly sent signals to my penile nerve for erection and to my surprise I found that I have already got instant hard on. I came out of kitchen with glass of water in hand & sat on the bed. By this time Ritu had adjusted her nightie in a way that the baby started suckling milk & very small part of her fruits was visible for me.

But for a Bachelor like me even a glimpse is enough and I was getting a eyeful. She was looking towards her baby and I was looking at her fruits. She turned her face towards me and caught me staring at her breasts. She smiled I exchanged smile. Now I found that she is very comfortable with me. And by now only I had this new feeling for her in my mind.

Anyways we started talks as usual and suddenly talks turned to breastfeeding. "Having Kids isn't a easy Job, I have to feed him 4-5 times a day" She said. "Yes of coz" I replied. "So how long breastfeeding is required" I asked "its upto a woman how long she can, I breastfed Guidya for 3 years, those were initial happy years of my life". She replied.

"So doesn't you get hurt when baby bites" I asked. "Yes but not in initial months until the dents are there, in case of Gudiya it was very problematic, She was kind of mad for breast milk and didn't opted for any other meal than milk. I had to feed her every now and then, sometimes in some places where I didn't found it comfortable there too I had to feed her."

Suddenly in between this she found that baby is done with her one breast as soon as he unleashed baby from her nipple she found that baby was still hungry. And for me it was a complete eye ful of her ripen fruit, Oh my God! It was awesome piece of flesh, Full white with Pink aroleas, Erect Wet Nipple and a drop of her milk just now came out of your breast & now waiting to fall down.

She immediately placed her hand below the nipple so that milk doesn't spoil her clothes. Baby again started to cry a little. She turned her face towards me and again caught my eyes staring at her fruit. "abhi iska man nahi bhara hai."(She is still not satisfied) She said, I smiled. And she had a kind of different smile on her face.

I was watching all this and she knew that I m diligently watching all this with all the curiosity. She slowly place the baby on bed. Now she put back her breast inside and pulled other breast outside. She rubbed the breast for a moment, perhaps to mobilize the flow of milk. Picked the baby again, put on lap and lashed baby to her nipple. Baby started suckling.

This time she was a bit careless, I don't know perhaps intentionally she kept her whole breast open for my eyes and turned her face towards me. I was watching her fruit. "So do you have milk all around the day" I asked. She laughed a bit. I smiled. "Haan"(yes) Her voice was different this time. "Kabhi kabhi to itna ki baby pita nahi hai aur inme itna dard hota hai ki."(Sometimes this much that baby does not drink I get pain due to them) She said.

"Tab kya karte ho"(then what do you do) I asked. "Tab, hmmmm…. Kya kar sakti hu. Wait karti hu ki baby kab piyega". (then what can I do. I wait when the baby can drink) Her voice was entirely different this time and I caught this point. "Aaccha tumhari koi gf hai kya"(Alright do you have any GF) she asked. "No" I replied. "To kabhi kabhi to Gudiya abhi bhi piti hogi"(So does Gudiya drink it sometimes) I asked. She smiled "Nahi pagal.... ab wo badi ho gai hai. Haan kabhi kabhi...."(No Mad....Now she is has become big... Yes sometimes...)

She laughed very loudly..... "kya"(what) I asked. "Kuch nahi"(nothing) she replied. Then after few seconds she said "Jab Guidya doodh piti thi to kabhi kabhi Jeetu bhi rat ko pita tha...."(When Guidya drinks milk then sometimes Jeetu also drinks in the night) she laughed like anything... and I too laughed..... "Sach"(Really)) I asked.... "Hmmmm". By this time her baby was done and slept. She kept the baby aside. and looked out for breast.

Drops were coming one after one and she kept her hand below her nipple to avoid milk drop on clothes. "Koi kapda hai kya"(do you have a cloth) she asked. I handed out one old cloth. Her full breast was outside her maxi dripping milk. "Jaise abhi Baby ne pura dudh nahi piya aur mujhe dard ho raha hai....."(Like now baby has not drank the complete milk and I am getting pain) she said. "oh" I said. "Ab pata nahi kab piyega aur tab tak mujhe yeh jhelna padega"(Now I don't know when he will drink and till when I must bear this pain) she said.

"Kuch aur nahi kar sakte"(Nothing else can be done) I asked. "Jaise"(like) she said. "Aap doodh haath se nikal do ya koi aur pi le"(You can remove the milk with your hand or someone else can drink) I asked. "Nahi pagal haath se aur dard hota hai, Aur Jeetu ab utne interested nahi, Aur kisi se mai yeh bat keh nahi sakti."(No mad with hands it pains and Jeetu is no more interested and I cannot tell this thing to anyone else) Immediately baby turned and was about to fall down. I quickly stood up and hold the baby.

In between this I was about to fall on her and accidently I brushed with her open breast. "Ah' She said. I sat down. We both were breathing heavily due to this. I sat down and don't know from where I got the courage. I asked "Kya mai aapki help kar sakta hu"(Can I help you). "Chal pagal"(Move it Mad) she laughed and hold my hand. She took my hand in her hand and I felt her warmness.

She guided my hands to her fruit. I kept my hand on her boob…..
OHHHHHHHHh !!!!! it was so soft and warm there…… I slowly
pressed it. We made a eye contact for mutual consent. I kept the
baby aside and put my head on her lap. "Ruko abhi"(wait now)
she said. "Pehle darwaja band karo"(First go and close the door) I
stood up and closed the door.

I came back, sat on the bed, she spread her legs parallel on the
bed and made way for me to place my head on her lap. She
smiled, now her fruit was touching my cheeks and milk was still
dripping. She picked my head in her hands and asked for a kiss.
I lip kissed her for around 2-3 minutes. She rolled her fingers
through my hair and placed my head at right place in her lap.

Now she said first kiss me on my fruit except nipple……I started
giving gentle sweet kisses in slow with long timings to ignite
the hungry woman inside her. I gave her kisses all around her
fruit except the nipple……"Ab nipple per kiss karo(Now kiss on
my nipple) … long kiss" I gave a long kiss on her nipple… She
closed her eyes taking deep breaths and sweet moans.

Suddenly she put her hand on my pants where my dick was
semi erect and started rubbing there. Now she opened her eyes.
"To tumhe dudu pina hai, naughty"(so you want to drink milk
naughty) then she put her nipple into my mouth and I started
suckling warm milk… Guys it was amazing like Buttermilk
without sugar / salt but the erotic feeling of having such milk
from the breasts a woman of dreams was awesome,

warm and soft touches of her breast on my cheeks were adding
to this. I put my hands on his other breast inside the maxi and
started slowly pressing it.. She closed her eyes and I was continuing my enjoyment of suckling and rubbing. Her hand was
on the other side finding my zip to reach my tool. All this continued for few minutes.

Suddenly I found some noise around the door and she sensed
that Jeetu is around. I stood up. She closed the nightie and
picked the baby to reach the door. Jeetu parked the car, open
the door & was there. He couldn't sense what scene was inside
the room few minutes back. Ritu & me exchanged smiles and we

both knew that a new spark has come in life without saying a single word.

I exchanged hello with Jeetu and Ritu and Jeetu climbed the stairs to reach their apartment on 1st floor. Guys this is just start of my adventure with Ritu. Ritu & I satisfied our carnal desires and she taught a lot to me about women and told me hidden secrets. I miss Ritu a lot in my life and waiting for somebody to fill in the Gap.

14. *Preeti*

My name is Kiran. I am 28 and I am from India. It has been five years that I migrated to USA. I had been busy exploring the new world and settling down. I built a home in the southwest on a 10 acre property. Now that the initial excitement is over and I have settled down I found myself lonely with nothing at hand to do. Because of the estates I inherited from my father I don't have to work so you can imagine I have abundant free time at hand. I started to think more and more of my life back home in India.

The village I used to live in was like stuck 100 years back in the past. We have vast lands and farms with scores of servants working under our family for generations. Our immediate family lives in a fortress-like home. The home has extensions which houses my extended family like uncles, aunts, grandparents and cousins etc. This complex is then surrounded by an irregular circle of all sorts of living quarters for dozens of farmers and servants whose livelihood depends on us.

Our family was very traditional with one exception -- my mother had the final say in everything. She was very loving to everyone, very caring. Once one of our farmer's wife died; he was devastated beyond description -- that is what mother said. Then mother let him sleep with her in her bed for more than a month. My father had to spend all those nights right on the edge of the bed; he even fell a couple of times. Mother said we always should help the poor. Then my mom let the farmer go when he was fully relieved of his grief.

I started thinking about starting my own family. " I think I should marry someone from my own village. Someone very gentle, caring and giving, innocent, untarnished." I immediately phoned my mother; within a week she had the right girl for me. Her name was Preeti. We married in a rush using telephone and courier to exchange documents and I sponsored her to come to America to live with me; my mother came along to help me in my new life. I had two surprises at the airport. One -- I saw one of our villagers, Devraj, carrying luggage following my new wife and mother. He was one of the older family servants but mostly used to work on farms. He was getting old -- in his 50's but looking a few years older. Tall, dark-skinned but skinny, somewhat mal nourished. He used to walk with giant leaps with his long legs. The other surprise --- my mother was carrying five year old girl. She was walking ahead of Preeti and Dev in the airport arrival terminal, her left breast hanging out while the girl was suckling on it. The girl was irritable probably because of the long journey; mother was holding her left breast close to the nipple with her right hand slightly squeezing the nipple between her index and middle finger and fruitlessly trying to place the nipple in the her mouth. The girl was shaking head back and forth causing the nipple to squirt drops of milk all around. My mind raced to my past. I have suckled on these nipples countless times, not only when I was a baby but also more recently. Mum says maternal milk is better than any other tonic in the world. When I used to come back from a game or after a long business trip, I would always find my mother standing in the front courtyard with her boobs hanging down with the weight of the milk ready for me to suck on. Sometimes me and my father would suckle on each breast after combined business trip. Mother had to keep up her milk production as we were eight brothers and sisters plus my father; on top of that mum would help poor servants once in a while after they were very exhausted working in hot weather. She would let them suck on her nipples for a few minutes while she was supervising their work. Sometime she would ask one of the farmers rub her in between her legs; mum says it makes her produce more milk.

My thoughts were interrupted by my mum's familiar voice. I wanted to hug my new wife standing close by but she was shy being in public. I grabbed some of the luggage, stuffed everything in a taxi and got everyone home. In the taxi my mum introduced the girl to me as my sister born soon after my departure for US five years ago. I always have thought very highly of my mother but the arrival of this new girl made me immensely proud to have a very fertile mother who never gets tired.

Next morning everyone woke up late. Preeti had been asleep all night like a kitten; I did not disturb her as I knew she was very tired after the long journey. In our bedroom Preeti was sitting in the reclining chair gazing through the windows into the backyard while I was reading newspaper.

Suddenly I saw uneasiness in her eyes; I followed her gaze and saw our servant Dev in the backyard standing close to a flower bed. He had removed his sarong (piece of cloth used instead of a trouser) and was standing legs comfortably parted. He was holding his dick at its base peeing into the flower bed. Beyond his fist his dick was hanging further out and down ending at the abundant foreskin which was hanging loose; a forceful stream of piss jetting out. The veins on his dick were shining in the early morning sun. Two heavy balls hanging low in his long and large wrinkly nut sack were jiggling sideways as he was easing himself over the rocks spread around the newly landscaped area.

Preeti, while holding one end of her long sari (Indian dress) ran to the backyard. For the first time I had a good look at her. She was a few inches taller than me and had a slender frame but had a big booty – a little too big; someone else might even call it oddly big. When she would run her hips sway sideways while jiggling at the same time creating a scene from which you can't take eyes off. I rushed behind her. She ran straight to Dev who was still pissing. "What are you doing Dev? You ruined all the flowers. Tell your pee thing to stop." Dev's pee stream stopped. Preeti held him by his wrist and led him inside. I was following. She continued to talk. "Don't you know flowers are living things and you can't pee on them. Let me show you where to pee. I am sorry if I scared you. Did your pee thing get hurt when you had to stop peeing?" Dev nodded his head in affirmative. With that my wife felt so guilty. She looked at me for help. Then said sorry to Dev and held the base of his dick with her two fingers to help his pain. They were ahead of me. I could see from behind Dev's two heavy balls still jiggling and swaying. Preeti's hips were swaying in harmony as well.

She led him to our master bath still holding his large beef-stick with her two fingers and stood him by the toilet. "Ok now, pee in this thing. It is called a toilet". Dev wouldn't pee. His dick twitched a couple of times and became semi-hard. "Why are you not peeing now. Tell your big pee thing to start again." She looked at me for help. I went closer and kneeled down. Preeti was already on her knees on the floor. Now she was holding the old man's dick which was now between me and her face. She moved it closer to me asking what to do. I saw the foreskin peeling backward and the big mushroom like head popping out. Preeti looked worried thinking she had hurt his dick. She really wanted to teach him how to pee in a civilized way. Dev said, " Preeti Ji (Ji is a word indicating respect), may be if you shake my dick, it might start peeing". Preeti still holding the base of his dick in her two fingers started shaking it side to side. We were not suspecting this but his plum like dick head hit my face then Preeti's while she was waving it. She seemed not to care. She had her eyes focused on pee-hole eagerly waiting for the piss stream. Dev's dick continued to get slapped on her face. Still looking worried she said, "Look Kiran, it looks like I did something terribly wrong. First he was unable to pee and now the head of his pee thing has grown bigger; the whole thing is hard. It is even twitching. I don't know what to do?" Then she answered herself, "may be if I squeeze his hanging sac the pee would come out". She cued me to hold the 12 inch dick while she started fondling the nut sac. I started rubbing Dev's dick trying to cure it while Preeti was pulling on the nut sac. Then she paused; I saw her carefully palpating her discoveries -- the two balls. She was deeply involved. She held the two balls, then rubbed them together; then held his nut sac towards the top and shook the balls sideways. She continued to fondle his balls in all possible ways she could think of; then took his dick back from my hand and expressed her new idea, " Kiran, can you please piss in the toilet to show him how to pee?" I felt embarrassed deep inside but couldn't say anything. I unzipped my pants and took my penis out. It was about a quarter the size of Dev's. I pulled on my dick a couple of times but it wouldn't get hard. But I did the job; I started peeing right away. Preeti got excited, and started rubbing Dev's cock more forcefully and encouraging him at the same time, " look Dev, look look; this is how you pee in a toilet. See how your boss is doing. Come on, you can do it. I am sorry I caused all this trouble for you. I am sorry.". Poor Dev; I felt sorry for him too. For no fault of his he had to go through all this. Then he said, " Preeti ji if you don't mind can I say something." "yes of course". " Preeti ji, you rubbed my dick so much it has gotten dry. Can you please spit on it." My wife immediately responded and started spitting along the length of his dick, then rubbing her spit all over it. But it would get dry again, so she started rubbing it with her tongue instead of her hands. I was impressed with her talents. I thought not only she is so caring and giving she also seemed to have natural nursing skills. My wife's ideas seemed to be working. Dev's started to growl and encouraged my wife to continue

licking his dick. Then he surprised me when he started saying bad words

for my wife. I don"t know why. She was helping him but he said things

like she was a dick sucking slut, a whore and a bitch to be fucked. He

even said he would fuck her in her ass. I think he momentarily became

delirious because of pain or something. Then he held my wife from her hair and directed her mouth so she could also wet his nut sack. She eagerly

started sucking his balls holding each one between her lips and pulling down until it would pop out. Then suddenly he howled like a mad man and

thick ropes of dick juice started coming out of his pee hole and landed in the toilet. He continued to express his desire to fuck my wife in her ass. After that he seemed to calm down and came to his senses. My wife was finally happy to have cured him. We left him there with instructions for chores around the house and proceeded to kitchen to get some breakfast.

Later that evening I was sitting in the family room by the fireplace while my wife Preeti, was sitting beside me. She was recollecting what happened that morning.

Thank you Kiran, for helping me fixing Dev's dick by peeing in front of him.

Oh, that's okay.

But tell me, why his pee thing is so long and big and yours is small.

It is not called a pee thing; it is called a dick or cock. Also penis.

Okay, but why is yours smaller than his?

I don't know; I guess not all men are born equal.

Will yours grow bigger when you reach his age?

No; I don't think so. This is the maximum for me.

You are lucky, Kiran. You have a small protected penis. Poor Dev. His is so big and long. I bet when he is walking around his cock is getting hurt by slapping on his thighs or even bumping into furniture and cabinets. And his thighs are so hairy. I wonder if his cock will get all scratched.

Yeah, may be.

And he has to be careful with his hanging balls too. They might get caught in the holes in his charpai

(traditional indian bed made of ropes).

Don't worry honey. There is no charpai in America. He left his in India.

Still.... but what was he saying about fucking my ass? What does that mean?

I think he wanted to put his dick into your ass.

You mean my shit hole.

Yes.

Really! Why? Why would he want to do so?

I don't know for sure but may be his thinking was not straight at that
time as he was embarrassed. You were making him to pee in front of us all. Or maybe he was happy with you helping him and he just wanted to express what he could give you in return. Poor thing. He has no money; what else he can offer except his cock. And he has no education so these were the best words he could come up with. I apologize if you found him rude.

Mother, who was sitting close by on the kitchen table, was listening to our conversation, came over to join us. She brought cups of tea and put them on the coffee table. She put the little girl (she was named Raveena) in the play area, pulled her left boob out and hanging over the coffee table squeezed her boob to pour milk in the cups. Then she came over to me saying that I had become so weak from eating foreign food; she pulled out her other breast and asked me to suck on it. While I started feeding on her boob she sat beside me.

She explained to my wife: Sometimes men want to do this for a change. They just want to explore women's assholes. We in our family always try to help the needy, the poor and the ailing. If we could help someone, then it is good for everyone. I am glad what you did this morning. First you saved the flowers from Dev's pee and then educated him on how to pee in a civilized way. You also did a great job fixing his aching dick by sucking on it and on his balls. As far as my son's small dick is concerned, it runs in the family.

I continued to suck on mum's nipple.

Preeti: I feel so sorry for Dev. But I am glad at the end he felt better. I am afraid it might hurt his dick again if I let him put it in my ass. And I don't even know if it would go in. It is so big and I have never done this before. I don't know.

Mother: Don't worry; that is why I came with you. Dev used to work on the farms not inside our house in India, so I don't know him much. I don't know how much he likes fucking assholes or how many times he has done this in the past. But we will see.

Preeti turning to me: Kiran, I never knew these things before. Now that Dev wants to put his cock in my ass to express his gratitude, what do you think I should do? If I say no would I hurt his feelings?

Me: It is possible. He is new in this country and left his wife and kids back in India. In a sense he came all the way just to help us. And he is lonely here. All these things can make a person emotionally weak.

Your "no" might disturb him to say the least.

Mother: We should try our best not to say no. This is against our family values of good will to all humans and living things. And plus there is no downside to having someone's dick in ass. Lots of people do it for pleasure but you, Preeti, will be doing it for a higher purpose.

Me: But Mommy she is my new bride and I have not even had any sex with her yet. And I too am worried about the size of Dev's cock. It might be very painful to have

Preeti's ass stretched with that thing.

Preeti: I am not worried about my suffering. But I am concerned Dev's
dick might feel squeezed and get hurt while probing into my shit hole.

Mother: My son, you will have your bride for you all your life. But the issue at hand is serious. We cannot afford to hurt any-one's feeling and Dev is our own and only servant. And if Preeti's ass feels a little pain it is still worth a good cause. And Preeti to answer your question, I am sure Dev would be able to stretch your ass enough to make things easy for this dick. And in fact many men feel happy when their dick gets squeezed in an ass-hole.

Preeti: Is that right? Kiran, will you enjoy if you put your penis in my ass?

Me: Hmm, I never thought about that before.

Mother: Every man is different, Preeti. Different things make them happy. Some of them like licking their wives' pussies. Some even like to see their wives suck other men's dicks.

Preeti: Kiran, did you like when I sucked on Dev's dick?

Me: It certainly was interesting.

Mother: He certainly liked it. He is just being shy. I can see it in his eyes. But at this time we should check on Dev to make sure he has healed well from this morning accident.

Then she shouted: Dev come here.

By now I had stopped sucking on mother's nipple and was snug-gled close to her. I love her warmth.

Dev came and sat on the ground obediently.

Mother: Preeti told me what happened this morning. Are you okay now?

Dev: Yes, just a little redness and soreness on my balls but otherwise I am fine.

Mother: I need to check; ultimately I am responsible for what happens here.

Dev took off his sarong and stood in front of mum and me, for mum to examine him. Mother looked happy and worried at the same time. She held his massive meaty dick which was now limp. She closely examined it up and down and then resting it on her shoulder started to examine his balls. She fondled his balls, rubbed them and kept on pulling and releasing them for quite some time. Since I had my head resting on mum's shoulder, Dev's dick was right in front of me. It smelled of sweat and piss. It was twitching slightly in response to mother's examination.

Finally mum said, "On the whole he is okay however, there seems to be some early skin damage reflected by the redness of the foreskin. Preeti, did you suck a lot on the foreskin?"

Preeti: Yes aunty; I was just trying to help.

Mum: That is okay. Next time if this happens just pull the foreskin
back and lick on the head of the dick. The head can sustain more trauma.

Preeti: Ok aunty.

Mum held her tiny hand and put Dev's cock in her hand. Mum said, "Preeti take a look at Dev so you can see the damage." Mum holding Dev by his dick led him to the other sofa where Preeti was sitting. It was quite a scene... my Mum holding our fifty four year old servant by his dick walking him across the family room to my wife so she can examine his hurt dick.

Preeti caressed the foreskin and apologized to Dev one more time.

Mum: In order to avoid further damage, Dev will not wear a sarong or trousers or underwear etc. In this way, fresh air will heal his dick. This is like his own home anyway and just like he is helping us with chores, we should help him too.

With this she tossed his sarong under the sofa.

15. Neelima

I am Aryan, 27 years old staying in Delhi. The story I am going to tell is few years old. At that time I was in college. I joined a college and due to heavy demand of hostel rooms, I couldn't get a room in the hostel. So I took a room in the nearby location and started staying there. It was a family of four, husband, wife, a son and a daughter.

They were having a shop and father and son used to sit on the shop and their mom was working as teacher in some school. The daughter Neelima was in class 12 and was around 5'3? Fair, long black silky hairs, big eyes and must be 34-30-36. Her size must be around B. As I used to come back from college at around 2 and her mom used to come around 4,

So everyday it was just she and me in the house, but I never had any courage to talk with her. We just used to watch each other and some time a small smile. One day when I was sitting in my room after coming back from college, she came in my room and asked if I could teach her some math as she was having some issues in solving her math questions.

I was really happy and accepted it immediately. So from that day onward I started helping her in her math problems. We used to work till 4 and she always left before her mother came, so her mother never knew that she was coming to my room. I just had a bed, so we used to sit on bed and study there only.

Initially we used to talk about math only, but slowly she started opening up and started talking about other things. Now she also started wearing some sexy dresses also. I always got the hard on when teaching her. One day while talking she asked me if I had a girl friend. I was shocked and she smiled, I told her that I like a girl but never had courage to talk with her.

She asked me about the girl and I told her that if I tell you about her looks and you may feel bad. She promised that she wouldn't mind. And I described her that I like this girl who has a very lovely smile and big eyes and is little shy and come close to my room. She was surprised and asked who she is as she knows all the girls from the neighborhood.

I slowly hold her hand and told that it's you. She just lowered her eyes. I slowly came close to her and hold her chin and lifted her face up, she had closed her eyes and was smiling. I felt really happy. I slowly pulled her close and hugged her tightly and whispered in her ears "I love you". She hugged me tight and said the same.

I kissed on her neck and licked her earlobes. She started taking heavy breath and I slowly moved my hand and hold her boobs trapped in her T-shirt. She tried to stop me but I hugged her tight and planted a kiss on her lips. Oh God, her lips were so juicy, I can't explain it. I started sucking it and sometime later she also started responding back started sucking my lips.

Then I slowly tried to remove her T-shirt, she looked into my eyes and looked at the door. I closed the door and came back. She hid herself in the blanket. I took the blanket and threw it away. I slowly removed her T and started kissing her neck and belly ad squeezing her boobs. She started moaning. I removed her bra and the most beautiful pair of boobs was in front of me.

I just hold them and started sucking one. She pulled my head towards her boobs. I started rubbing her pussy in her capri and slowly removed her Capri now She was in her black panty and was looking like a sex goddess. She looked at me and pointed at my cloths. I removed my cloths and became naked in one minute. She was surprised to see my 7 cock.

She hid her face in her palms. I started kissing her moved my hand in her panty and started rubbing her pussy. Her pussy was already wet with her juices. Then I moved down and kissed her boobs and licked her belly button. Then I hold her panty with my teeth and pulled it down. Now she was baked in front of me and I was looking a real pussy first time in my life.

She had some hairs across her pussy. I started licking her legs and moved up and kissed on her pussy. She holds my head and moved it and said it's bad. I told her it's the fun and forcefully started licking her pussy. After some time she got relaxed and started enjoying it. I inserted one finger in it and started finger fucking her.

She was moaning heavily and threw her juices. I licked them all and continued licking her. She got hot again. I moved up and she opened her legs and I put my cock on her pussy and I told her that I would pain a little first time and she nodded her head. I made a small push and it was too tight and didn't go in. I tried again and it was too tight. She looked at me started laughing.

I felt really bad, and this time I opened her pussy a little and put it there and made a push and 2? Of my cock went in and she screamed with pain. I closed her lips with my lips and stopped there. After 2 minutes I made a bigger push and it all went in, a stream of blood came out and she was in tears, but couldn't scream as her lips were closed with mine.

She was screaming that take it out, it's hurting. I consoled her and told that it's only a matter of few minutes then you will have the real fun. After few minutes when she got little relaxed I started making small moves. After some times she started enjoying and started responding back to my moves by moving her ass. I fucked her deep and hard for next 10 minutes.

She came twice during that time and when I was about to come and told her, she said don't came inside as she may get pregnant. So I took my cock out and spayed it on her belly. Then we lay there on the bed and kissed each other passionately. It was already more than 3 and her mother had to come by 4, so she said that she has to take a shower,

So she left and after that we had sex many times. I fucked her in all her holes. I taught her blowing so she blew me out many times which I enjoyed the most. After few months I got a room in the hostel and moved to hostel and could never get a chance to fuck her again.

16. Rahul

My name is Rahul, I am 19 yrs old and am quite attracted to matured ladies specially who are friendly and thinks life is for once , and a person can only live up to his / her given time , and want to enjoy fully out of it. One of such incident happened with me when I was staying in Raipur. And I was far away from my home. I was staying there in rented house of a community with other peoples staying over there. As I was very good in getting familiar with different peoples, I faced no problem in getting familiar with peoples around me staying in the community.

My neighbors were well behaved towards me though they were all staying with their respective families. There was a neighbor as such who were very much liked me. They were only two of them with a 2yrs old son. I used call them as aunty and uncle only, as they were quite an elder than me. Aunty was 10 yrs older than me and her husband was 10-15 yrs older than me. As my work was very demanding. I use to come home at late hours of the day, tired and feeling to have a good sleep.

These things happened many days and my neighboring uncle and Aunty watched several times. One day they invited me when I just came home; they invited me by telling that I can have my dinner over their place instead going out again. As I thought that was not a bad idea and also they were requesting i agreed upon. That evening we all enjoyed the dinner together and in the way we also became very familiar to each others. When finished I went to my house which was just beside their house.

A week later I was given the charge for night shifts in my workplace. So I use to come home by 9am. And resting for the whole day again at 10pm I had to leave. That week when my night shifts were on aunty use to sometimes take care of me for my breakfast and lunch. In the meantime we chatted a lot on different topics. These were all happening when uncle was out to his office. Once when I was sitting in her house, casually she asked what I do in the night shifts, do I really work or I look for fun.

I asked her what she really meant of fun. She replied that I should know that am not a kid. From that I understood what she meant, as the conversation kept on going we became frank in our approach, even she didn't hesitate asking me about my sexual experience if I had any. I said no. Aunt was sexually very attractive, she was fair in complexion, nicely curved figure. Especially her ass and her boobs, I use to stare at them very much as they can't pass by any male unnoticed and she was very soft spoken her smile was like an angel. Suddenly her 2yrs old kid woke up started to cry, she hurriedly went to that room and when returned she was breast feeding him, seeing that I was in state of shock and embarrassment. I tried to avoid seeing that as I already saw her one boob out of her blouse and the child was feeding onto it.

Though it shocked me but it also aroused me too, as I saw her big swollen white boob was out of her blouse while the other one was covered in the other cup. It seemed as she was not wearing bra because she had to feed the child often. She was absolute ignorant of me and was roaming free in front of me and acted as if I was not there at all. Slowly I gained some courage, started to watch what in fact was offered to me. I can clearly see her cleavage, her naval area but she was totally ignorant of my presence. Suddenly she asked me what you are looking at Rahul. I thought the ground beneath my feet shocked. I shuttered, but she said, Rahul, it seems that you never saw a child's breast feeding. In return I just afford to give a smile to her as the baby slept. She quietly kept him on the bed and returned to this room. And asked me did you like that? I just nodded my head in appreciation, and only I knew how I said yes to her, my heart was throbbing inside as she was staring right into my eyes. I tried to leave her place but she held my hand smilingly urged me to stay back for sometime more, as she felt lonely in these hours of the day. So, I stay back. She then started to play games by quizzing me. How I feel with elder women? Do they attract me sexually? What is my choice of woman?

When she asked the last question I replied I can only dream a woman like you who is attractive in nature and soft spoken. Hearing this, she was impressed and was smiling looking into my eyes. Then she asked me how I look at her, I said as friend who is elder than me. Then she said do you like to do a favor to your friend, I said sure. She then holds my hand and said do I look attractive to you? I said yes, off course you are attractive. She smiled in return and gave me kiss on my forehead.

Then she said Rahul I started to like you too, and I want you to make me happier. As she said that everything was clear for me, I decided to agree on her offer. So, I nodded my head in return. She smilingly, hugged me kissed me gently all over my face. In return I hugged her quit tightly and felt like her boobs were getting smashed on my chest, it felt really good, as the soft bosoms of her flattened on my chest.

In the meantime things were getting a bit heated up. As we kept kissing and hugging each other, our kissing developed in a passionate tongue twisting kiss. We both were searching for each other's tongues and sucking it passionately. Then I broke the kiss and said what was in my mind, I said her that I wanted to feel her heavy bosoms as they attract my imagination. She happily opened the buttons of blouse and the two bosoms were set free.

They are big swollen and soft. I touched one of her tits and she rolled her eyes back. Then lowered my mouth on her and started to suck I thought some milk will flow out of her tits but it's not , then she laughed back and taught me not that way. She sat on the bed and told me to lay down my head on her couch. I saw two big tits hanging right over my face to be sucked like a baby.

She then, put her one tit into my mouth and told me to take

more of it in mouth, until the whole areole was in my mouth, and said to suck now, wow what a thing her warm sweet milk from those fleshy boobs was flowing into my mouth. I kept on sucking while squeezed the other one. I squeezed the nipple hard and it became erect. While I dried up this one, I started to suck on the other boob. By this time she started to unzip my pant and pushed it down to my knees, and slid her one hand inside my underwear.

She was playing with my tool, caressing it softly while moving the skin up n down on my shaft. She asked me how you keep this huge cock inside. She was caressing with my balls. Then I got up and she bent over my lap and took the full length into her mouth, sucked it hard, very hard indeed. I felt like I will cum in her mouth there only. As I said her I am Cumming she didn't moved her head and eventually came in her mouth she swallowed my cum as much as possible. I was then lying over there, on her bed and fondling with her tits.

She touched my cock and my balls caressing them griping my cock in hand and moving them up n down motion. Suddenly I felt I was hard again. This time, I undressed her totally, goodness gracious what a sight to see. Below her boobs there starts another world of beauty. Her navel was deep , curved smooth white hips , nicely curved thighs , a protruding fleshy buttock , and between all these a glistening plumpy hairless love triangle. Phew! I thought that was enough to kill a man in an instance.

She, was standing nude in front, I held her tightly against my body we were pressing onto each other's body. I made her lay down on the bed on her back. We kissed deeply, as our tongue played on our mouth swirling in. simultaneously squeezing her boobs. Then moved down, sucked both her tits, squeezed some milk out of those. Swirl my tongue deep into her navel. At this she started to moan slowly and was pressing my head for more. Then, moved further down and between her fleshy thighs, I licked I her thighs bite them, licked her pubic region. I put my hands under buttocks and she spread her legs apart. Licked her asshole, and then slowly licked her pussy. Pressed my tongue harder inside and parted her pussy lips. Jabbed one index finger into her asshole while I sucked her clit. By this she was arching her back up and then falling down. Holding the back of my head she was pressing my head for more intense and deep sucking on her pussy. She was moaning quit loudly and I was afraid that it may just wake up her kid.

As my action was kept on going she was thrusting her pussy on my face and was shaking violently. Then she came scream-ing….right onto my face I drunk her juices as much as possible. But my erection by that time was painful. She jumped up from her lying position and bend over my dick she took full of that in her mouth and sucked it hard. When she moved her head it was glistening with her saliva. She pushed me to lay down on my back. And squirted over my dick it entered in her as it pushed its head inside her.

Her mouth was opened and was looking at the genitals. She started to squirt over slowly then became faster and faster. And she bent forward offering me to suck on her tits while she kept on pumping on my dick. I took one tit in my mouth while squeezed the nipple of the other one harder and painful. Sucked both the tits alternatively. Then she got up and changed her position in doggy style and told me to hump her from back as she like this position very much. I settled myself behind her and pushed my dick inside.

Humped her so furiously that she buried her face on the bed. And with each thrust she was jerked ahead. She was grinning with pain while her face was buried in the bed. As I was very much fond of her ass too. They were nicely shaped like two globes placed side wise. Fair in complexion and was shining be-cause of the sweat. I pulled out from her cunt. She tried to look over her shoulder thinking what happened by that time I place the tip of my cock at the entrance of her brown eye.

It didn't require any lubrication as my cock was already slip-pery because of her cunt juices. I shoved it inside her asshole and her head thrusted backward. Grinning in pain, she tried to suppress her screaming by pressing her lips together. I was able to enter the head of my dick only and it got sort of locked inside as her sphincter gripped firmly on my cock. I started to push inside slowly and entered all my full length. She was urging me to stop that. But her urging felt in deaf ears.

I kept on pumping her ass. At one point I pulled out and that left ass gaping. When the gap was slowly getting to close. I pushed in again. I stood up on my feet and while half squirting position I was humping her ass from behind like a mad dog. I reached ahead to cup her tits. Squeezed them hard. Pinched the nipples hard. And saw her looking at my face over her shoulder. There was an expression of pain in her face , but she was enjoying and was meeting my thrusts by giving back thrust.

I was about to cum and wanted her to drink all that down her throat. So, pulled out and while standing onto the bed I hold her chick up right at the tip of my cock and in anticipation she opened her mouth and discharged loads of cum into her mouth she sucked the tip hard and drank all the juices. We were so exhausted, that we laid there for about an hour or so. Then we, both cleaned up our selves. And I went to my room as she kissed me and hugged me and thanked me. Later, I came to know why she was that desperate.

Her husband used to have a quick fall problem. And over that he was very much ignorant to sex and her sexual feelings. Whenever he felt the urge, climbed onto her comes within 5 mins. And falls asleep. She couldn't bear it after her 3yrs of married life. Things were driving her crazy and then she found me. It's sad but, at the end I promised her to keep her happy and she doesn't require going to other males for her needs. That kept her happy. And kept her family life just like a happy family.

As the day progressed I was getting attracted deeply with her. And we shared a good bondage between us. In times I use to go to her house while her kid was awake. But at the same time we need to do something to settle the fire. So, we used to have few quick sessions than longer ones. One day I saw her in the kitchen her kid was playing in the other room, so I thought of quick fire.

She was cooking I grabbed her from behind rubbed my dick on her ass. Pressed her boobs. Lifted gown from the back I gave her good oral session.

Other day, when she asked for milk for my coffee I said yes and when went to the kitchen I came following her and lifted her blouse from down sucked her tits and drank a lot of milk. One I told her to bent down over the kitchen sink and lifted her gown from the back and fucked her hard and came in her, while her husband was in the bathroom and her kid was sleeping. We enjoyed both very much.

And kept both of us happy. I was then planning to move out of Chhattisgarh. But before leaving we did all sort of things. But unfortunately she moved to Delhi few months before. Anyway, she is still in touch with me via e-mails.

17. Ricky

I am Ricky here I'm sure all of you like eating Chaats(snacks), during rainy season for that matter I like it in any season. So the story goes like this, this paanipoorivala I go to have his wife helping him in his shop. She is really hot. At first I never used to notice her cause you know these Rajasthani women who take pallu on their head and keep their face covered so their face can't be seen lekin they forget to cover other parts of their body which I feel is strange. However whenever I go there I started noticing her curves while having the chat.

Whenever I used to stare and our eyes met I used to see some kind a anger in the eyes so I stopped going there for a while and when I went after a week she was inside the shop and as soon as she saw me she came out of the shop to serve me which was strange I kind a liked it very much. Guys forgive me I really forgot to give u her stats her figure was too good when I say Rajasthani u must have thought she is hugely built as if a gas cylinder ready for explosion but let me clear this lady is a mother of two but she is very much in shape a bust of 34 (which I came to know is 36c when I Slept with her) and a nice waist of around 30 and her ass is the most beautiful its 38 and it sways whenever she walks around and that walk really gives me a hard On.
Now whenever I went to the shop I used to see that she would leave her other work and come and stand and watch me watching her and used to purposely show me most of her parts. However we never spoke to each other it was only exchange of smile while paying her or while accepting the plate from her this continued for almost 3 months.
And then I got some courage and started visiting her shop when

her husband was not around that is during the day time as there was no much work he used to get things ready for the evening. So here when we started talking to each other. And when I used to talk to her she would be sitting below the counter so nobody can see her from outside and when I went to talk to her she would adjust her pallu so that I can see her cleavage and her deep navel very clearly.

And my she used to look like a sex goddess to me we used to often crack jokes and whenever I did that I used to hit her on her shoulders. I know she liked it very much one day while I cracked a joke instead of hitting her shoulder my hand accidentally hit her breasts on the side. They were really soft like jelly I know she felt the shivering waves as I felt it in me we stared at each other for god half minute and I said I'm sorry galti se lag gaya(it bumped by mistake).

Her reply completely shocked me she said bade buddhu ho itne din se main dikha rahin hoon aap itne mahino se dekh rahe ho aaj chu liya to main bura kyon manoongi(Big dumbo you are. From so many days I am showing you and from so many months you are looking at them. So today you touched them then why will I feel bad) . I couldn't believe my ears and I said that its very soft she smiled and said aur ek bar choona hain(want to touch them once again). I said why not she said wait for some time. She went inside and she came back there was no much difference in her appearance.

She said aapko yeh acche lagte hain na kyonki maine aksar aapko inko ghoorte huye dekha hain(You like them a lot since I have seen you a lot of times staring at them). I said yeah I like them a lot.

She said ab dheere so chuye na(Now touch them slowly) and I touched it she had removed her bra and I could feel her tits I slightly pinched the tits and she said aap bohut badmaash ho (you are very naughty)

I instantly got a hard on which she noticed and she touched it. It was a gr8 feeling I was on cloud nine at that moment.

This continued for a week and then one day I asked her can I see u in your birthday suite and she smiled and said I would love to but thinking how and what if somebody comes to know I told her to make some plans so that she can stay at home in the morning and if her husband can come to work instead of her she said she will try and I started kneading her melons she was a bit high at this moment and took her pallu down and touched her belly button she started breathing heavily.

I was out of control however as it was a public place I stopped and told her that she has to try the plan she said we will have fun on Sunday which was three days ahead of now and she told me that she would give a call to me so I gave her my mob no she asked me to follow her to her house so that I know her house when she goes home today. I readily agreed and when she left the shop to go home I was following her and I saw her house and I started returning back with the thoughts of fucking her in all the holes on Sunday.

These 3 days for me was like 3 years days were not passing by at all and she also did not come to the shop for 2 days I was a bit worried and on Sunday at around 8 in the morning I got a call from her saying that she would be ready at around 10 I said fine and I was really happy to fuck this sexy lady, As planned I reached her house at around 10 and she opened the door wow she looked out of the world in the navy blue saree which was matching her white skin.

And all her stats were clearly visible she had purposely worn her saree below navel so that I could see it. And she had worn a low back blouse without bra while I followed her inside her house I was watching her swaying ass and her back and the side view of the jumping melons it was too much for me to handle at once.

She said she will get tea for me I held her hand and pulled her on the sofa and said thai wanted milk which is warm she understood what I said and she said aapke samne pada hain jab chahe moo marlo. I slowly put her pallu down and kissed her on her forehead, Kissed her on her eyes and then on her ears and then lips. We lip locked for around 15-20 mins I came to know while kissing that she is really naughty when it comes to sex she put her tongue in my mouth while lip lock and I was feeling on top of the world.

I kissed her neck and she left a very low hiss I knew that gets turned on when I kiss her on the neck so I started kissing her vigorously on her neck on both sides and back now she was uncontrollable she was pressing my head towards her neck and I was continuously kissing her and while did that I was kneading her melons and pinching the tits she was giving out cries loudly now uuuuuummmh. Aaaaahhhhh. Ummm.

I really liked her moans and I unbuttoned her blouse and removed it I had never seen such stiff and round white boobs with pink small tits with large areola it was awesome she had the perfect breasts and really soft the feeling I got was something I can't describe in words. Now I slowly cam down kissing and sniffed her armpits and kissed her armpits then the side of the breasts and then I took one of the breast in my mouth and was constantly kneading and pinching the other one. She said.

Mujhe nanga kar do aur chod do mujhe meri foodi phad dalo bohut din se main is ke liye tadap rahin hoon(Make me naked and fuck me..tear my pussy. Many days have passed since I am yearning for this) . I obliged and got her naked while doing so I saw her clean shaved pussy with pink lips awesome it was. I felt as if this was an award anyone can get for their hard work. She said ab chodo mujhe main aur intezaar nahin kar sakti I told her to relax as there was much to cum or shall I say come. I started licking her tits with stiffening my tongue continuously and also started fingering her she was going crazy.

And she was like ab nahin aur mat tadpao aajao(Now don't and don't make me suffer come now) when she said this fastened my fingering and I could see that madness on her face. And then slowly I left her breast and put my tongue on her pussy at first she hesitated as she had never been licked before as she told me later. I licked her and started biting her clit while still fingering her now she was getting of the sofa in the rhythm I was fingering and licking her she said she can't take it anymore and she came with a shiver. All her juices were flowing on my nose and tongue and fingers I licked them nicely and also made her lick it.

Now she was ready for the next set of excitement she unbuttoned me and I was fully naked and she saw my tool and was really happy. Well I have a 7 inches and 3" thick cock. She said aaj to mujhe bohut maza aayega ise lete hue meri choot poori bhar jaayegi(Today I will have a lot of fun taking this.My pussy will be filled up with this) . I guided her mouth towards my penis she said she can't do it as she doesn't know how to do it as she has never done it. I told her to lick it as a ice-cream candy and she obliged and she began kissing and sucking it

I told her to lay down in 69 position and once again I started licking and fingering her as I was doing that I sucking became wild and started enjoying it a lot and fastened my fingering and licking. She started moaning loudly aaaaaah ummhhhhhh isssssss. She was going crazy now and she started stiffening I could realize that she is going to cum gain I continued and she scratched my ass with her fingers when she came.

Then I slowly made the attempt to go inside her pussy which was highly lubricated with one stroke I entered her fully lubed cunt and I started stroking her she put a pillow under her back so that I have easy access I thrust deep into her. She said aur andar faad do mujhe. Maine aisa kabhi pehle mehsoos nahin kiya rukna mat chodo mujhe aur zor se zor se(More inside tear me. I have not felt like this before.. don't stop fuck me more harder... harder . I fastened my thrusts and started going deep in her I could see a nice grin on her face while I was pumping into her

I grabbed her boobs and was licking and sucking them while constantly ramming her pussy mercilessly. After about 20 mins again I could feel her pussy walls stiffening she was going to Cum again I was on the verge too. We both came together and then I removed it from per pussy and put it in her mouth for her to clean it she cleaned it nicely and then we took rest for some time as the show was not over yet.

We lay besides each other she was playing with my now limp cock and I was kissing her on her neck. she saw that my now limp cock was getting stiff slowly she started stroking it up and down and started licking her neck from both sides I wanted to finger her again but this time I had something else in mind. I told her spread her legs wide and I started playing my fingers around the pussy and went near her ass she immediately was turned on and started making moaning sounds I slowly rubbed the areas around her ass with light fingers.

Now my cock was ready for another round I told her to get some butter she obeying got it and I rubbed it on my tool and put some on her asshole she was shocked and she started begging not in the ass as she has never done it and it is going to pain she said meri gaand ko baksh do woh is ke liye tayar nahin hain(Spare my ass it is not ready for this).

I consoled her nothing going to go wrong and I pinched her ass and slightly gave spam on her ass cheeks we was begging with a no I started slowly pinching it and made stand in doggy style I took some ice from the freezer she had and rubbed it on the buttered ass she was jumping in excitement and then I slowly entered her ass it was very tight tough. I knew im going to enjoy this like hell

I slowly penetrated her ass she was shouting no no no I spanked her ass and and entered in one big shot she cried out loud maaaa-aaaaaah I started stroking fast and while doing so I was pinching and the circling my fingers on her areola. Now I could feel that she is enjoying it and slowly I was going in and out in her ass she started giving out moans and I fastened my rhythm after a good 20 mins I was about to come and I told her that I am going to fill her ass with my jizz she readily agreed and I came in her ass.

Her ass was completely filled with my juices. I was shivering with the pleasure of conquering a virgin ass. I took my tool out and made her clean it with her tongue she cleaned it nicely. Now I was tired however my desire of filling all her holes was still pending I had filled her pussy and her ass her mouth was the next.

I was tired so I thought I will take some rest before the next round so I had her make tea and she made while she was still naked and while she was preparing tea I was rubbing my tool on her ass. We had tea and she said she never had oral sex in her life. However she said that she enjoyed it very much today for the first time in her life or else the routine was her husband would lift her saree fuck her till he came and slept. Can you imagine how boring that is?

Now I was ready for the next round and I gave my tool in her hand and told her to stroke it she thought all was done and said phir se aap thakte nahin hain kya. Kya khaate ho sand ki tarah kare ja rahe ho(Again….dont you ever get tired. What do you eat that you keep doing it like a bull)

I told her meri jaan(my Love) there is more to cum hehehehe!!!. She started stroking my cock then I said ab mooh main karoonga(Now I will do it in your mouth).

She said chi chi main nahin karoongi ganda lagta hain(I will not do its dirty).

I said try you will love it for sure.

She hesitantly said.. Ok and then I stroked my cock in her mouth and she started rubbing her hand around my balls and I started taking my fingers through her hair and caressing her. She licked and sucked the cock nicely I never felt she was a first timer. After good 30 mins I came in her mouth and told her to drink the entire juice she readily agreed and said maine socha ganda hoga lekin yeh accha hain thoda namkeen hain(I thought this will be dirty but this is good and salty).

And she said ab to aap jab bhi kahe main mooh me le loongi aapke lund ko(Now whenever you say I will take your cock in my mouth). I was really happy how the day went it was a Sunday a fun day and my god I think I had too much fun. But to my shock she said that she wanted another round of hard fucking a quick one as she had to prepare lunch and give it to her husband I readily agreed. And we had nice quickie and she was fully contented. She told me that now she will not let her husband touch her instead I would be the owner of her pussy and I can fuck her whenever I want and she will do whatever I say. I was really happy with this. After this episode we have had sex almost every day after that. Now she comes to the shop only in the evening and in the morning before I leave to work I make it a point to fuck her and only then go to office.

18. Pushpa

Its Pushpa here 8 years ago this story happened in Bombay. I was newly married with Rajesh and we were enjoying our days and nights. Rajesh is very smart and gentle person he got all the things in his little age. He has very attractive personality. After marriage I became a great fan of Rajesh because of his qualities. Rajesh is a businessman his business is related to import-export. So for this he usually makes visit to abroad and his client/suppliers are mostly from Arabian countries. And in these dealings he usually met them in hotels and office. Sometimes he welcomes his clients with call girls, because almost all Arabians are great fan of Indian women and all these things are normal in business dealings.

After 8 months of my marriage once Rajesh said to me that today you arrange the guest room because one of my clients from Dubai is coming for dinner and after dinner he will stay at our guest room and will enjoy with a call girl. All the time Rajesh made these arrangements outside but at that time due to Bombay Bomb blast there was very much checking in hotels. So for security purpose Rajesh made all these arrangements at home. So I made all the arrangements for them and was preparing dinner. On 7 pm they came I saw first time any Arabian sheikh. He was almost 6-2 in height and have 42 inches chest, will be of 42 years age and have lust in his eyes. They came in and sat in drawing room at that time I was in blue sari and a matching sleeveless blouse. They were discussing some business points. On 9 o'clock Rajesh told me to arrange dinner before that they had taken scotch.

So I called our servant and said him to arrange all the things, after arrangement I called both of them for dinner. Rajesh introduced him that, this is Mr. Rahman and this is my wife Pushpa. We said hello each other, then Rahman said you are very much lucky Mr. Rajesh; you got such a beautiful wife. We all smiled on his comment. Then we started to take dinner in between Rahman asked, what about night arrangement Rajesh answered yes I called someone but why she did not come till now? Ok I just call her and Rajesh went to another room for making phone to a call girl in that mean time Mr. Rahman said you are really a beautiful lady and have a marvelous figure I just smiled but I felt his thirst eyes on my body, he was watching my mountains and depths. I felt some shy but suddenly Rajesh came and said Mr. Rahman I am very much sorry the call girl is not coming because of security checking. In these days here the conditions are very much tight due to bomb blast. Mr. Rahman said Oh god now how I spent my night this would be very difficult for me. After completing the dinner both of them went to guest room and I went to bedroom.

After 2 hours, I think it was 12 in night Rajesh came in to bed room and asked me dear Pushpa do you love me? I replied why are you asking like that? He replied first tell me, then I said yes then he said please do one thing for me. I asked what? Then he told me please understand the whole situation. Mr. Rahman is our client, so it is our duty to please him t I questioned, but what can I do in this situation. Rajesh replied you can do everything. Mr. Rahman is very much impressed with you and he is saying if you sleep with him only for one night he will gave a biggest contact to us. Please try to understand. I shouted on Rajesh, I am your wife and you are offering me like that shame but Rajesh said quietly Please try to understand my darling he was very much requesting me then he told me if we will not agree then Mr. Rahman will break the contact and we will on road after that, because of this typical business dealing at last I got agreed and said Ok after listening my Ok Rajesh became very happy and went to call him.

After 15 minutes Mr. Rahman came to my room with Rajesh. Rajesh told him Mr. Rahman now Pushpa is only for your enjoy and he went to the guest room. Now Rahman closed the door and came near to me and said actually I was praying to god, how can I get you and god gave me a chance. Then he said you are really a beautiful lady and he took me in his arms I was silently presenting myself to him he lifted me like a doll and threw me on the bed I got little fear but what could I do? After that Rahman dropped all his clothes except his underwear. Then he came to me and opened my hairs, then he put his lips on my lips and started kissing passionately his kisses were very hard and rough during all that time he was slipping his palm on my butt and squeezing them passionately, he did my whole face wet by his kisses in between he was saying something which I could not understand I think he was speaking some Arabian language. Then he pull my sari. And his hands were moving on my whole body and I really say, in starting I was feeling hate but now I was also feeling wet and was eager to lie under him. I just heard before about the wildness of Arabians but now I am feeling myself at that time I was in petticoat and blouse and perhaps 1/2 hour had spent oh god this time was too much for my husband and in this time we did complete sex so many times. But Rahman just undid my sari now I was fully aroused and started slowly moaning but he was quite. He lied beside me and asked to arouse him now it was my chance although I was feeling shame in starting but now I had gotten fully aroused. And I started to move my hands on Rahman's body up and down he closed his eyes I started kissing him. His chest was hairy and color was very fair, his thighs were very tight moreover he was a complete man. I kissed his nipples and naval now he started moaning ohh-hh....aaahhaaahhhhh yeeessssss youuu blooooooooody biiiitchhh Indian. Now I wanted to see his big Lund(cock), which was trying to come out of his underwear. I fixed my fingers in the strip of his underwear and he lifted his hips and helped me to do him necked. Now what a glorious seen was

sympathy my hands were caught by Rajesh and boobs were in his mouth Rahman hold my waist and put his cock head on my butt hole I just cried by pain but as soon as I opened my mouth for crying Rajesh entered his cock in my mouth and I could not cry. In the mean time Rahman put his cockhead on my butt hole and pull my waist towards him but could not enter his cock into me then he asked to Rajesh have you some butter in kitchen because her hole is very much tight Rajesh told yes I go for take then Rahman told him no no I will go and he left the room then I begged to Rajesh Please save me I can't do that Then Rajesh said me darling Why are you not understanding why are you trying to get Mr.rahaman angry?

Then there were no other way and there was no one to save me so I just left myself free after coming Rahaman I made myself in bitch position Rahaman told yes Rajesh do work on her breast Rajesh started to squeezing my boobs then Rahman applied some butter on my butt hole and some on his Lun then he put his Lun on my hole and applied some pressure I was feeling a lot of pain but I was not reacting at the same time they counted one, two, three and Rahman pushed his cock forward and Rajesh push me backward and now something was inside my butt hole after a few seconds Rahman pull his cock little outside and again they did same one, two, three and now I think his half cock was into my butt hole then They both gave some jerks after a while Rahamn told Rajesh now it is moving easily so you leave now and see the show Then Rajesh once again kissed my boobs and left me and sat on sofa now I was in Rahaman's hand he told me Pushpa darling now It will be more enjoyable for you also now assume you and me like a bitch and dog and move to and fro then I also thought while it is being with the permission of my husband then why should not I enjoy with this Arabian cock. And I started to give support to Rahman he was now increasing his speed and I also joined him. My boobs were moving to and fro I was tired but was happy after 20/25 minutes he loaded my butt with his cum and then I got relaxed. Now this was 3 am in the night. Then Rahman told Mr. Rajesh I got satisfied now I want to sleep Rajesh replied Ok let us move but I told loudly I am not satisfied they both look at me in surprise. I was told you want to take my ass I gave it to you but now I am interested to take your 10 inch in my pussy because I never took such a big thing in my pussy. Rajesh shouted at me what the hell!!! Rubbish… you only give that how much we want from you

But Rahman said, "Quiet! No Rajesh she is correct you may go I will enjoy with her".

Rajesh got silent now he was helpless and he went to guest room then Rahman closed the door and abused Rajesh. I told him yes come on and fuck me now I am in love with you then he came near to me and his palms were moving on my whole body I was also kissing him. Then I lift my hands to tie up my hairs and gave him full look of my ripe mangoes and was successful to attract him on them. He came near and took one tit in his rough hand and another tit in his mouth he was really sucking my nipples like a baby. I was smiling and was pleased that at last I made him mad of my boobs. After some time he changed his mouth and hand position on my tits. Although Rajesh is also my boob lover but after feeling passionate sucking of Rahman I forgot Rajesh and thought it will be better if I become a sex-servant of Rahman in comparison of being wife of Rajesh. After getting satisfied with my boobs he told me let us do 69. I agreed and climb on him and put my pussy on her thirst lips and took his tool in my mouth I was kissing his tool like a banana and he was fucking me with his tongue. He entered his thumb and finger into my pussy and found my clit and took it in his mouth. I was in heaven no doubt he was a complete man.

I said Rahman, "I am coming"

He replied, "no problem"

And I came on his face most of my cum he drank after that he got lied me on bed and came in between my legs I spread my legs and gave a full look of my pussy he entered his cock in my pussy with little barrier because I was habitual of only 5 inch of Rajesh so my pussy was tight but this Arabian man has just double of Rajesh. After inserting he started to move to and fro and I also tied his waist with my legs I started moaning myself really he was giving me full pleasure. He fucked me at least for half an hour then he told me I am coming. I just ignore his words and told him yes yes yeeeee hhhhhh please be fast and fast again he told it may be risky if I come into you but I replied Rahman It will be my fortune I will like to become mother of your child instead of that bastard and after listening my words he gave me full length rapid jerks and loaded my pussy. After that we both got tired I told him you are my dream man he asked why? I replied because I like brave persons and you are like that.

He asked me how? I replied with smile you fuck me on the bed of my husband, in front of my husband and with the help of my husband this is what????? He also smiled and kissed me and squeezed my boobs and left the room next day he left India now we are normal after that Rajesh got some great dealings through him and yes also now when Rahman comes to India (rarely once in a year) He does not stay at hotel and Rajesh does not arrange call girl for him and really that time spends very pleasurable for me Now I have two kids of Rajesh but also Rahman and me love each other and I cannot understand which type of love is this can you?

19. Anjali

I am a working professional and stay in Bangalore. My Name is Rajesh. This is my story with a girl in my office. Her name is Anjali. We both joined the same company as freshers and were in the same training batch.

Bangalore was a new city for both of us and soon we became good friends. After few months while working I bought a bike and then we used to roam around in my bike. We both were quite free and open with each other and occasionally used to share naughty jokes and talks.

She was quite comfortable with me and there were many times when we held hands while crossing roads or she had placed her hand on my shoulder while sitting on my bike. All this was casual friendly gestures and there was no hanky panky involved in our friendship. But everything changed that one day.

It was Friday morning and I had absolutely no mood to work. I was trying to time pass and pinged Anjali. "Oye kya kar rahi hai"(Hey what are you doing) She replied "Kaam karne ki koshish kar rahi hoon. Par (Trying to work. But)not in mood. I am already in weekend mode."

I thought Bingo. I asked her. "Hey let's make some plan. How about a movie after we had lunch. I can leave early."

She said. "Am ready...Let's go"

We asked some common friends but all of them had some work and it was not possible for them to leave early from office. So we two decided to catch some movie in the Forum Mall, which is the most popular mall in Bangalore. We reached there by 3PM, but to our surprise not a single ticket for any watchable movie was available.

"Ohh Shit...Not a single ticket..What you want to do now" I asked Anjali.

"No Idea Rajesh. You tell...We can just chill around as well" She said.

"Hey.. why dont we go for a drive towards Old Madras Road. I have heard there is some Dhabhas on the way. We can have something there and then come back."

"Yup...let's go.." She said.

Thus our journey started. Who knew that not getting the movie tickets would make this day so memorable. I was cruising my bike on the empty Old Madras Road. Cool air was breezing against me and Anjali. She had come closer to me as it was getting difficult to talk due to the air noise. I could see the sun going down the horizon.

The entire sky was crimson with lovely romantic effect. She was holding my waist and her boobs were touching my back occasionally. Even though we were not official lovers but some chemistry was going on in those moments. After covering quite some distance, we stopped by one Dhabha for tea and snacks.

The sun had gone down taking away the colour with it, but now clouds had gathered making the sky dark purple. The weather was slowly getting cold and it was getting dark and cloudy. We still had some time for dusk but today clouds were deciding the time for us. We felt it's better to leave as it could start raining any time. While our drive back Anjali was sitting really close to me.

I guess she was feeling cold as she had worn a thin Sleeveless chiffon salwar suit. We were almost nearing Bangalore and it started raining heavily. We were on the road with no shed nearby where we could take shelter. After some distance I saw a tree. I stopped my bike under it. We both tried to save ourselves from the rain in that small tree but we were already quite drenched.

Anjali was shivering in the cold. Her salwar suit was totally wet and sticking to her entire body hugging her voluminous figure.

For the first time I noticed her with a different feeling. She had a slim waist and good size firm boobs. Her hands were thin, slender and looked very soft. She was shivering and I could see the goose bumps on her arm. She had a round face with dark eyes.
It looked more mystic because of the kohl that she had applied. Her lips were thick and properly accentuated with lipstick. Small water droplets dropped from her lovely nose to her lipstick laden lips. She clasped my hand firmly while it thundered heavily. "yaar bahut thand lag rahi hai"(Friend I am feeling very cold) She said making chattering sound with her teeth.
I came close to her. My arms were crushing her arms. The small tree could not do much to save us from the torrential rain and we both were drenched till our bare bones. Not even a thread of my underwear was dry and I could say the same for her as well. It would have taken another 20 minutes drive to my house which was nearer. Her PG was much further.
"Anjali, I think we should leave. Yahan ruk ke koi fayeda nahin hai.(It's no use to stop over here) It doesn't seem to slow down."
"Haan(yes) Rajesh. Chalo...Chalte hai. Mujhe bahut thand lag rahi hai."(Come on.. Let's go.I am feeling very cold) we started again in the rain. She was holding my waist and had buried her face on my shoulder. It is difficult to drive in situation when such a lovely girl is so close to you and your visibility is almost nil due to rain.
Somehow we reached my home. I stay in a 2 BHK flat with one more person. We both have our separate rooms. I opened the door as my roommate had still not come. "Anjali, take this towel and go and change else you will catch cold." I handed her a towel and showed him the restroom. "Change?? Kya pahnu mein(what do I wear)...you want me to be in towel for rest of the evening"
She was shivering and smiling at the same time. "At least kuch pahenne ke liye toh do(At least give me something to wear)."
"hmm..I can get you some clothes but the problem is neither it will be your style nor size.." I joked. "Are yaar kuch bhi lao....sab chalega..(Come on friend get anything ...anything will do) I

can't be wearing at least this for sure for a single more second"
She laughed. I gave her a T-shirt and pyjama. She went inside the
bathroom.

I also changed to shorts and T-shirt. I went inside the kitchen
to make some tea. We needed that badly. She came out with
the towel wrapped around her hair. She was wearing the pyjama
and T-shirt that I gave her. The T-shirt was quite loose for her
and was giving little-little peek of her melony boobs.

She could not wear her inner garments inside for obvious
reasons and without bra her big boobs were jiggling in the T-
shirt. The ass was also properly visible with the pyjama sticking in her ass creek. Needless to say I was having all kinds of
thoughts and it was getting difficult to control my emotions. In
fact this was first time when I was looking at Anjali from a totally different perspective.

She is no more a friend with whom I used to hang around.
Suddenly I was feeling a kind emotion which I had never felt
towards her. I wanted to caress her in my arms. To pamper her,
to play with her hot body. But I could not jump into all this
as I was supposed to be a cultured man and should control my
emotions.

But Carnal desires are hard to keep and I started looking for
ways to come close to her. I could not resist myself and went
to the rest room that she used. Her clothes were hanged in
the hanger. She had hidden her bra and panty below the salwar
kamiz. I took them out and sniffed. The panty smelled awesome. I imagined how it would be to smell her vagina directly.

Her bra was smelling like the perfume she had used. I came out
and we sat down on the couch with Tea cups and switched on
the TV. It was still raining heavily outside. Suddenly I remembered, it is almost time for my roommate to come and I did not
want to spoil those precious moments with her. So I called up
my roomie.

See my luck, he was also stranded in one of his friends house and
told me he would not be coming back that night. I was elated
but didn't show it. "My roomie is also stuck in rain. He is not

going to come tonight." I said to Anjali.

She was watching the TV. "I don't know when this rain will stop. How will I go home Rajesh" She asked me with concern.

"Hmmm....Let's see.. Once the rain stops I will drop you." I consoled her.

"Actually yaar(friend), I am starting to have a headache because of the cold. Want to go home and sleep for some time. You have a disprin." She said.

"No Yaar(Friend). I generally do not keep disprin as I was getting habituated to it. If you want to sleep you can go in the room and sleep."

"No its ok, Not that bad also." She said.

"Tumhara sar daba doon kya?(Should I press your head) I think you will feel better." I asked her. She just smiled and didn't said anything, which I took as yes. I went and stood behind her. She was still sitting on the couch. As her T shirt was quite big, I could see her cleavage well enough. I felt like putting my hand inside and grabbing one but resisted.

I started massaging her forehead. I was massaging her slowly, applying pressure just above her eyebrows. Then slowly using my thumb I massaged behind her ears. She seemed to enjoy it. Her eyes were closed and she was making sound like haaa-aaan...aaahhhh. achha lag raha hai... after that I brought down my hand to her neck and shoulder and started giving her a shoulder massage.

Now this time effect was different. She didn't move. I knew she was liking it as she didn't ask me to stop but at the same time, she was not saying anything either. I slowly massaged her neck and shoulder. I could see goose bumps in those areas. She was still not moving. She just kept on changing the channels one by one.

I slowly moved my hand to the front and massaged below her neck slowly. I still could not make myself to take my hands inside her T-shirt. I slowly sat down on my knees. Now my face was reaching her shoulder height. I could smell the perfume that she had applied. It was same that was smelling in her bra.

Some fruity smell and that was driving me crazy.

Thoughts of her bra and panty started coming to me and I could not control my hard on. All my good boy fundas(principles) went out the window. I could not think of anything else and I moved my nose against her neck trying to smell the perfume. I felt the goose bumps against my nose and lips. I kissed her slowly on the neck. She folded her neck further back.

I kissed her again and this time I inserted my right hand inside her T-shirt and touched her left boob. He skin was soft like satin. I slowly explored her boob with my hand. Her nipples were hard like nuts. She wrapped her hand around my head while I kissed her neck again. This time I gave her a wet kiss. Slowly I moved up and licked her ear lobes. This time she went crazy.

She clasped my head and pulled my hairs. I kept licking her ear lobe while exploring her both the boobs. After sometime she could not take it anymore and she held me by hair and removed my head. She turned back and looked into my eyes. We looked into each other for some time. No one spoke anything. I held her cheeks and slowly planted a kiss on her lips.

She closed her eyes and kissed me back. The kiss slowly grew more passionate and then we were exploring each other's mouth with our tongues. We were in a situation from which there was no looking back. I also joined her in the couch and made her sit on my lap. We kept on kissing. I inserted my hand again inside her T-shirt and squeezed her boobs and kissed her on her neck.

I pulled up the T-shirt to reveal her juicy boobs. It was white and smooth with hard dark nipples. I licked her nipple. She could not take this and pushed my mouth away from it. I held her hands and again groped one boob in my mouth and started sucking it. She was going crazy. She started caressing my hair. One by one I was sucking her boobs and slowly I removed her T-shirt.

She was very shy to be like that in front of me. "Rajesh...please light off karo...mujhe sharm aa rahi hai"(Please turn off the lights..I am feeling shy) She said hiding her boobs with her hands. I held her hands and guided her toward the bed in my room.

She lied down covering her with the blanket. I was thinking whether I should fuck her or not as I was not having the Condom.

Suddenly I realized that I should look into my roommate's room. He has a steady girlfriend and she used to come and stay with him as well. I went searching in his cupboards. Didn't get anything. I was thinking whether I should go out and buy a condom but that was not possible as it was raining heavily. Then I looked under the mattress. Yes. There it was.

Three packs of Extra Pleasure condom. I went back to my room. She had already switched off the lights but still I could see her in the light coming from the streetlight in front of my window. I removed my T Shirt and went inside the blanket. As soon as I went inside she hugged me and planted a kiss on my lips.

We started smooching again and this time she was more free than before. She was exploring my back and chest and I was squeezing her boobs. I then get on top of her and started kissing her from her neck. I sucked her boobs and pinched her nipple.

"Oouuch..Rajesh tum ye kya kar rahe ho" (Rajesh what is this you are doing)

"Tumhare boobs ko taste kar raha hoon." (I am tasting your boobs)

"Achha...toh kaisa laga taste"(Alright .. then how was the taste) She asked.

"Bilkul rasgulle jaisa" (Just like the Rasgulla sweet)

"Ragulle ko ab nichorna band karo...sara ras nikal jayega...waise bhi we don't have protection. Fir mein badi wali rasgulli ban jaungi tab.. (Stop squeezing the Rasgulla sweet... All the juice will come out.. anyways we don't have protection. The I will become your big Rasgulla sweet.)

" I was still sucking her boobs. "I have everything....I am always ready..." I said..

She pulled my head in front of her and asked. "Achha....toh kitne rasgulle pahle kha chuke ho??"(OK.. So how many sweets have you eaten before)

I looked into her eyes "Anjali, tum pahli ho.(Anjali you are the first) And this condom is thanks to my roomie and his GF"

Listening to this she pulled my head and kissed me hard. I held her hands and put it behind her head. Her armpits were clean shaved. I licked them. She could not take this and was trying to cover it but my grip was hard and she could not do anything.

I slowly moved down and kissed her navel and explored the navel area with my lips. I moved further down and kissed below the navel. I inserted my hand inside the pajama and squeezed her hip. I then held the elastic of pajama and removed it completely. I could see her trimmed pussy in the slight light that was coming through the window. I kissed her thighs and legs.

She was moaning like anything. I then planted a kiss on her pussy. She shivered.

"Rajesh wahan nahin...bahut lagega"(Rajesh not there...it will hurt a lot)

She cried. I did not listen to her. I licked her pussy lips and she went crazy. She was trying to fold her legs but the way I had positioned my head did not let her cover her love hole.

My face was totally on top of her pussy and she could not do anything apart from pulling my head and hair. I licked her pussy lips again and this time I plucked one vaginal lobe between by teeth. She was now not able to control herself and was shouting.

"Rajesh Pleeaaaase.....don't do....mar jaungi(I will die).....wahan nahin(not there) pleaaaaase....Tum upar jo karna hai kar lo(You can do what you want on the top)....wahan nahin(Noth there)...please"

But how can you stop in such a moment. I held both her legs, kept it apart and kept on licking her pussy lips. After some time she started liking it and moved her legs to open her pussy more. I kept on licking and exploring her pussy. I inserted my lips inside her vagina. The salty taste was driving me crazy. I was licking the pussy and also inserted one of finger inside her.

I finger fucked her and then inserted 2 fingers and then finally 3 fingers and increased my motion of finger fucking her. She was going crazy and making sounds. "Ohh Rajesh....aaaaaahhhh......nahiiiiiiiinn" After some time she came and my finger was filled with her juices. I got up and wore the condom. She spread her legs to make way for me.

I planted my cock on her pussy and pushed. As it was so lubricated by my sucking and finger fucking, my cock went inside easily. I started stroking her slowly. She was also moving her hips to match my motion. I kissed her softly on her lips. She opened her eyes and brought her lips near my ear and whispered. "Rajesh You know what..." I stopped for a while and asked "What?"

She said "Please don't stop. Continue" I started stroking again and this time with more force. I was stroking hard and hard and she was moving her butt with my motion. She wrapped my body with her legs and I was almost in peak and was about to come any moment. I was stroking hard and hard with full force. I shouted "Anjaliiiii.....I will come soon....very soon..."

She clasped my head and shouted. "Come dear come... Please come...I want to come with you...because u know what...."

"What?"

"Because...I loooveeee you sooo muuuuuch"

And with those words echoing in my ears, we both came together. We had our moment of love in that love making session. We were very tired after getting drenched and with so much of activity.

We kissed each other and slept for a while embracing. When we got up she slipped into the Tshirt that I was wearing. It covered only till her thighs. We ordered Pizza as it was quite late. I asked her will it be a problem if she stay in my house for that night. "Obviously not baby" She laughed and planted a kiss on my cheek.

She called up her PG and made some excuse. In the meantime Pizza came and we had our dinner. As we already slept little, we felt quite fresh. I looked outside the window. The rain had stopped and could see the moon peeking within the dark clouds. I looked inside, one moon was sitting in front of me and I had the full night with me...

20. *Priti*

My name is Priti. I lived with my mother till about two years ago when I got married. My mother was a Matron with a very big Hospital in Delhi till she retired a few years back. We had a house quite close to the Hospital and the Nurses Hostel. Due to the loyalty of my mother to the hospital the directors of the hospital contracted her for five years extendable as warden of the the nurses hostel.

She also took classes for the nurses -epecially the new nurses and those wanting to go abroad-. The old hospital building had been converted to a nurse's hostel and the operation theatre was used as a class room. My father a vascular surgeon in the same hospital had lost his life in a road accident after about 10 years of married life. I was 7 years then.

My Mother never remarried. As her work timing and my school and later college timings did not coincide I had a set of keys of the house and her office (in the event I had to make use of the printer or the computer of her office). My Mother was a Malayali woman 5 feet 7 inches, well endowed and a little on the plumb side.

Being a mother figure there were quite a flow of young nurse coming to her for help - whether it was domestic trouble, love gone sour, or academic. Mum had time for all. The story I am going to narrate happened when I was in senior class - about 15 years old. One day I returned from school early for some reason which I cannot remember.

As I had expected Mom to be in office I entered the house using my keys. As I was walking to my room I heard my Mom saying "Come do not cry. We are all here to help you. I will help you. No harm will come." The sound was from the drawing room. I went straight to my room, but after changing my uniform, curiosity got better of me and I tiptoed to hear more of the problem and who it was.

From hiding I saw Mom had her arms around a young Malaysian trainee-nurse and the girl had her face resting on Mom's huge breast. Mom had on a long 'T' shirt that she wore in the house (same as me) which meant she had nothing on underneath -also same as me. The trainee had on a short skirt and blouse. She was about 5 ft tall.

After a while Mom kissed her on her forehead and then held her face with her hand and first wiped her tears and then kissed her on the eyes and then the nose. They both smiled at each other. Mom then kissed her lightly on her lips and hugged her tight. The nurse did not seem to mind. Mom then lifted her face and kissed her full and proper on her lips and continued to do so for a while.

No resistance as yet. Mom again kissed her on the lips but this time I could see she tried to put her tongue into the nurse's mouth. There was a bit of resistance and the nurse moved away but Mom held her and again pulled her close to her. "Come sweetheart, I won't hurt you". She smiled and moved close to mom. Her back was towards me.

Mom then put both her arms around her body and started to kiss her. At first the nurse remained like a statue but a while later she also put her arms around Mom. They were in a clinch and stood up as Mom's hand started to wander all over her back. Mom then pressed her arse cheeks first with one hand then with both hands. They continued to kiss each other.

The nurse was also moving her hand but her body had screened my view. Mom then put her hands under the skirt of the nurse. I could see she had on Baby blue panties. Mom had got one palm under her panty. They stopped kissing and broke the clinch. Mom stepped back and opened the button of her T shirts. The nurse immediately put her hand in and pulled her right breast out.

It was for the first time I had seen them. I knew they were big but I never imagined them to be so big. The nurse after playing with it for a while started to suck it. It may have got a little uncomfortable for Mom so she stepped back and pulled the T shirt off and threw it on the sofa. She was now as naked as the time she was born and bald around her pussy too.

The nurse again began her sucking - now alternating between Mom's left and right breast. After a short while Mom took of the blouse of the nurse and her bra. I could not see her breast as could only see her back. Mom then bent down and started to suck her breast. While sucking her breast she removed the skirt of the nurse and then got on her haunches.

The nurse had a cute little dimpled arse. First mom held her arse cheeks and started to suck her cunt, but later holding the nurse arse with one hand started to finger her own cunt. It was hairless and big. What was very prominent was Mom's cilt. It was large and thick -perhaps the size of a new born child. Mine were big but no way close to Mom's.

Mom had put her two fingers inside and was frigging herself very vigorously. The nurse pulled her up and pushed Mom on to the sofa and spread her legs. She then got between her legs and started to lick her cunt. Mom was responding to her licks, when she suddenly got up and said "let us go to my bedroom."

(I got a bit of a problem as my panties were at my knees - I was also frigging my self - and it was difficult to move fast enough to hide.) Luckily, they started to collect their clothes and I managed to hide. In Mom's bedroom, Mom placed the nurse on the bed and spread her legs. It was the first sight I got of the cunt of the nurse. It was small and very cute.

She was devoid of any hair also. Don't know whether she had shaved or naturally had none. (That day I decided to find out for myself at a later date). Mom then mounted her and placed her own mouth on the nurse's choot (cunt). I could see her licking her and with her legs spread she was also tongue fucking her. When she was sucking her cilt she would put her finger into her cunt.

The licking and sucking from them both was making a storm - not only on the bed but in my body, I had meanwhile discarded my panty and was profusely leaking - ; the nurse now started to move her hip up and down to match Mom's tongue movement. Mom stopped to lick and got of her. 'Are you climaxing, my love" " yea, do me more my little baby" the nurse said.

They both changed position with the nurse on the top and now Mom's cunt facing me. Mom's cilt had really got enlarged and the nurse was sucking it like she was sucking a cock. She was frigging Mom'cunt with two fingers of one hand and using three fingers in her arse hole. (I thought I would die today as I was climaxing so many times)

Soon both Mom and the nurse were moving their hips at full steam and climaxed together and then lay sucking each other. "Baby you are really good" Mom said, "We should get together more often". "Whenever you want me I am ready."With such a large cilt like yours, I have become your slave" the nurse said and continued,

"I will never go with anyone but will be only for you" "No do not make such a promise. We cannot keep this promise. When I got married, my husband and I promised to be faithful to each other - this was after the ritual promise around the fire. Yet on the third day of our honeymoon, we had swapped partners.

They were a Russian couple holidaying in Goa and then at a party given by them there was free-for-all. It was great fun. I'll show you, on condition you do not talk about it with anyone. I must have sex at a regular basis with anyone -man, woman or animal for that matter, so I cannot be faithful to one and would like you to be like me also.

With that Mom went to the cupboard and brought out a steel safe. She opened it with a code and took out some photos. "See these are from our Honeymoon. That is my husband. See his cock - it is nice and big and thick. Standing next to him is the Russian woman, really busty then me and the Russian with the thin long cock.

This is me sucking the Russian while his wife sucks my cunt

and my hubby fucks her. These are pictures of the party. This Negro was good with the largest and thickest cock. He took my arse virginity." Mom kept showing the pictures of the party. The nurse found a large double headed dildo.

The photos were forgotten and Mom and she then put the dildo into each other's cunts and started to fuck each other -the climax came soon enough. "Is it time for your daughter to return?" Fuck her I want to suck you once more" Mom replied. "I would like to fuck her someday" The nurse said. "So would I" Mom giggled and said.

She then got down to the business of sucking her. Once she climaxed again the nurse said she better be going as she had to go on duty and started to dress. Mom kept her panty after wiping her pussy with it. At the door they again got into a clinch and sucked each other's tongue. Before leaving Mom again got on her knees and kissed the nurse's honey box.

21. Kareena

I here am Mrs. Kareena Bose. Don't be surprised but I'm 37 years old and stay in Mumbai. My husband is a rich businessman having not enough time for me. Actually he isn't interested in me coz he complains that I'm too big down there. You see, I have a big cunt. He just can't satisfy me with his dick. So he just blames me. But, I don't care. I have stopped having sex with him. But my sex life hasn't stopped. I have my own means. This is a true story, believe it or not. Let me warn you. All those who are disgusted by sex with animals, do not read this. This happened a few years back when we had gone to the States on a holiday to visit family friends. They stayed in Texas, actually they owned a ranch.

Now, Sita, my husband's friend's wife was a good friend of mine too. I confide in her a lot and she knows about all my sexual escapades. Now, through all my sexual incidences with different men, none really could satisfy me and bring me to a fuckin' orgasm. My best partner was my 11 inch vibrator. I needed something better than that. The next morning, just roaming around the farm with Sita, my eyes settled on a big, white stallion servicing a mare. The horse's massive dick going in and out of the mare's cunt sure got me excited. Seeing the mischievous look in my eyes, Sita could guess what was going on in my mind. Well, lucky for me she thought that the idea was great and decided to join me. We just had to wait for the right time.

We soon got it. The men had to go and attend a seminar and they decided to leave us behind (as if we wanted to go). These people left early morning and we waited for the maids of the house to involve themselves with the daily chores. We left the house on pretext of riding the horses. We took two stallions: I rode Whisper, the dream horse and Sita rode another brown horse called Lightfoot. We rode till the farthest end of the meadow where there stood a barn-house. It was far away not to be seen from the house. We went inside the barn house and closed it from inside. We tied the horses to the stumps. Lightfoot was kept a bit far away so that he wouldn't interfere with our stunt.

Now, Whisper needed to be aroused in the right way so that he could be ready for the act. I started stripping in front of him. So did Sita. Off came our tops and skirts. There we stood in our under-clothes. I went close to Whisper and put his nose between my breasts so that he could smell my fragrance. I unhooked my bra and let my breasts go free in front of him. Sita took a jar of water and started pouring it over my cleavage. Whisper licked the flowing water. His tongue wandered all over my breasts. The sensation of his rough tongue on my nipples made them hard like marbles. Oh, what a feeling!! I wanted Sita to experience it too and we repeated the same thing with her. I pulled off Sita's panties. She tried to push Whisper's face towards her cunt. It was hard but she achieved it after a little while. Now, I could see Whisper's dick getting hard. The smell of Sita's wonderful cunt was doing its job. The horse gave it a few wet slurps of his tongue. It took some time of caressing and coaxing to get Whisper's dick to its royal hard position at its fullest length. We had to find out a way to get it into our pussies. We dragged a small bench under Whisper's stomach. It was just about the right height. I took Whisper's dick in my hand and gave it a slight rub. By the way, it was 11" in length and 3" in girth. I had to use both my hands to engulf it. Sita bent down and gave it a lick with her tongue. Whisper started neighing. I was sure he was also feeling good. I allowed Sita to go first. I would say I was a bit selfish. You see, I wanted him to cum in me. So I wanted to go last. I bent down and started licking Sita's pussy. Had to get her well lubricated for the penetration. I made her cum with my tongue and then inserted my fingers in her cunt. I spread her juices nicely around and then told her to get ready. She got on the bench and raised her cunt so that her pussy lips just touched the head of Whisper's dick. I had to assist Whisper in getting it in. Sita forced open her lips with her fingers while I rubbed the tool and tried getting it in. Whisper started responding and the tool glided in with some effort. Sita gasped by the size of it. It sure was tearing her cunt. After some time, Sita got accustomed to the rhythmic up and down motion. It was slow at first but then she picked up speed. I also had to do something and went for Sita's breast. I flicked my tongue over her nipple. Moans escaped Sita's mouth as she became more and more ecstatic with Whisper pumping into her. The combined efforts of Whisper's dick and my tongue got Sita cumming in minutes. Whisper also by now had gotten into the act and co-operating fully. Obviously, it was his first time to fuck two sex-hungry females lusting for his massive dick. After cumming once more, Sita decided to let me have the pleasure. Oh, how I was waiting for this moment. Sita lubricated my pussy with her own juices. I got on the bench and guided Whisper's dick in my cunt. Wow, was it big!! I guess I had met my match. I started my up and down motion on his dick. Now, Sita started licking my breasts. I couldn't believe it. I was really fucking a horse. My first orgasm ripped through me and I cummed screaming out with pleasure. Now I had to make him cum. I wanted him to spurt his jism inside me. I increased my speed. He soon reached his hilt. I came to know coz he too increased his speed of pumping into me. Oh, how much I wanted his cum inside me. Not long, not long. Whisper neighed out loudly and started cumming. Load after load of hot cum were being let go in my cunt. I also cummed at the same time. My cunt was big but not so big enough to hold a horse's cum. It overflowed my cunt and ran onto my thighs. Sita was masturbating and she too couldn't hold on for long. We both were screaming out and Whisper too was neighing. Luckily, we were far off from home not to attract attention. After some time, Whisper's limp cock slipped out of my wet cunt. I was exhausted. I got down from the bench and joined Sita on the ground. Ummmmmm, we were thoroughly satisfied. Thanks to Whisper. I got up and kissed him. It was certainly a great experience. We dressed and rode back home. Our husbands came home late at night. They had no idea about our episode. I returned back to India and resumed my life. This secret was a secret till now. Now, it is out to the public. I don't care if my husband reads it too. I want him to realise that I can do without his dick.

22. Prena

I am Bharat here and I am going to tell the hot fling that between my mom and a nasty guy at my rural village. When this happened, I was 11 years old but I still remember it clearly. I am the only son of my parents. My dad is a business man and my mom was a housewife. Besides my parents, the only relative I had was my blind grandma living at my dad's birth village. My grandma was home sick and refused to leave the village. So, she stayed there with a maid. The fun began when the maid had to leave for some reason. Now, about my mom, my mom's name is Prena and she is the best looking woman I have ever seen in my life. She was a professional dancer so she maintained a lovely figure. After my birth, she quit dancing and became the perfect housewife. Her skin was milky white and her hair was pitch black that covered her entire back. She has very pretty lips which anyone can kiss forever. Her ass is big and round. She used to wear saris and that made her butt more beautiful. It was the perfect match with her lusty figure. Although she maintained a lovely figure, the sign of her age could be found on her belly. She had a little touch of fat on her belly which made her even more sexier. But her greatest weapon would be her breasts. They were huge. The blouses would do a poor job of covering them because of their big size. They were like juicy coconuts. The sight of her cleavage would make anyone mad. I always wondered how she danced with those things on her. Maybe that's why she was so famous among my dad's friends. She was a 41 year old sex bomb. Still, she maintained a very ideal life.

Now, let me jump to the main stuff. One day, we got a letter from my grandma telling that she needed someone to look after her for a month as her servant had to leave for a month. My dad asked my mom to do that. My mom was more happy to do that. She and grandma always had a special bond. As it was my holiday, my dad told me to go with her. So one fine morning we left for our village. Our village house was ok. It was made of bricks. The only problem it had was that the bathroom was not attached to the main building. So if someone needs to do something they have to go out of the house. With our house a friend of my grandpa called Reddy lived. He was very friendly with us and was a good family friend. His wife passed away and his two sons lived abroad, He was all alone. He was a rich man and had influence over the village. He used to come to my grandma's place a lot. His house had a joining door with my grandma's house as my grandma used to live alone. When we arrived there, he was quite happy to see us.

Reddy: "ahh, at last all of you have come, I missed you all. Welcome home."

Dad: "thank you chacha. Hope you are doing all right?"

Reddy: "yes my boy, I am fine. How are you Prena? "

Mom:" I am fine Radii "

now when Reddy was talking to my mom, he was looking at her in a different way. Although my mom and dad didn't notice, I looked at his eyes and saw that they were stuck at my mom's boobs. More importantly, I saw a bulge on his dhoti. At that moment, I just ignored it and went inside the house with everyone. Grandma was very pleased to hear us. After dinner we all got together to do a little chat. Grandma was talking about the bathroom problem. As it was not attached with the main building, it was very hard for my grandma to use it. My dad told grandma that he would make an attached bathroom for her very soon. We stayed up until 10 pm and we chatted with Reddy uncle. At 11pm Reddy left our house and we went inside our rooms. My mom and grandma were staying together in one room but me and dad slept on the balcony as it was very hot. My dad went to sleep instantly but as it was a new place for me, I was having trouble going to sleep. My dad started to snore loudly. Man, this guy can really sleep. He wouldn't wake up even if an atom bomb explodes around him. I was awake and was looking at the sky. It was a very beautiful night. Who knew that the most remarkable event of my life was about to happen that night?

After about two hours, I heard the sound of grandma's door opening. It was my mom in a lovely yellow sari. Man, she was a sex bomb. I guess she was going to the toilet. She came near to me and checked whether I was sleeping or not. My mom was very caring of me and it would make me mad if she finds out that I was awake. So, I pretended to be asleep. She came near me and kissed me on my forehead. Then she got up and started walking towards the bathroom. I got up and watched her as she was going to the toilet. Everything was normal. Just that moment I saw a very weird thing. Reddy was hiding behind the big mango tree beside the toilet. I was sure that he was up to something and my instinct told me that something was about to happen. I decided not to wake up my dad and I was wondering why he was hiding like that but I got my answer pretty quickly. As soon as my mom entered the bathroom he came out behind the tree and took place behind the toilet wall. I was watching very carefully as he was looking towards us. After sometime, mother got out of the toilet. As she turned her back to lock the bathroom door, Reddy jumped on her back and put his hands on her mouth. My mom was about to shout but he was too strong for her. He kept one hand on her mouth and he wrapped around her belly with the other hand. He told her something and my mother stopped fighting. Reddy had an evil smile on his face. He told my mom to walk. He was still holding her from behind and in the shinning moonlight; I saw a knife on his hand. He smelled her hair like a dog. My mom looked at us helplessly. They entered Reddy's house through the joining door. Now, I got up and started to follow them. Reddy's house was bigger than ours. He took my mom upstairs. I was staying in the shadows and following them. Reddy took mom to a room and locked it from inside. I quickly followed them and stood behind the door. I heard my mom cry. There was a small hole on the window and light was coming through it. I peeped through the hole and saw the sexiest scene in my life. My mom was in Reddy's arms and Reddy was trying to kiss her face. Mom was trying her best to avoid her ugly lips but it was a hopeless try. He planted a number of moist kisses on her beautiful sexy face. After some time, he pushed mom onto the bed. Surprisingly the bed was covered with flowers. It was decorated for a Suhaagraat(honey moon).

Reddy: Stop fighting Prena, if you do as I say, there will be no problem.

Mom: what are doing Reddyji; i am like your daughter. Please release me or I will tell everything to my husband.

Hearing this, Reddy started to laugh loudly.

Reddy: you will tell your husband? Well, what if your husband never wakes up from sleep my lovely?

Mom: what are you talking about?

Reddy: Listen Randi (whore), if I want, my men can burn down your house in an instant. I am the most powerful around here. No one can touch me. So cooperate with me or your son and husband is done for, understand?

Hearing this, mom started to cry. Reddy was such a perverted asshole that he started to laugh. He then came near to mother and hugged her again. This time mom was really silent. Reddy held her face to admire her beauty. He looked at her with lust and planted some passionate wet kisses on her lovely luscious lips. He started to lick her whole face. I was getting aroused to see this hot action. My modest mom was sucked by an ugly, fat black man. While kissing, he started to squeeze her ample buttock. His hands started to roam on my mother's sexy butt. Her ass was too big and round for his hands to cover. As this position was not suitable for ass roaming, he bent down and kept his mouth on her big ass. He started to smell her ass area and was giving small, lusty bites on her ass globes. Mom was trying to keep his head from her ass but it was of no use. He wrapped her belly with his hands and was smooching her buttock. After 15 minutes of ass loving, we went up and went for her boobs. This time, he didn't try to bite her boobs; he started to squeeze her breasts. My mom's breasts were so big that one hand wasn't enough for one breast. He then used both of his hands to feel her boob completely. He held each boobs a number of times. Finally he gave a little bite to each boob and released her. He stepped back a little and with a swift motion, removed the dhoti from his body. He was completely nude. Her chest was covered with white hair. His belly was huge and ugly but the thing scared my mom was his cock. It was almost 10 inch long and was fully erect. It was pointing towards my mom. He started to massage his cock and sat on the bed. Then he told my mom something really weird.

Reddy: Prena, go the bathroom, you will find some clothes there. Wear it with your mangalsutra and don't try to escape or anything. There is no window there. Hahahaha.

Hearing this, mom entered the bathroom. She was sobbing quietly. She knew that there was no escape. This ugly mad man is going to make full use of her. As mother went inside the bathroom, Reddy got up and inserted a cassette into the player and took a bottle form the table. The sign of victory was all over his face. He drank a little from the bottle. My mom came out from the bathroom and I couldn't believe what I saw. She was dressed in a red sari. She looked like a newlywed wife. She was looking dam sexy. The sight of my sexy mom seemed to freeze Reddy. He just started at her for a moment. My mom was completely silent.

Reddy: come to me my bahu.

Mom: please Reddyji, please don't do this. Please I beg of you.

Reddy: Shut up Randi (whore), look at my cock. This is hard just because of you. I will enjoy every inch of your body my darling. Now come to me, I won't say it again.

Mom came near him and stood at the edge of the bed. Reddy got up and put his face on her lovely fleshy belly. He agian started to feel her ass. He then started to kiss those sexy pieces of flashes around her belly. He inserted his tongue on her bellybutton and was sucking very hard. Although my mom was completely against everything, her body was not listening to her mind. Her eyes became closed as she was receiving this love treatment from this ugly man. Reddy then again kissed her ass globes, breasts and finally kissed her lips again. He then released her and leaned against the wall. He started the player and a Hindi song started to play.

Reddy: Prena, I once saw you dance my love and that was the beginning of my lust for you. How did you manage to dance with such big ass and those round boobs, tell me?

Mom: Please Reddyji.

Reddy: I bet all your husband's friend wanted to fuck you right? How many of them have you fucked?

Mom was really silent now.

Reddy: Tell me Randi (whore), how many guys have sucked on your lovely tits?

Mom: I only have my husband as my lover. No one has done anything to me besides my husband.

Reddy: Really? I don't believe it. How the hell your husband satisfies such a piece of sex goddess like you? Well, truth or not, get ready to get the fuck of your life. But we will do that later. Now dance for me my Randi.

Mom was out of words and stared at Reddy. Reddy again told her to dance. As there was no choice, my mom started to move a little. Her ass was sawing like crazy and Reddy was looking at her with his mouth was open. Her jiggly breasts actually made him drooling. My mom was looking too hot. Even a dead man would get erection by looking at my mom dancing. Her big coconut shaped boobs were jumping in a rhythmic motion. They would jump up and down or sideways. The blouse mom had to wear was too small for her love balloons. They did a poor job of covering her boobs. Suddenly Reddy called her. As mom went near him, he pulled off her sari in a swift motion. Mom was in her Sari and petticoat. Mom tried to cover her boobs with her hands Reddy just overpowered her and freed her boobs from mom's hand wall. Reddy stick his face in between her breasts and started to smell her boobs. Mom had her eyes closed the whole time. Reddy was again giving small bites on her boobs. The blouse became all wet from his saliva. I think there wasn't any part left on my mom's boobs that Reddy hasn't sucked. Reddy kept on biting her tits for good 15 minutes and then again told her to dance. My mom was in a dance. She couldn't believe that this was happening to her. This time Reddy told her to pay more attention on her ass. Mom started to move her ass in a very seductive way. Reddy was stroking her penis very hard. This dance show was becoming too much for him. Suddenly he got up from the bed and stopped the player. My mom stopped dancing. Sweat was covering her whole body. Reddy then sat on a sofa near the bed and told mom to come forward. Again, as mom came near him, he did his best to feel her boobs and ass sucking and squeezing away. Finally he planted some wet kisses on her lips and told her to bend on her knees. Mom knew what was coming and there was sign of fears on her lovely eyes.

Reddy: You danced quite lovely my dear. Now your reward is my dick. Suck on it real good.

Saying this, he held her head and pushed it forward towards his dick. His 10 inch penis was inch away from her lips. He then started to tease her with his dick. He touched her eyes with his dick head. His dick's head was shinning with Precum. He then kept his penis on her lips and started to move in a circular motion. After doing this sometime, he finally rested her prick and gave it a little push. My mom had to open her mouth widely to accommodate his huge tool. Reddy gave a loud moan of pleasure. First he held his dick in that position for a while. My mom was trying to stop him by holding his hands but it was of no use. He simply pushed his cock and more of the meat entered her mouth. Half of the cock was in and mom's mouth was fully stretched. He then withdraws his tool and pushed it again. He started to mouth fuck her. He held her head and started to push it back and forth. I guess with was giving him much pleasure because with every stroke of his cock in my mom's mouth, he would give out a loud moan. Mom was having a hard time to keep pace with Reddy's vicious strokes. She was actually gagging and was trying her best to stop him. But Reddy was too powerful and was filled with lust. He simply ignored her weak protest and kept on mouth fucking her. He started to pump more of his cock in mother's mouth. Guess mother was not used with deep throat. Slowly Reddy pushed his whole 10 inch Lund (cock) on my mom's lovely mouth. His pubic hairs were touching her nose. Mom now really started to struggle as she started to hit him. Reddy was simply laughing and kept his whole cock on her mouth for some more time. Then he withdrew his whole meat from her throat. It was shinning with my mom's saliva. Guess he wanted to give her some breathing space. Again he pulled her face and simply inserted her penis on her mouth. Reddy now told my mom to use her tongue and told her that it was her time to do all the things. I saw a glimpse of tears on her eyes. Reddy told her to use her hand and tongue both. Mother had nothing to do but to oblige to this mad man's desire. She started to stroke his penis. His penis was so huge that she had to use both her hands to hold it. Reddy told her to kiss her cock tip while stroking. So mom kept her lips on top his cock and with each stroke she was giving a small delicate kiss to his cock head. This sensual feeling was giving Reddy tremendous pleasure. Reddy told mom to lick her cock like an icecream. Mom started to suck his penis with her tongue. She sucked every inch of his dirty penis. She would suck sideways and took his penis on her mouth to give a deep throat. Slop slop slop slop was the only music that was going on. After sometime mom stopped sucking and remained silent. Then Reddy guided his balls to her mouth. His balls had made a huge round shape because of all the excitement. He told her to take his balls in her mouth and treat them good. My poor mom opened her mouth and took them on her mouth. She sucked on them for 15 good minutes.

Reddy: Ahhhhhhhhhhhhh, lovely my bahu (daughter is law). You know how to use your lips. Now enough of the teasing, I am going to rip you apart now.

Hearing this mom again started to cry and begged her stop all this. Reddy simply ignored her and made her stand up. He kept his hands on her blouse and again started to feel my mom's huge coconuts. Suddenly he inserted his fingers inside the blouse ripped apart the blouse. Mom was not wearing a bra and her breasts jumped out from the blouse cage. My god, they were huge and beautiful. Reddy was speechless. He was just stunned to see my mom's beautiful breast. Soon he was back to reality and sticks his head in between them. He started to sweep his face with my mom's breasts. He then started his licking again. First he went for her right boob. He opened his mouth and took my mom's right nipple and a huge portion of breast into his mouth and with the other hand he was feeling her left boob. He was squeezing it like crazy. He started to chew his nipple. Mom was in pain and pleads him not to do that. But moms cry just spurred him on. He began to bite her with more passion. He took her left nipple and was pinching it. Although my mom had no desire for this man, her body was reacting very differently. This ugly man's touch made her nipple very hard. With each bite, mom's breasts seemed to get bigger and bigger. Reddy was still kissing her breasts like crazy. First he was taking a large portion of breast into his mouth and was biting very roughly. Mom was giving out moans with every bite and it made Reddy laugh. He knew that my mom was in his control fully. He continued his biting. He would kiss and lick the area where he was chewing just before. It was like consoling that breast portion. After sometime he started the same routine with the left boob. Biting and chewing while feeling up mom's right boob. My mom had her eyes closed. She was totally helpless. Guess she never experienced this kind of love before. Finally, Reddy kisses both her long and hard nipples one more time and paused for a bit.

Reddy: ahhhhhhhhhhhhhhhhhhhh, heavenly, just wonderful. It would have been nice if you had milk in your breast. I could suck your tits forever Prena.

Mom remains silent.

Reddy: When you are going to take your next child? I will be there to clean up the milks from your tanks. hahahahaha. Tell me, when.

As mom was still silent, he came forward and squeezed her

breasts hard. Mom cried out in pain.

Mom: Please Reddyji.

Reddy: no no, not Reddyji. Call me swami, Randi (whore).

Mom: please Reddyji.

This time he gave a hard slap on her ass and told her say him Swami again.

Mom: No swami, we are not planning to have any more kids.

Reddy: Really? Then I guess I have fill up your pussy. I have to taste your breast milk one way or another.

Saying this, he again hugged my mom and started to kiss my mom. Reddy told her to cooperate with him. So mom also started to give him small kisses. Reddy's hands were moving all over my mom's body. After sometime Reddy removed the petticoat form my mom's body. She was only wearing a black panty now. God, mom looked simply stunning. Her thighs were fat and flashy. They were milky white and that black panty was in a total contrast with them. Then Reddy told her to get on the bed. Mom was now terrified and realized that it is better for her to listen to this man's order. She got up on the bed which was covered with flowers. Now Reddy told her to lie down and saying this he jumped up on the bed. The bed cracked a little as he was a huge man. Reddy then straight went for her pussy. He ripped the panty and her royal pussy became visible to him as well as to me. She had pubic hairs on her pussy that was doing a good job of covering her pussy. Guess she was never fucked that regularly. Reddy now held his with his left hand and kept it near the pubic jungle. He then started to move aside her pubic hairs with his cock. He was really enjoying this teasing. I looked at my mom. She was frozen. She knew what this monster can do to her. Finally, Reddy managed to open a way to my mom's pussy. In one word, it was just marvelous. Her pussy was small and pussy lips were pink. My mom was completely wet. Her pussy lips were glistering from all the sweat. Reddy went down and started to lick her pussy madly. Now mom was shivering from all the pleasure. She was moaning loudly but Reddy was a selfish bastard. He gave attention to her pussy only for a couple of seconds. He then started to bite her fat thighs. His head was completely lost in between her valley. After sometime, he got up and told mom to get ready for the final session. Now mom was really terrified. She looked at his monster and told him not to enter that. Reddy simply ignored her cries and told her to spread her legs wide. Mom still was begging him. He got impatient and with his hands pulled her legs apart. Mom's pussy became clearly visible now. Reddy got on top of her. His weight nearly crushed mom onto the bed. He looked at moms face and told her to get ready. He guided his tool in front of her vagina kept in on her pussy door. He started to rub her pussy with his cock head. Finally he kissed mom on the lips and gave a dam hard push. Mom screamed loudly in pain as half of his cock was lost in her pussy. Reddy kept his dick in her pussy and paused for a while. He started to move his hips in a circular motion as he was trying to make room in my mom's pussy. Mom was crying in pain. His thing was too much for her little love hole. Mom told her not to enter anymore as she would die. She was crying and begging for her life. She told Reddy that he can do whatever he wants with her but forbid him not to enter anymore. An angry look was in Reddy's face but he also got the idea that my mom can take him no more. He then pulled out his cock except for the tip and entered her again. He was slowly giving her strokes. He was pulling out the whole thing and was ramming it in again. He was slowly building up his pace. ahhhhhh ooo-ooohhhhhhhhh ahhhhhh mmmmmmmmphhhh ahhhhhh was the sounds coming out of my mom's face. Now he started to fuck her real hard. He was removing and entering her cock very rapidly. With each stroke mom's breasts were jiggling like crazy. The bed was making a squeaky sound because of all the wrestling. Reddy was like a crazy bull crushing my modesty mom. He was bucking his hips like a released bull. With every stoke mom was making a small puppy like sound. Oh ah oh ah oh ah oh ah hmph. Then Reddy told her something. Now she put two fingers on either side of her pussy and was pulling it apart, trying to take him in properly. This went for 30 long minutes. Reddy used to bite her breasts from time to time. It was wonderful to see mother's bouncy boobs bounce up and down so violently and she was moving her head side to side. Reddy then paused for while and got off from her. He then lied down and told mom to ride him. Mom got up and positioned herself on top of his cock. She made her legs bent like a frog to take only half of him. As her pussy was touching her cock head, to me and moms surprise, he kept his hand on both her shoulders and gave a dam hard push. With that stroke, the whole cock was in. Both mom and Reddy gave out loud moan. My mom was impelled fully. His balls were touching her ass flesh. He said don't worry bahu (daughter in law), it is all in. Now jump on me. My mom was lying on him helplessly. She got herself up and started to ride him slowly. She carefully got up and again Reddy gave me hard push. This routine went for few minutes. Mom was now jumping by herself. She was slowly getting up and letting her get impelled by his cock. I could see Reddy's cock covered with my mom's cum. I guess she cummed many times. Reddy was also giving strokes from bottom. His balls were getting slapped by mom's ass checks worth every stroke. Mom's wet pussy and Reddy's dick made a plop plop plop plop sound. The whole room was filled with the scent of cum. Reddy was now resting and let mom do the rest. He was slapping her butt from time to time. He occasionally got up and hugged my mom and kissed her wildly. Mom was still crying slowly. Reddy most of time kept his hands on her breasts and was pressing them wildly. He boobs were moving in all directions. After 30 minuter of horse riding, Reddy told her that he was about to cum. Hearing this mom was trying to get down from him but Reddy made her stay in that position.

Mom: please don't cum inside, please please, this is my fertile season and you will make me pregnent.

Reddy: really? Then I must cum inside you.

Saying this he hugged my mom tightly and started to give damm hard strokes. My mom screamed with every push and was jerking like a fish. She was cumming over and over. Fianlly Reddy gave a deep stroke and started to moan loudly. Take take he was saying. He was cumming inside her. Man, he cummed for like half a minute. Cum started to leak from the sides of her pussy. He made sure that she was fully filled. My mom was just speechless. They stayed that position for a couple of minutes and then Reddy broke off the hug. Mom laid down on the bed. She was too tired to even move a muscle. Reddy then went to the bathroom to freshen up.

After 10 minutes, Reddy again fucked my mom, this time in doggy position. Now mom was really stretched and was easily taking the whole prick inside her. Reddy again cummed deep inside her. Seeing this, I left the place and returned to Grandma's place. I thought mom would return now. I looked at the watch and it was 3 am. Man, Mom was fucked for straight 4 hours. Surprisingly mom didn't return then at about 5 am. I heard the joining door open and mom coming towards the main building. She was limping a bit. She was wearing the same sari she was wearing before she was taken by Reddy. She was still crying a bit. I felt sorry for her but couldn't help the feeling that Mom was banged hard by Reddy. I was hard and was desperately in need of jerking.

The next morning, dad left us there and told us that he would return in a month. Mom didn't know what to answer. She just nodded a little. Reddy was jumping with joy. He told dad to take his time and told that he would look after his Mom and wife. I don't about my dad's mom but I do know that he took care of my mom. He fucked her every single night and even in day times. Once he fucked her right in the middle of the kitchen. He thought that nobody was around. Ha-ha, I saw the whole thing hiding. My mom had no other choice but to become the play doll of Reddy. All the fucking made my mom pregnant. Dad was so happy that he was going to have another child. Only me and my mom knew the secret. I will never forget the fucking of my lovely mom.

23. Nekta

My name is Amit and I am a 61 year old Gujarati bachelor businessman from Mumbai. I am a fit person health wise, as I exercise, do yoga and eat right and keep myself active as far as my life style is concerned. I am sure all of you might be astonished by my age and may be wondering that I am just trying to fake with my age, but in real life I am 61 years old. I have never got married, but still believe that a human being can still have an active sex life without even getting married and also at any age.

Generally I am extremely busy with my business work having a business of my own and travel a lot around the world, so being unmarried never hurts me, but to be honest I have had an occasionally active sex life back in the past. My policy in life is not to live till 100 years without a sex life, but instead I'll live 50 years by having a highly active sex life. One thing I never understood about my charm that I am a bachelor but I find women are easily attracted to me. When I was a teenager I had realized that I had a mole on my on the foreskin of my penis, later in my life I had read a book on Mole Theory which had mentioned that it indicates that the person will have a fulfilling sex life and will have more than one partner, which absolutely came out true in my later life when my sex life started long back without even getting married. Honestly, I never take drugs like Viagra, as I generally have no erection problem, as I drink a lot of pomegranate juice which is supposed to be a healthy supplement for men's sexual health. One thing I must say that being a rich businessman helps you to get women, no matter how old you are. Whenever I have a good interaction with decent women that leads her to my bed and eventually to sex. I have read so many real life stories here, so I decided to share my sex life with all of you. Current I am enjoying my sex life with my 36 year old married girlfriend, who is wife of one of my business associate Sahil.

Therefore, I am keeping my name and my girlfriend's name secret, as you all will understand the reason for discreet names. My girlfriend Nekta is a 36 year old Sindhi lady who is happily married to Sahil for past 12 years and have a 7 year old child. Nekta is a very fashionable lady with shoulder length dark brown highlighted hair; she has a light wheatish skin tone that makes her look very sexy. Now about Nekta's figure she has a great physique with well toned body shape, probably with a figure 36-33-38 figure. Even after she is married and has a child, I can say that she has maintained her looks and physique in an excellent manner. I have been having an affair with Nekta from past 3 months and to be clear with all my readers, Nekta and me are just having sex affair and she and I have no intentions to break her family. Basically Sahil is very friendly with me socially and that's how Nekta and me know each other closely. One time Nekta was waiting for Sahil at my place and we had great conversation with each other, as Nekta knew me for a long time and she was not shy of me at all. In the conversation with her sexy looks she asked, "Amit I wonder why you are still single even after you are a handsome looking matured man. I would have had no problem being your wife, if I was single", Nekta said and smiled. At that time I smiled and said to her, "Nekta, I am unmarried, but still women want me at this mature age, isn't that weird". She looked at me and said, "Amit you are rich, charming person with good looks and perfect physique even at the age of 61, so women will get charmed by you". There was a moment of silence and hesitation in both of us to speak the next step.

Then jokingly I said, "Nekta are you attracted to me and started laughing", Nekta smiled and said, "Yes Amit, I am, if you like me then you can say it to me., but keep it a secret from Sahil, as I want to have my own fun filled life". Nekta mentioned that her life with Sahil is happy, but she would like to explore new things and add spice to her life in a fun way. Friends how can I say no to a young sexy lady who wants a handsome old man like me and more over when it was past 2 years since I had sex. I smiled at Nekta and gave her a kiss on her cheek, she laughed at me and said, "Amit common you can kiss me on my lips." I was really overwhelmed, as I never thought that I would ever have an affair with Nekta, though always I had the lucky charm of attracting women. Now I held Nekta in my arm and kissed her on lips for few minutes. Then Nekta told me, that as Sahil was expected to come, so we should be decent. In few minutes Sahil arrived to pick Nekta, we behaved normal in front of Sahil. Now Sahil did not know that his wife was my girlfriend. The next day I called Nekta on her cell phone and decided to meet up secretly in a Coffee shop. We met in the evening and that where, Nekta mentioned that she always had a fantasy to have fun with a guy double her age and my looks and personality attracted her. I mentioned to Nekta that meeting up in a hotel would be a danger to the secrecy of our affair. Therefore, Nekta agreed to come to my house to have a good time with me. Nekta was also had a circle of Kitty party friends, so she had no problem making excuses to leave her house. Nekta and me we met secretly for few days having long conversations and spending romantic moments knowing each other well in order to get intimate. Few days later I gave Sahil an assignment to fly to Europe for business. Now Sahil flew out on Friday early morning for a week and that was the night when we planned to start our sex life. Nekta decided to come to my house at 7pm after leaving her child at one of her friend's house, so she could enjoy the whole night. Now I came home from office by 5pm and freshened up and from 6pm onwards I was excited, as my thick manhood was getting to enter Nekta's vagina. My penis has become very sensitive with my aging process, as my penis gets ticklish sensation inside a vagina. At 7:15pm, my door bell rang and when I opened and saw Nekta standing in front of me wearing a gorgeous blue salwar-kurta, with blue nail paint on her long nails and with a white platform heel shoe on her feet.

She also had a designer bindi on her forehead, just looking like a sexy young lady. Now we both sat on the sofa and spend some romantic moments talking and drank some beer. Now after an hour, I kissed Nekta and asked her, "Nekta darling, bedroom mein chale?"(Lets move to the bedroom), she smiled in a naughty way and said, "Yes sweety lets go". Nekta sat on my bed and I closed all the windows and curtains in my bedroom. Fortunately, I live on the 11th floor and the walls are sound proof, so there was no risk of anyone hearing us. Now I sat on the bed and held Nekta's chin and my lips touched her soothing moist lips and in no second we were kissing each other on lips and we slowly went into French kissing with our tongues exploring our mouth. Aaaaaaahhhhh it was just like heaven. Now Nekta said, " Amit darling u are a good kisser" and by saying this we again started French kissing and my hands slowly went to her thighs and now she took my hands off softly and said, "Well friends I am sure you all can very well imagine that how tough it was for my penis to control its erection when I was going to bang Nekta on my bed. Nekta and me we both sat on the bed and we were kissing very passionately. I could feel that she was not only thirsty for sex with a 61 year old guy, but was enjoying my company.Now I removed Nekta's kurta and her black bra was looking sexy on her tits.Now Nekta untied her salwar and pulled it down.Oh my! She was looking so hot in her black panty. She had a well shaped physique. Now we were passionately making love on my bed. Nekta started moaning softly, 'Aahhhhhhhhhhhh darling, it feels good'. So I unhooked her black bra and kissed her tits and then started licking and sucking her brown pointed nipples and she moaned loudly Aaahhhhhh......I started pressing and kneading Nekta's sexy round tits and she was enjoying it and was moaning and telling me, 'Darling I find you sexy and dirty old man, press and massage my tits, they are really hard, as there's a lot of sex filled in it. I now started kissing all over her soft silky tummy and our bodies had become hot along with heavy breathing. Now I started tickling Nekta's vagina over her black panty. Now I started circling my index finger on her pussy over her panty. I saw Nekta slowly closed her eyes and was moaning,'Oooooohhhhhh, Amit it feels so good, do it, don't stop, 'Ouch darling choot mein gudgudee ho rahe hai. (My pussy feels tickled)' I could smell the female fluid from her pussy as she was getting wet because of the tingling sensation she was getting in her womanhood due to my tickling. We again started making love, as I was kissing her pinkish lips and she was inserting her tongue in my mouth. I was now coming down to her tummy area and got busy kissing her stomach and this made Nekta really excited and she was moving her legs. Now I took her left smooth silky legs in hands and ran down my lips kissing it.....Wowwwwww it was smelling Vanilla-Sugar body wash, I was so much turned on by her sweet odor.Slowly I ran down my lips over her panty to kiss and arouse the area in and around her vagina.While I ran down my lips.....

I should be saying, Wow! It was an awesome feeling kissing the vaginal area, as I could smell the sweet female odor from her pussy and her panty was wet near her vaginal opening. Now Nekta pulled me up and planted a kiss on my lips and we were kissing very passionately and in the mean while I again ran down my lips over her silky tummy. Now Nekta was moaning "Uuuummmmm I want more sweety".Now I slept on my back and Nekta now waved her hairs up sexily and slowly laid her fingers on my underwear and slowly pulled my manhood. As a result my thick manhood popped out and it was hard and also very hot. Nekta said, "Wow! Dirty old man your penis has turned so red". Well being a fair complexioned man made my penis turn red while I made love to my married girlfriend on my bed. Now she covered my penis with her sexy lips and was enjoy licking and sucking my manhood like a bar of chocolate. After a little while she slept on her back and now I removed her panty. Nekta had little bit of trimmed vaginal hairs which always turns me on in a woman.Ohhhh her vagina was so wet and lubricated. Now Nekta spread her legs and in the meantime I was enjoying eating her pussy. I was circling my tongue in and around the clit and the pussy lips and loads of salty pussy juice was flowing into my mouth. Now me and Nekta were ready for the real sex action. I spread Nekta's legs and slid a pillow under her hips and I once again stroked my thick manhood with my fingers and inserted straight into Nekta's vagina. Aaahhhh it felt so great as I was having sex after 2 years. Now I was moving slowly and kissing her lips passionately. I increased my speed a little bit and Nekta started increasing her moans. I realized that Nekta was very much hot in bed as she was also moving her body along with me to create double pleasure. Now my fat penis was going in and out from Nekta's vagina so her moans were building up,Oooooohhhhh Aaaaaahhhhhhhhhh,Aaaaaaaa-aaaaaahhhhhhhhhhh,Ohhhhh Amit darling u dirty old man, fuck me,Aaaaaahhhhhhhhh.I now increased my speed and by now we both were moaning in great pleasure. I was pumping my penis in and out and Nekta was screaming as hell.......Oooo-ooohhhhhhhhhhhhh,Aaaaaaaaaaahhhhhhhh,Aahaaaaahhhh-hhh. Now my penis was getting sensitive inside Nekta's vagina, so I pulled my penis out in order to avoid ejaculation. The moment I pulled my penis out from her pussy, Nekta grabbed my fat penis and started giving me a blowjob.This was exciting me as she was also tasting her love juices too.

By now I was ready to fuck Nekta in another sexual position. Now I slept on my back and Nekta sat on my penis facing me as a result my penis was in her vagina and now I held Nekta's hips tight with my both hands.............and to my feelings it was a tremendous sensation, as my penis was more sensitive to women-on-top position. Nekta started moving back and forth in order to ride on me. Slowly Nekta started stroking her hips.......Aaaaa-aaaahhhhhhhh it was a great sensation for my 61 year old penis. I should be honest enough to say that Nekta was so good in shaking her hips while riding over me, like I was holding her hips tight and she was shaking her gaand (hips)...Aaaaaahhhhh-h,Ohhhhhhhhhhhhhh. Now it was time for me to do some erotic action, so I asked Nekta to stop and I now elevated my both legs a little bit and now Nekta leaned on to my face and we were kissing each other's lips passionately. In this position now I started pumping my fat penis in her pussy and Nekta was moaning loud, 'Aaaaaaaaaahhhhhhhhhhhh, Ooooohhh, Aaaaaaaaahhhhhhh , Mazzza Aaa raha hai Darling , aur zorrse chodo mujhe jaan'(I am having Fun, fuck me harder honey). Nekta was leaning on me and while I was fucking her, with my left hand's middle finger I was tickling her asshole and then inserted my finger inside her anus...... Friends you won't believe me how much she was enjoying my finger in her anus and Nekta was screaming more loud, 'Aaaaaaahhhhhhhhhhhh, Aaaaaahhhhhhhh, Oh yea, Aaaaaahhh-hhhhhOoooohhhh dard ho raha hai darling, aur zorse karo.'(Its paining darling, more harder)) I told Nekta to go slow in this position, as my penis had become sensitive.While continuing Nekta said, "Darling mera paani niklega (that she was about to cum)". Therefore, I was going slow and in seconds I felt hot liquid hitting my penis and as a result I was screaming loud, "Aaaahhhh, Aaaaahhhh,Aahhhhh, Ohhh I luv ur juice hitting my penis" and Nekta shivered and moaned out of pleasure. After reading my above line you all can very well imgine that I went for a decent amount of time fucking Nekta and inserting my finger in her anus at the same time. Now I felt as a result of Nekta's gaand (hips) wiggling on my penis, my sperms were tickling inside my penis just like as if worms were inside my penis and my testicles. Now I told her, ' Nekta darling sperms are tickling my penis real bad.' Nekta demanded me to cum in her mouth, as she was ovulating and chances of her getting pregnant were high, if I shot my semen in her. As a result she slept on her back and I sat on her tummy and tit fucked her for a moment with my ticklish manhood and now I inserted my red fat penis in Nekta's mouth while sitting on her chest.Now I was mouth fucking her but it did not last very long, as in no time my penis bursted out my semen in Nekta's mouth, Aaaaaaaaaahhhhhhhhh what a relief, I moaned loudly, as I had sex after 2 years. It was such a wonderful scene where I see all my thick love juices in Nekta's mouth. Nekta was now spitting a little bit of juice on my penis, as her mouth was full with my sperms. All of you can imagine that I the intensity I shot all my semen. Now we washed up all our sex juices and fell in each other's arms for a short nap. After we woke up after an hour and a half, we started making another round of hot love just to arouse each other. Now as a result Nekta and me we both were ready for another round. This time I entered her from behind in Doggie style and I was again in full motion. Ooooohhhhh it was fun doggie style with Nekta, as she was also stroking me at the same time I was slapping her hips real hard, in order to make it rough sex and Nekta was enjoying it sooo much. Now again we changed positions, as now I entered Nekta's vagina from the side-rear entry position where she kept her right leg in the air and I was playing and stimulating her clit with my middle finger same time while fucking her. This went on for few mins and I was now ready to cum. Nekta wanted me to cum on her tummy this time, so my wiggling sperms blasted on her tummy. Now as the sex procedure goes, Nekta felt like peeing, so she went to take a piss immediately. I am not sure that, if you all know that it's normal for a girl to take piss after having sex. After this Nekta and me cleaned up and then Nekta smiled and said, "Amit darling you are my dirty old man who was awesome in bed, as you know all the right moves to satisfy a woman. We kissed each other for few minutes, then she was cuddling with me in her arms. Now for a little while I tit fucked her, then after that I slept on my back by spreading my both legs, as Nekta wanted to suck my manhood along with my balls. Wow....

I should say, she did great, as Nekta was sucking my testicles in her mouth for a long time just like a vaccum.Now this gave my penis a great sensation and out of pleasure I said, "Bitch suck me dry Aaaahhh",and finally I threw my sperms in Nekta's mouth. We then slept for a long time in each other's arms. Later Nekta dressed up and then she went home in the morning. This was the first time sex in our affair. After that every day we had sex, till Sahil returned after a week. Nekta and me have sex two or three days in a week. In the meanwhile we have had many fantasy positions and foreplay during sex and I also use sex toys on her and especially she demands me to insert my finger in her anus while I am fucking her on Woman-on-Top position. Friends you all can understand that I have had sex with Nekta uncountable times in past two months. Along with this I have given a promotion to Nekta's husband Sahil, so he is happy with his position and does not know about Nekta's affair with me.

24. Rajini

I am Kishore. To tell about me I am fair and had a normal youth body. My age is 26. I completed my PG. The incident which I am going to narrate is happened during my PG college days. I completed my PG in Noida. Since it was business school our class is packed with all type of age grouped peoples. Among the students there was a girl called "Rajini" who is around 32. She is married and have 8 month old child. Her husband is a business man and most of the time he use to move to Bombay or other cites for business trip. So most of the time she use to be alone in her home with her child. Now I narrate about her character and body. In our college all girls are allowed to wear all king of dress. But she use to come only in sari which is always transparent. Such that through blouse we can easily find which color bra she is wearing. She had a very good structure of 38d-28-30. Through her boobs size you can easily understand how big it is. Since she give birth to a child 8 month before her blouse look always wet due to her milk. Since it is a PG college it crowded only during the first 20 days of the beginning of the college and during exam time. So Within that 20 days I had a very good friendship with her. Since I was younger then her, her husband did not mistakes our friendship.

The days pass and one day she called to her house for taking notes for one subject which I can score well in it. So I had gone to her home at 7 o'clock in the evening. When I entered the house she welcomed me. She was wearing only a nighty at that time. I can easily see her points in her boobs from out side the nighty due to the nighty is that much trace. I entered the house and sat on the sofa. She gave me coffee which she prepare only for me since north Indian peoples won't drink coffee. After having the coffee she sat in front of me with a chair and in between us there was only a small stool. We started to take notes. Suddenly the child cried due to hungry. She told me to take notes alone and gone inside to give milk to her child. With in 5 to 10min she came back. But she doesn't notice that she have not closed her front zip in her night. By without knowing she came in front of me and sat on the chair. Now both of her 38d size boobs are clearly visible to my eyes. Now I was totally disturbed and I could not able to take notes. The boobs were very whitish and her nipples were very beautiful. Now I slowly asked about her husband. She told that he has gone for a trip t Bombay and he will come after 1 day. I got some courage. Now I slowly asked about her personal life. Now she was disturbed and told me not to ask anything about it. Now I got the answer clearly that she doesn't like her husband.

In the mean time her milk from her nipples made wet her nighty some what which any one can easily view it. The time goes and its time for me to move away from the home. I told her that I am moving. But surprisingly she told me to say in her home for that night due to that we can take some more notes. I told her that I will take dinner outside and I will come back. She told that she will prepare for both of us. The we went inside the kitchen and started to prepare subjii. I cut the vegetables and give to her at that time mistakenly touched her body slightly. Both of us realized that some chemical reaction had take place. Again suddenly I mistakenly touched her boobs. This is so soft. They are very big. By holding by breath I asked for some milk. She asked me what for? I told her to give first. Then she gave me the cow milk. I don't know where I got the courage and I told to her that I need breast milk. Now tell me what my situation is and what she told to me. Everyone will surprise to hear what she told to me and what she did for it. By giving a positive smile to me she removed the nighty. Now she was standing in front of me with only panties. Here nipples were inviting me to suck them. The boobs were very big due to she was giving milk to her child. I like her boobs very much and I could not able to control my feeling. I placed my hands on her boobs. I was so soft. She slowly responds to me and her to touch me. I squeezed here boobs gently with here milk peeping out of her nipples. I give her a lip kiss and we continued for about 10 min. I asked here does she like's me. She responds me with deep kiss. And by that time see was holding my tool and playing with it. I told to her that I need her breast milk totally. She told me that after taking dinner that she will give to me and I can drink it.

I agreed and we prepared the dinner and we had it very fast. By this time she was wearing only panties. Could any one thing what will be my tool size. My tool arouse to around 8'. I could not control and while washing the hand I scattered some water on her boobs. She understand my feeling and she to do the same and I caught hold her total body. Now I kissed her from her forehead and to the neck. Then I took her to the bed and I made her to lie down on her bed. The I took her right boobs on my mouth. I squeezed her boobs to get more milk. Now I got a flow of milk from her boobs and it taste to me very sweet. Then I was sucking it for around 20 to30 min. Then I took the next breast and started to suck it. By this time she was taking care of me like her child. That is she was slowly combing my here and try to hold my tool. But my tool is already over tempered. The around after a hour I drank all the milk from her breast. The she start her work. She enjoyed with my tool by sucking it and then I inserted my tool into her pussy. I gave her a good stroke and with in 15 min cum on her mouth. She tasted it and told to me that she want some more. I told to her that I need milk for that. Since she had already given all of her milk to me, she could not able to give milk to me so she told to me that she will give me in the morning. The we were so tired and we slept together in the same bed in the nude form.

In the morning I opened my eyes around 9 o clock during that time she was feeding her child. At that time she had take bath and wearing saree. She looks dam sexy and woke up and walks near to her. At that time I was nude my tool is totally up. I lay by head on her tight and try to open the blouse. She told to me that she will give it only if I agree to give my total cum on her mouth. I agreed. She opened the blouse. Since the breast was very big it falls on my face. The feeling was very nice. It's like a pillow is dashing with my face. Then she told to me that her child had finished taking milk. So I can take both of her breasts for her milk. Now she opened her blouse totally and her breast was hiding inside her pallu. So I remove her saree and I saw two boobs which are so big inviting me to suck it. Since I could not able to see it in the night now it was totally visible. The I suck all of her milk from her both breasts and gave my tool to her as during the night. The after we had the sex I told to her that I need her milk till it stops from her breasts. She agreed to me and I continued. The day passed and we continued and her husband got promotion with transfer to Mumbai. So now I am missing her very much

25. Lal

I am Rohit Sharma, 21, doing my engineering in Bangalore...I stay here with my mom...However the following incident took place during my stay in Delhi... this incident is about 10 years old, when I was about 12 years old... I lived with my widowed mom...My dad had died when I was about 1 yr old. Since then mom had been working in an MNC and had taken good care of me. My mom Neelam was 34 at the time of this incident. Now let me describe her features. Mom was about 5`6 ft in height. She had quite a fair complexion. Now about her beauty...she had very long hair which fell up to her ass when she kept them open. Mom had really big boobs and generally wore low-cut blouse which easily exposed her big boobs and deep cleavage (Now don`t ask me about her exact figure because I am not a damn tailor or something!!!) Now, whenever we walked through a public place, men definitely stared at mom`s huge boobs and I knew, she liked it!!! Mom wore beautiful coloured saris (actually I heard from her that dad never liked the idea of a widow wearing white dress just because she had lost her husband), but she had a habit of wearing her saris below her navel...I guess she just liked to flaunt her belly...Although she was not a born flirt, she definitely liked male attention!!! Now coming back to the story, in class VI-th I didn`t have a good friends-circle...As a result I had scored poor marks in the final exam...

So in class VII-th, mom decided to put me into one of the good schools in Delhi itself...After doing some research, mom finally sorted out 12 good reputed schools. Then we started to visit them one by one. But as I had got very poor marks in my class

VI-th finals, so all the schools refused to admit me...Till now out of 12 schools, 10 had already refused me...Mom was really frustrated. Although she didn`t tell me anything, I knew she was very upset...It was Saturday... Mom and I prepared to go to the 11th school. Mom had some hope regarding this school as in the advertisement it had stated that it had around 25 seats available for class VII-th. So we started for the school. When we reached there we saw that there was a notice board outside the school which displayed in bold letters, THE ADMISSION FOR CLASSES VII-th AND VIII-th HAVE BEEN CANCELLED DUE TO UNAVOIDABLE CIRCUMSTANCES...WE ARE SORRY FOR THE IN-CONVINIENCE IF ANY CAUSED Mom was really shocked to read this...She couldn`t react!!! We returned home...Mom was very quiet that evening...All her hopes had been washed away...Only one school was left now and we had heard that it was a very strict school...The next day that was Sunday, mom spent half of the day sitting alone and thinking...At night, she told me that the next morning we would go and visit the final school. So the next morning I got up early...Mom was already dressed up and asked me to hurry...I hurriedly took bath and got dressed...Then when I looked carefully at mom, I found something very un-usual...She was looking more beautiful than usual...She was wearing a semi-transparent sari which was excessively below her navel...She had let her long, black hair loose, which fell on her ass. She was just looking like a sex-goddess!!! I can bet that seeing her, even a dead-body could get an erection!!! Anyhow we then started off for the school...We reached there by 9 am...The principal`s office was on the first floor of the main school build-ing...The corridor was empty as the school had already started and classes were going on...We reached outside the office and sat down on the bench...A lady in her late 20s was sitting with her kid who was around 4yrs...I guess even she had come for her son`s admission...

Few minutes later the buzzer rang and she was called in...She quietly went in with her kid...Meanwhile mom was getting im-patient...She got up and started walking in the corridor and then went over to the notice board and started reading some article on it (You know how mothers are!!! They are always curious about the things that irritate you the most!!!) Anyhow I was sitting alone...Suddenly the door of the principal`s office flung open and the aunty came out with the kid...I was wondering that how could their meeting get over so soon...Anyhow, the aunty slowly said to her kid, Baby, can you stay here for some time while I finish the meeting??? The child innocently asked, Mamma, can`t I come in??? The aunty said, No darling...don`t worry...I will be back in five minutes...ok??? The child innocently agreed...So she again went into the office...I was just wondering that the child was so small that he could hardly understand the meaning of the word 'Principal'...So why she had to go alone??? Time passed but the aunty didn`t come out...Mom was getting impatient every minute and so was the child...Almost half an hour had passed...Mom was still roaming around...Suddenly the door opened and the aunty came out...But there was something very strange...I observed that there was something different about her appearance...When she had gone in, her sari was well kept but now it had wrinkles all over it...It looked as if she had worn it in a hurry...also her hair was well tied but now it was partially scattered around her face...she was sweating and nervous and somewhat looked tired...she then picked up the kid and started leaving when I saw another strange thing...There was something on her hair just above her left ear...It looked like some white jelly...I was shocked...I couldn`t believe that it could be the THING that I was actually thinking!!! I just thought to myself that there was nothing such as I was thinking and it was just me who had a dirty mind!!! Well the buzzer rang again and I called mom and went into the principal`s office...! As we entered I saw that the principal was drinking a glass of water...After he finished drinking, he looked at mom...He was definitely impressed to see mom...! He looked at her from top to bottom, carefully observing her boobs...His eyes got struck when he looked at her bare abdomen...he just licked his lips and then asked us to sit down...Before moving on let me first tell you about the principal, Mr.Lal...He was a man of about fifty years of age.

He was not very tall but taller than my mom...He was neither too fair nor too dark...He was quiet a well built man...Now let me come back to the story...He started the conversation by asking my full name...He then asked me how much I had got in my previous class...He didn`t look quite happy hearing my result...He then said to mom, Well Mrs.Sharma, I am sorry to say, but it seems your ward is not very interested in studies... Mom said, Actually it is somewhat my fault...I can`t give him much time and he doesn't have his father... Hearing about the absence of my dad, Mr.Lal`s face suddenly brightened up as if he had got an opportunity to fulfil his dream...He then said, well I can understand, but I am really very sorry, I can`t admit your son... Mom started to plead to him...On much request he handed over a brochure to mom and asked her to read it...Now while mom was reading it, I saw that Mr.Lal was staring at mom...He was constantly gazing at her boobs through her semi-transparent blouse...I think mom noticed him but she didn`t react...Mr.Lal then continued, as you can see that your ward has received much less than what the minimum criteria our school has put forward...So I believe you can understand my helplessness...I am sorry, I don`t think I can do anything about this problem...I hope you can understand my helplessness... Mom was quiet for sometime...Suddenly she dropped the pen that was in her hand onto the floor...As she bend down to pick it up, I saw that she intentionally put down the palloo of her sari exposing her huge boobs and deep cleavage...Seeing it, Mr.Lal`s eyes almost popped out!!! (Actually mom always thought that I was too innocent to understand ANYTHING...) He couldn`t take his eyes off her boobs and deep cleavage...He continuously stared at her big boobs and deep cleavage...Even some portions of her black bra were clearly visible!!! After sometime mom put back the palloo of her sari and sat down...Mom then continued, ...so are you still sure you can`t do anything...? Mr.Lal got up from his seat...He came around and sat on the table just in front of mom...His hard-on was clearly visible to mom...It was just inches from mom`s face...mom just stared at it for some time and then looked at him...Mr.Lal continued, ...so Mrs.Sharma, it seems you are really quiet interested in admitting your son in my school and as you know that every problem in this world has a solution so I think we could talk about this sometime later as I have an urgent meeting now...How about dinner at your place tonight??? Mom smiled at him and immediately handed over him our address and telephone number... He said he would be there at 8 pm....While leaving, Mr.Lal said, ...well...I am looking forward to an eventful time tonight... After that both mom and I came back home...! In the evening mom prepared the food by 7 pm...She was looking very excited...! She then entered into the bathroom to get changed and dress up...I observed that mom was taking much more time in dressing up than she usually took...

When she came out I saw that she was looking absolutely gorgeous...She was wearing a yellow sari with a matching yellow blouse...She had kept her long hair loose which fell up to her ass...as usual she was wearing the sari much below her navel...She was looking really hot and sexy!!! She just looked like a seductress!!! I said to her, ...mamma, you are looking very beautiful!!! Mom just smiled at me and thanked me for the compliment...I wanted to pee so I went to the bathroom...I saw something strange there...I saw that there were lot of hair on the basin...the hair were much thicker than usual...I just thought that she must have shaved her arm-pits which she frequently did and so without bothering much, I came out...It was 7:30pm...I was watching TV and mom came by and sat beside me...I saw that she frequently glanced at the wall clock...After every five minutes she saw the time on the clock...She was looking very anxious and impatient...It was looking as if she was just waiting for her lover to come and take her to eternity!!! It was almost 8`O clock now...Mom was getting impatient every minute...She got up from the sofa and started to move around in the house...At around 8:10 pm, the door-bell rang...I opened the door...It was Mr.Lal!!! He wished me and then came in...When he saw mom, he was definitely stunned...He looked at her from top to bottom and then said, You are looking very beautiful, Mrs.Sharma!!! Mom just blushed and thanked him...She then asked him to sit with me in the drawing room while she arranged the dinner table...After setting the table she called us... Mom started serving food...First she served the rice to me and then went to the other side of the table to serve it to Mr.Lal...I observed that while she bend a bit to serve the rice, her palloo slipped off from its place, exposing her big boobs and deep cleavage...Mr.Lal was stunned to see her huge boobs...He almost lost control over himself and took his mouth near her breasts and almost took one of her boobs in his mouth...He however controlled himself and mom also hurriedly put back her palloo at its place...After having dinner, they started to chat in the drawing room while I started to watch TV...After sometime mom came and said to me, beta your sir and me are going to my room to discuss about your admission, so don`t disturb us...and it's quiet late so you should go to your room and sleep Mom kissed me and went to her room while Mr.Lal followed her...I smelled something fishy!!! So I quickly switched off the TV and tiptoed into my room...Well my room was just adjacent to mom`s room...Our rooms were separated by just a common ventilator and to my amazement it was somehow open...

As it was on one corner so I guess mom had forgotten about it...My room was completely dark while there was light in mom`s room...As a result I could see everything going on in her room while she couldn`t see me!!! Now after mom entered the room, she just locked the room by closing the door-latch and switched on the A/C as it was just too hot...Both of them then sat on the bed and started to chat...They were laughing...I guess mom liked his company...After sometime, mom just got up from the bed and went towards the other side of the bed...Mr.Lal quietly followed her and went and stood just behind her...suddenly he put his arms around her from behind and hugged her... Mom tried to move away but he held her tight!!! He then put his lips near mom`s ear and said something to her which I couldn`t hear!!! Then he slowly kissed on her neck once...Mom just tried to move away her neck...He then started to plant small kisses on her neck to which mom didn`t protest...After kissing her for some time I saw that Mr.Lal put his hand on mom`s bare, white, smooth abdomen to which mom suddenly shook a bit...He started moving his hands all over mom`s belly and kissed her all over her neck...I saw that he then put one of his fingers inside mom`s navel and started to rotate it...Mom just twitched her head from one side to another and made a noise like sss-ssssssssssshhhhhhhhhssssssssssssssssssssss...I guess she liked it!!! After all,, she had not been touched by any male other than me for about 11 yrs!!! After sometime, Mr.Lal took his hands up her belly and slowly put it on one of her breasts from top of her palloo...Mom caught his hand and tried to move it away from her breast but he was too strong for her...Mr.Lal suddenly pulled down the palloo of her sari and caught mom`s boobs in his hand..A slight moan of hhhhhhhhhhhhhmmmmmmmmmmm-mmmmhhhhhhhhh escaped from mom`s mouth!!! Mr.Lal now turned mom around towards him...Suddenly, he put his lips with mom`s lips and forcibly started to kiss her...Mom resisted all his efforts by trying to pull her lips, but failed...She was just shaking but after sometime her movements became slow and I think she gave up and started enjoying the kiss!!! Mr.Lal then said something to mom...

He came and sat at the edge of the bed while mom came and stood close to him...His face was just inches away from mom`s big boobs...Mr.Lal pulled down mom`s palloo...He then stared at her mammoth boobs with wide open eyes...Suddenly he buried his face in between mom`s deep cleavage and started to play with her boobs...He rubbed his nose all over her blouse-covered boobs...Meanwhile mom had closed her eyes and I saw that after sometime her hands automatically went behind Mr.Lal`s head and she started to pull his head more into her boobs...After sometime, Mr.Lal put his mouth on one of mom`s boobs and started to suck the blouse itself...Mom moaned, nooooooo......

pleaseeeeee......noooooo.... but he didn`t listen and sucked on the other boob too...I saw that due to the heavy sucking, mom`s blouse had become wet...He then put his hand on the hooks of her blouse and started to open them...mom tried to resist a bit but finally gave up...After he had opened all the hooks, he tried to pull-off the blouse...I thought that mom would resist it but surprisingly she herself put her hands up and helped him in pulling off the blouse...Now mom was only in her black bra and petticoat...Mr.Lal then started to remove her bra to which mom didn`t oppose at all!!!

When he pulled off her bra, her two big boobs were in front of him...They were really round and big...Her areola was very dark and her nipples were really long...They had become fully erect by now!!! I knew Mr.Lal wouldn`t be able to control for long and as predicted, soon he put his mouth on one of mom`s boobs and started to suck it hungrily...Mom initially tried to push his head away from her boob but I think soon she lost control...now she herself pulled his head more into her boobs and after some-time she started to moan like ...oh While he sucked one boob, he squeezed the other with his hand...Suddenly, Mr.Lal caught one of mom`s nipple between his teeth and bit her, due to which mom suddenly screamed like After sometime he did the same to her other boobs...Mom`s boobs had now become red with his heavy sucking...There were even clear marks of his teeth on her breasts!!! Mom now looked very very sex-cited...She couldn`t control her feelings anymore!!! Mr.Lal then got up from the bed...He then suddenly pulled mom`s sari due to which it came off completely...Mom was now only in her petticoat...Mr.Lal then started to kiss mom on her neck while with his hands he started to open the knot of the rope of petticoat...After some struggling, he was successful! As he left the string from his hands, her petticoat fell down on the floor...Mom herself stepped out of it...

Now she was only in her black panty...She was looking really sexy...Mr.Lal then said to mom, Ok slut...now lie down on the bed... When mom didn`t react to his words he became angry and said, hurry up bitch, I don`t have much time!!! Mom then slowly got on the bed and sat down...Mr.Lal came near her and suddenly he grabbed her head and locked his lips with hers... Due to the sudden force, mom fell down on the bed...Mr.Lal was kissing her vigorously while mom was struggling to free herself from him...He caught one of her boobs and started to squeeze it really hard...Slowly and slowly mom became calm and it seemed now she was enjoying the kiss and breast-squeezing...Mr.Lal then unlocked the kiss and started to suck her boobs...He started licking all over her neck and slowly progressed downwards...Mom was moaning like ...... aaaaaaaasssssssseeeeeeeeeeee..........but she didn`t resist him...Mr.Lal now reached up to her panty...He put his right hand on her panty and started to play with it...Mom`s moans increased now....She started panting in excitement...Mr.Lal tried to pull down her panty but mom tried to resist his efforts by closing her legs...

But Mr.Lal forcefully pulled apart her legs and in one pull, pulled down her panty completely...Mom was now completely naked...Well, both me and Mr.Lal were shocked and surprised to find out that she had a clean shaven pussy!!! (Now I understood what took mom so long in the bathroom and what those thick hairs were!!!) Anyhow, Mr.Lal laughed and said, So bitch...it seems you were expecting a real hard fuck from me, huh....! Mom just kept quiet...Well guys, mom`s vaginal lips were really red in colour just like a teenager`s pussy!!! Mom`s pussy lips were shining from her vaginal juice...I thing Mr.Lal had made her really hot!!! Mr.Lal then put his one finger on mom`s pussy and immediately mom moaned like hhhhhmmmmmhhhhhhhhhh and closed her eyes. Mr.Lal put his first finger inside mom`s pussy and mom suddenly groaned like aaaaaahhhhhhhhhhhhhhhaaaaa......He started to rotate his index finger inside mom`s pussy...mom was moaning loudly like aa After sometime Mr.Lal took out his finger from mom`s pussy...He then put his head down to her pussy...He took out his tongue and touched her pussy lips with it and mom suddenly moved and moaned like waaaaaaaaaaahhhhhh...but she didn`t protest at all which surprised me...Mr.Lal then again put his tongue on mom`s pussy and started to lick it...Mom started panting and shaking...She was also moaning like. As the speed of Mr.Lal`s licking increased, mom`s moaning also increased...now she grabbed Mr.Lal`s head with both her hands and pulled it more into her pussy...She was mad with lust...She was also moaning loudly like aa. After about 15 minutes mom`s moaning became tremendous...Probably she was about to cum!!! And after few seconds, suddenly she screamed likeoooooohhdddddd!!!!!!!! and she came...She ejaculated a lot of water from her pussy which hit Mr.Lal directly on his face...

He drank up mom`s pussy juice...Mom was now too tired...She laid on the bed motionless as if she was dead...Mr.Lal was laughing!!! He then got up and wiped off his face...Mr.Lal then went and sat beside mom...Mom still laid motionless...Her eyes were closed...Mr.Lal looked at mom from top to bottom...Then he bend down a bit and took out his tongue and licked mom`s face and planted a kiss on mom`s lips...Mom didn`t respond to his kiss and just laid motionless...Her face was shining with Mr.Lal`s saliva!!! Mr.Lal then started to lick her neck...Mom just moved her head on the other side giving him more space to lick!!! There was a faint smile on her lips...She slowly put her hand on Mr.Lal`s head and buried her fingers into his hairs...She slowly started to caress his head just like a mother caresses her baby`s head! Mr.Lal soon got down a bit to her boobs and took one boob in his mouth and started to suck it...Mom now again started to moan. While sucking mom`s boobs, Mr.Lal put his one hand on mom`s pussy and started to move it over her vagina...Mr.Lal`s teeth marks were very prominent on mom`s breasts...her breasts had now become red with the continuous sucking!!!! Mom was breathing heavily now...she had now become hot again...After sucking her breasts for some time, Mr.Lal got up from the bed...Mom also got up and sat at the edge of the bed...I think she thought it was all over!!! But suddenly Mr.Lal said to mom, Ok....now it`s your turn... Mom couldn`t understand him...So she just gave a blank look at him...Mr.Lal then said, come on slut...now give me a blowjob!!! Mom was just shocked to hear it...She opened her lips but just said, Bl...bl...Blowjob... Mr.Lal was surprised to hear it...He then said, come on slut...don`t tell me you have never done it before... Mom said, ...I never did it even with my husband.... Mr.Lal burst out into a laugh and continued, What!!! You mean I would be the first one you will suck!!! Mom just stared at him...Her face had become red now...Mr.Lal impatiently said, What...come on...suck me slut...hurry up.... When mom didn`t move, he became angry and threatened, So don`t you want to get your son in my school, bitch...Come on...do it now... Mr.Lal took mom`s hand and placed it on the button of his trouser...Mom`s fingers were shaking probably because she was very nervous! Somehow she opened the button...Mr.Lal pulled down the zip of the trouser and it automatically fell down on the floor...He slowly stepped out of it...Now he was only in his underwear! Mr.Lal`s huge erection was easily viewable...It made a tent in his underwear...At the tip of the tent, there was a big wet spot which showed his pre-cum...Mom was really stunned to see his huge erection...Mr.Lal then impatiently said, Come-on slut, take off my underwear...hurry up... Mom slowly put her hands on his underwear...She nervously pulled down his underwear...As soon as she pulled down his underwear, his penis sprang out like a angry tiger towards its prey...Mom was stunned to see his huge dick!!!

Although it wasn`t much thick, but it was almost 7&1/2 inch long...Mom couldn`t say a word...She just gasped slowly like, huuuhhhhhhh!!! She was definitely shocked by its size!!! She just stared at it with fear in her eyes!!! I think dad`s cock was much smaller!!! Mr.Lal also had really huge balls...His cock was covered with some hair...He then said to mom, what are you waiting for, bitch??? Come-on, hold it with your hands!!! Mom couldn`t move...All she did was just stared at his huge cock... When mom didn`t move, Mr.Lal himself took mom`s right hand and placed it on his dick...Mom just looked blankly at his face...Mr.Lal then said, come on, now pull back the foreskin...Hurry up slut! Without any more words, mom put her fingers at the tip of his penis and slowly and very slowly pulled back his foreskin...Now the head of Mr.Lal`s cock was exposed to mom...It was wet and shining with his pre-cum!!! The head of his cock was also very big with a purple border...Mom just stared at it with fear!!! Mr.Lal then continued, Ok bitch, now take out your tongue and lick it like a good slut!!! But mom didn`t move...He became angry and shouted, ...hurry up slut, now lick it...or else forget about your son`s admission!!! Mom was helpless...I could clearly see there were tears in her eyes but she somehow controlled herself... She slowly took out her tongue and touched the tip of his penis...As soon as her tongue touched the tip of his cock, Mr.Lal moaned like ooooohhhhhhh-h...........yeeeeeaaaaaaahhhhhh!!!!!!!!!!!!!!!!!!! Mom immediately pulled back her tongue...I think she didn`t like the taste of his pre-cum...Mr.Lal again became angry and shouted, What's wrong bitch!!! Come on...lick it...don`t you want your son`s admission in my school... This time mom without saying anything more, took out her tongue and with a very slow speed she started licking his erect cock...Mr.Lal interrupted her by saying, start licking from the bottom, slut... Mom obeyed him like his slave and put her tongue at the bottom of his cock...She started licking it and slowly started coming up...I don`t think she liked it much but she continued her act...She was licking his cock just like a dog licking its master!!! I think mom slowly started to like it and soon she was licking his big dick with more enthusiasm...Soon she reached the head of Mr.Lal`s cock which was constantly oozing juices...Mom slowly licked it...Mr.Lal was moaning like oMr.Lal soon stopped and took a deep breath and told mom, Ok slut...now take it in your mouth....come on suck it... Mom slowly opened her mouth and hesitantly took the head of his cock in her mouth...She started to suck it like a lollypop!!! She however couldn`t take any more than his head in her mouth...Mr.Lal said, come on...take it completely in your mouth like a good slut!!! I saw that mom was trying her best but was unsuccessful as his cock was too big for her mouth!!! Mr.Lal then suddenly put his hand behind mom`s head and without any warning pushed his dick completely into mom`s mouth!!! Mom`s eyes were wide open...She tried to scream but couldn`t as his cock was blocking her mouth...All she could do was to moan like...

Mom was trying her best to take his huge cock out of her mouth but was unsuccessful...She had no choice but to suck his cock...Tears were rolling down her eyes...Mr.Lal was constantly thrusting his cock into mom`s mouth...Mom was really struggling to keep up with the pace!!! Mr.Lal was constantly moaning like, oooooohhhhhh.....yyyyyeaaaaaaaaahhhhhh.....sslllllll-luuuuttttt.......ssssuuuuuucccckkkkkk iiiittttttttttt......yyy-yeaaaaaaaahhhhhhh.......gggoooooooooooodddddddddddd-d.......ssssssslllllllllluuuuuuttttttttt.........yyyyeaaaaaaaahhhhhhh-hhhhhh!!!!!!!!!!!!! When mom was sucking and licking Mr.Lal`s cock, sounds were coming like, ssslllluuuuuupppppp.....ssssslll-luuuuuuppppppp....ssssslllllluuuuuupppppp...ssssssllllll-luuuuuuuuppppppppp!!!! All this continued for about 15minutes after which Mr.Lal suddenly took out his cock from mom`s mouth...Mr.Lal`s cock was wet and shinning from the mixture of mom`s saliva and his own pre-cum!!! Mom`s lips were also shinning from the same juice!!! Her eyes were red and watery... Mom seemed to be breathing heavily due to the oral torture...She seemed very tired by the continuous sucking!!! But she also looked a bit relieved because I think she thought that it was all over finally...But little did she know of the things to come!!! Soon Mr.Lal said to mom, Ok...slut...now get ready to get fucked!!! Mom was definitely shocked by his words...It struck like lightning on her!!! Her eyes were wide open and stared at him...She stammered and said, Nooooo......pleaaaseee.... Mr.Lal was angry and shouted at her and said, What do you mean by no, bitch??? Mom said, Please...not today...please...nooo...please... Mr.Lal was really annoyed now...He said in a cold voice, ok... bitch...I won`t do anything...But forget about your son`s admission in not only my school, but any school in Delhi!!! Mom was shocked...She knew he was a powerful man...She knew she

had no choice but to surrender...She said in a low voice, no...
Don`t go....OK..... Mr.Lal had smile on his face...He knew he had
succeeded!!! He immediately said, Ok...now go and get some
oil... Mom seemed confused!!! But without saying anything she
got up from the bed and walked out of the room towards the kitchen...Meanwhile Mr.Lal took out his purse from his trouser...
From his purse he took out a small packet almost of the size of a
tomato-sauce pouch!!! I couldn`t understand what it was...Soon
mom returned to the room and with a bottle of oil...Mr.Lal took
it and placed it on the table and asked mom to sit down at the
edge of the bed...As mom sat down at the edge of the bed, Mr.Lal
handed the small pouch to mom...Mom just stared at it...Mr.Lal
said to mom, ok...slut...now tear the packet and take out the
condom...

Now I realized what it was...Guys in those days condoms were
not popular...They had just then arrived in India and not many
people used it...In those days neither was there any awareness
about AIDS...So condom was just used to protect one from unwanted pregnancy...I think mom had never seen any condom
before because she just stared at it with amazement!!! Mr.Lal
said, Come-on....hurry up!!! Mom just fumbled with it and somehow tore the pouch...She took the condom in her hand and
stared at it...Mr.Lal now placed his rock-hard cock in front of
mom`s face and said, ok...slut...now put it on my dick and roll it
over... Mom did as told and placed the condom at the head of his
cock and rolled it over, covering his cock completely...Mr.Lal
now said to mom, ok...bitch...now suck it...this condom is
strawberry flavoured...you will surely like sucking it!!! and saying so he started to laugh loudly...Mom was scared by his loud
laughing and said to him, please don`t laugh so loudly...Rohit
might wake up... Mr.Lal laughed and said, So what...let him wake
up and see his mother sucking the cock of his principal...let him
see what a slutty bitch his mother is... Mom`s face became red
again with humiliation...Without saying anything, mom put
her mouth on his cock and started taking his cock inside her
mouth...She was sucking it hard...I think she liked the taste of

the condom...Mr.Lal asked her, so...do you like it??? Mom just looked into his eyes...Mr.Lal soon took out his cock from mom`s mouth and said, ok...slut...now it`s time... and saying so he took the oil-bottle and opened it...He took some oil in his hands and started to apply it on his condom-covered cock...His cock was now shinning due to the oil...He then said to mom, ok now lie down on the bed and spread your legs... Mom quietly laid down on the bed and spread her legs...Mr.Lal now got on the bed and placed his cock at the entrance of mom`s vagina...Mom looked very scared and said to him, please do it slowly... Mr.Lal started to rub the head of his cock on mom`s vaginal lips!!! Mom had closed her eyes...Mr.Lal then suddenly inserted the head of his cock into mom`s vagina...Mom immediately opened her eyes in pain and screamed like aaaaaaaaaaahhhhhh-hhhhhhhhhhhhhhhhaaaaaaaaaaaaaaaaa...... and started shaking her body in pain...Mr.Lal took out his cock from mom`s va-gina...Mom now looked really scared...Mr.Lal then took the oil bottle and took some oil in his hands...He poured some on mom`s pussy and then he started to rub his hands on her vagina and inner vaginal walls making it smooth for his entry!!! He looked at mom and said, Bitch...your pussy is just like a virgin!!! So after oiling mom`s pussy for some time, Mr.Lal again placed his cock at the entrance of her pussy...He slowly started insert-ing his dick into her vagina...Mom just closed her eyes in pain...but I think this time it didn`t hurt her much...

The head of Mr.Lal`s cock slowly vanished into her pussy... Mom just bit her lips in pain and pleasure...But just as the head entered, it couldn`t go any further...When Mr.Lal tried to apply a bit pressure, mom screamed like aaaaaaaahhhhhhhhh-hhhhhhh.......... it hurts.......pleeaaaaaseeee.......take it out... Sur-prisingly, Mr.Lal took out his dick from mom`s pussy...Mom had tears in her eyes and said, please....I can`t do it...it hurt-s...please... Mr.Lal calmly said to mom, don`t worry...it won`t hurt now... and saying so he again placed his cock at the entry of mom`s pussy...He then leaned forward and put his head on mom`s boobs and took her nipple in his mouth and started to suck it...He squeezed her other boob with his hand...Mom just looked at him...Meanwhile Mr.Lal adjusted his cock at the entrance of her vagina...Mr.Lal then left mom`s boob and started kissing her lips...He started kissing her hard...Mom also responded slightly!!! While kissing her, Mr.Lal suddenly, without any warning, pushed his hard dick into mom`s pussy!!! Mom tried to scream in pain but couldn`t because her lips were locked with his and she let out a muffled moan like mmmmmmmmmmmmmmmmmmmhhhhhhhhhhhhmmDue to the sudden pain mom tried to get up but couldn`t as Mr.Lal was on top of her...She tried to push him away but failed as he was too strong for her...Her body started shake with pain...She was shaking just like a fish out of water...She started throwing her hands around in pain...

She grabbed the bed sheet with her hand and pulled it...She was continuously moaning or screaming but the sounds were somewhat compressed...Mr.Lal was constantly thrusting his cock in and out of her body, although not with much force...After about five minutes, mom`s body stopped shaking and her moans also stopped...She had closed her eyes now...I thing the pain had now vanished and she was in pleasure!!! Soon Mr.Lal too unlocked her lips...Mom slowly opened her eyes...They were full of tears and one or two drops even rolled down from the side of her eyes...Mr.Lal continued his thrusts and mom again started to moan like...mmmmmmhhh......mmmmmm......aaaaaa........hhhhhhhhh.......mmmmmmm.........mmmmmm...aaaaaahhhhhhhh.....aaaaaahhhhhh....She now clearly moaned due to immense pleasure!!! But to her horror, Mr.Lal suddenly increased his speed and now mom again started to scream loudly like.....aaaaaaThis continued for about 15minutes after which Mr.Lal suddenly took out his cock from mom`s vagina...Mom`s vagina was leaking a lot of juices...I think mom thought that it was over now...But suddenly Mr.Lal said, ok...slut...now turn around and sit like a dog....I am gonna fuck you doggy-style now!!! Mom was shocked...She had no choice other than obeying him...But she definitely looked tired due to the heavy fucking...So she quietly turned around and sat in doggy-style...Mr.Lal quietly placed his cock at the entrance of mom`s cunt...

Suddenly he pushed his dick into her vagina...Mom screamed in pain like aaaaaaaaaaaahhhhhhhhhhhhhhhhhhhhhhhhhhhh.........uuuuuuuuuuuuuuuuuuunnnnnnnnnnnnnnnnnnnnnnn.......aaaaaaaaaaaaaaaaannnnnnnnnnnnnnnnnnnnnnnnnaaaaaaaaaaaaaaaa...... Mr.Lal slowly started to gain momentum and started to fuck mom harder...Mom was moaning and screaming quiet loudly...With every thrust, Mr.Lal`s balls started hitting mom`s ass cheeks and it produced a sound like.................'plat!!!'...'plat!!!'...'plat!!!'...'plat!!!'...'plat!!!'...'plat!!!'... .. Meanwhile Mr.Lal was also in lot of pleasure and was moaning like, oooohhhhh....yeeeeaaaaaaahhh.....ssslllllluutttttt..... yeaaaahhhhh.....ooooooohhhhhhh......ffffuuuuucccccckkkk.......ffffuuuuucccccckkkkk.....ffffuuuuucccckkkkk......bbbbbiiiittttccccchhhhh....you have such a ttttiiiiigghhhttt pppusssy!!! Mom was moaning and moaning and Mr.Lal also kept on banging her pussy mercilessly...After fucking her doggy-style for about 15 minutes, Mr.Lal suddenly took out his cock from mom`s pussy...Mom just fell down on the bed on her abdomen...she looked really tired...She probably thought that ultimately it was all over...But she was wrong....Mr.Lal soon said, come on slut...get up...the final act is still to go.... Mom was shocked and she turned around and looked at him in surprise...Mr.Lal said, ...yeah...now get ready to get your anus fucked!!! Mom was shocked...Her eyes were wide open and she immediately said, Nooooooooooooo.......nnnooooo.....pllllleeeeaaaaaseeeeee.... Mr.Lal interrupted her by saying, shut up slut...don`t you care about Rohit...Can`t you understand Rohit`s future lies in my hands...or I should say his future lies in my balls!!! And saying so he started to laugh loudly...Mom started to beg him by saying, ...no please...no...I can`t do it....I have never done it...please... Mr.Lal was shocked to hear her...he said, What! You haven`t done it before...you mean you are an anal-virgin!!! So I will be the first one to pop your anal-cherry!!!...

Mom again pleaded, No...Please don`t do it to me...please...I have heard that it hurts and pains a lot....nooo....pleeaaaseeee.....no.... Mr.Lal was in no mood to listen to her....He just said, pains so what...haven`t you heard that parents have to take a lot of PAIN in growing up their children!!!

So just turn around and sit in the doggy-style position... Saying so, Mr.Lal held mom`s hand and started to turn her around... Mom didn`t protest much, but she kept on saying, pleaaaseeee be slow....pleassee...pleaseee... Soon mom was again in doggy-style position...Mr.Lal then slowly started to examine mom`s ass!!! He started moving his hands all over mom`s ass...Sometimes, he even squeezed mom`s ass...After sometime, Mr.Lal took the oil-bottle in his hands and took out some oil...He poured the oil into mom`s ass-hole and applied some onto his fingers...After keeping down the bottle, Mr.Lal put his first fingers into mom`s ass-hole...mom suddenly moaned like aaaaaaaaaahhhhhhhhhh....Mr.Lal started to rotate his finger in mom`s ass-hole!!! Mom was constantly moaning in pain like aaaaahhhhhhhhhh....aaaaaahhhhhhhhh......aaaaaahhhhhhhhhh......aaaaaaahhhhhhhhhh.......Mr.Lal said, ...you have such a small ass-hole slut!!! How will you take my big dick in it...huh...? Mom just kept moaning in pain... After sometime, Mr.Lal took out his finger from mom`s ass and placed his hard dick at the entrance of mom`s ass-hole...His cock was absolutely rock-hard!!! Then as he tried to push his long dick into mom`s little hole, mom screamed in pain like aaaaaahhhhhhhhhhhhhhhhhhhhhooooooooo-oooooooooooooooooooooooooooooooo...........This time mom put her hand on his cock and tried to remove it from her ass-hole...But Mr.Lal pushed away her hand and again tried to insert it in her tiny ass-hole....this time mom even screamed louder like ooooooooohhhhhhhhhhhhhhhhh.........nnnnnnnnnn-nooooooooooooooooooooo............mmmmmmmmmmmmmmmm-m.......But this time the head of Mr.Lal`s cock went in amazingly...as his head went in, mom started to shiver and moan like ooooooohhhhhhhhhh........pppppplllllllllllleeeeeeaaaaaasssssssss-seeeeee.......take it out...pleaaaaaseeeee.... Mr.Lal suddenly withdrew his cock from mom`s ass-hole...Mom was a bit relieved and became quiet...But suddenly Mr.Lal pushed his hard dick back into mom`s ass-hole with a lot of force...Mom screamed at the top of her voice like oMr.Lal now started thrusting his cock in and out of mom`s ass hole!!! Mom was screaming with every thrust....She was begging him to stop like...ooooohhhh ppppleeeeaaaaassssseeeee......tttaaaaakkk-keeeee iiiitttttttt ooooouuuuuuutttttttt......pppppppleeeeeaaa-aaasssssseeeeee......uuuuuuffffffffffffffff......aaaaaaaaaahhhhhhh-h......ppppppplllleaaaaaasssssseeeeee...... But Mr.Lal went on ramming his cock into mom`s ass-hole...With every thrust, Mr.Lal`s ball`s hit mom`s ass hole and produced as sexy sound like...plut... Plut... Plut... Plut... Plut... Plut Mom was constantly screaming at the top her voice...Her screams were loud enough to arouse anyone... (now friends, I forgot to tell you that every floor of our building had three flats...Ours was the middle one...In the floor towards our right a family lived which had gone for vacation to Shimla and were suppose to return the next morning and the flat towards our left was temporarily vacant but a newlywed-couple were suppose to move in within a week...) So back to the story, Mr.Lal was ass-fucking mom and she was continuously screaming at the top of her voice like oh...pleaase...I can`t ...it hurts so much....pllleeeeaaaaasss-seeeee...ttaake iittt oouuuutttt.... Suddenly Mr.Lal slapped mom`s ass-chick with some force...Mom moaned and screamed like aaaauuuuuuuuuuuuhhhhhhhhhh....Mr.Lal started slapping mom`s ass-chick....Mom moaned with every slap!!! Mr.Lal was moaning like, oohhhh....ssssllllluuuttt....yyyooouuu haavvvee ssuuuccchhh aaaa tttiiigghhht llliittttttlllee aaaassssss hh-hoooollleee....sssshhiiiittttt....iittttt fffeeeellssss sssssoooooooo-ooo gggooooooood....yyyeaaaahhhh.... With every thrust and slap, mom screamed and groaned...By now her ass cheeks had become red with the slapping....Mr.Lal kept on ass-fucking mom mercilessly for about 20 minutes...Suddenly Mr.Lal withdrew his huge cock from mom`s ass-hole...Mom`s ass hole had become wide open due to the massive fucking!!! Mom fell down

on the bed due to tiredness...She was breathing heavily...Mr.Lal meanwhile pulled off the condom from his cock and threw it on the floor...He looked very sexcited!!! He hurriedly said to mom, oh slut...hurry up...kneel down on the floor...hurry up... Mom was confused and in the confusion she without understanding anything, nervously got down off the bed and sat on her knees on the floor!!! Mr.Lal quickly placed his hard dick in front of mom`s lips and said, come on...bitch...suck it...fast...oh... Mom without understanding anything, quickly opened her mouth and took his huge dick in and started sucking it quickly...Mr.Lal had closed his eyes in pleasure and started to moan like, oh...slut...yeaaaaaaahhhhhhh.....yyyyeaaaaaaaahhhhh.....hhhh-hhhmmmmmmmmmmmm.......ssssssuuuuuuuucccccckkkkk-kkk...... iiiiittttttttttt......yyyeeeeeeaaaaaahhhhhh!!!!!!!!!!!! After about a minute Mr.Lal couldn`t take it any more...
He suddenly took out his cock from mom`s mouth and sud-denly groaned like oohhhhhhhhhhhhhhh........gggggooooooo-ooodddddddd.......fffffuuuuuuucccccckkkkkkkkk-k!!!!!! ...............and before mom could even react his cock erupted like an angry volcano!!! Without warning, litres of sperm flew across and hit mom`s face directly...Mom was really sur-prised....she somehow closed her eyes and moaned in surprise like, Oh! God!...Mr.Lal`s cock started to erupt gallons of thick, hot, white sperm which flew across and landed on mom`s face... Mom moved back a little and as a result, lot of sperm fell on her big boobs!!! Well friends, I couldn`t believe that Mr.Lal could ejaculate so much of sperm...I am sure that even a porn star would have been ashamed in front of him!!! He just came in litres and within seconds mom`s face was completely covered with Mr.Lal`s thick, white sperm!!! Mom couldn`t move!!! When Mr.Lal saw mom`s face completely covered with his white sperm, he started laughing loudly and said, oh...shit...slut...you look just like a whore... Mom just got up...she tried to open her eyes but couldn`t as it was completely covered with his white sperm!!! She somehow picked up her clothes and started to walk towards the bathroom...I saw that mom had real difficulty in

walking probably due to pain in her ass due to the brutal fucking of Mr.Lal...she was limping as she walked towards the bathroom...I heard the noise of falling water and understood that she was taking bath...Meanwhile Mr.Lal dressed up and lit a cigarette!!! After about 15 minutes, mom came out of the bathroom...She was now properly dressed and was wearing the same sari...Mr.Lal said, ok...Mrs.Sharma, now I got to go... and saying so he started to walk out of the door...Mom silently followed him to the main door...After reaching the main door, mom was about to ask him, Mr.Lal...so when shall I....... when suddenly Mr.Lal caught mom`s arm and turned her and pushed her on the main door...Mom was stunned and before she could say or do anything, Mr.Lal pulled down the palloo of her sari and put his mouth on one of mom`s blouse covered breasts and started sucking it....Mom closed her eyes and moaned like, nooooo.....n-not...again...please..noo.... Mom just tried to push him away but I guess he was too strong for her!!! Mr.Lal sucked mom`s boob for about five minutes and then suddenly withdrew his mouth from mom`s boob...Mom`s blouse which had meanwhile dried, now again became wet due to his sucking...Mr.Lal then said, ok...slut...bring your son tomorrow morning sharp at 8 am!!! and saying so he opened the door and walked away!!! Mom slowly closed the door and walked towards the fridge...

She took a bottle of cold water and almost drank half of it!!! Then she slowly went to her room and lied down on the bed and switched off the light!!! Next morning at around 6:30, mom came to wake me up and said, Beta! Get up...We have to go to your school...hurry and get ready... Saying so she went out...I got dressed by around 7:15 and went to mom`s room...I saw that mom was combing her wet hairs!!! I was about to leave when suddenly my eyes fell on the foot of the bed...The condom that Mr.Lal had thrown away was lying there!!! An idea came into my mind!!! I slowly picked it up without letting mom know!!! (Well friends, before proceeding further, let me tell you guys one thing...When I was younger, I mean younger than what I was at the time of this incident, I didn`t know what were condoms...so

sometimes, rarely though, when I used play in the field I would find condoms on the field...so at that time I used to think them as BALOONS!!! But I never understood why those balloons were so BIG!!!) Now coming back to the incident, I picked up the condom and said to mom, mamma...why didn`t you give this balloon to me before??? Mom initially didn`t pay any attention to me as she was sitting in front of the mirror and combing her hairs...But when she suddenly saw my reflection in the mirror with me holding the condom, she almost jumped up!!! She was shocked to see the condom in my hand!!! She quickly took the condom from my hand and threw it in the dustbin...I said pretending to be innocent, mamma...why did you throw it away...I wanted to play with it... Mom just kissed me and tried to console me by saying, no beta...I will buy you a new packet of balloons...ok... I just said ok...mamma After having our breakfast, we started for the school at around 7:40 and reached the school at around 7:55am...We straightway went to the principal`s office...Mr.Lal was waiting for us...He asked us to sit down...He gave the final admission forms to mom and asked her to fill it up...While mom was filling it up, I saw that Mr.Lal was staring at her boobs with lusty and hungry eyes...After finishing the papers, mom handed them over to Mr.Lal...Mom looked really happy!!! Mr.Lal said, so Rohit...do you know something...your mom was really desperate to get you in my school!!! Mom`s face was really red with shame!!! Mr.Lal then said, Well your classroom is on the ground floor and your class teacher shall be Mrs.Malhotra... I got up and started to leave...Mom was sitting there...After that I started to move towards my class-room...But something in my mind told me that something was going to happen again...So I ran back and went towards the principal`s room...When I reached outside the room, I just looked around to see if anyone was around...No one was to be seen...So I looked through the key-hole...I saw that mom was still sitting and talking to Mr.Lal...I thought nothing was going to happen...
I thought that at least Mr.Lal wouldn`t have the courage to do anything in the school!!! So I decided to return...but this time

when I peeked in...I saw that Mr.Lal was now sitting on the table in front of mom...He said something and suddenly mom got up from her seat...Mr.Lal moved away from the table...To my surprise and disbelief, mom put both her hands on the edge of the table and bend down a bit exposing her huge ass!!! Mr.Lal suddenly started opening his trouser...Then he quickly took off his trouser...His cock was rock hard!!! He then took out his purse and took out a condom from it!!! He quickly put it on his hard dick...He slowly lifted mom`s sari and to my surprise, mom was not wearing a panty!!! Her clean shaven pussy was clearly visible to me...It looked somewhat wet!!! Mr.Lal carefully placed his cock at the end of mom`s vagina and then with a sudden thrust, his cock completely vanished into mom`s vagina...I saw that mom was moaning...Although I couldn`t hear anything from outside, but I could easily understand her facial expressions!!! Mom had her eyes closed and was moaning in pleasure...Mr.Lal kept on ramming his cock into mom`s vagina for about 15 minutes and then suddenly he took it out...He quickly placed his hard dick at the entrance of mom`s ass hole...Suddenly he jerked his cock into mom`s little ass-hole and mom, I think, screamed in pain...I could clearly understand from her facial expressions that she was I lot of pain...Her mouth was wide open and she was just shaking her head in both pain and pleasure!!! Mr.Lal was also in lot of pleasure...His eyes were closed!!! He was holding mom`s waist for support and continuously rammed his hard cock into mom`s ass hole!!! He ass-fucked mom for about 20 minutes...Suddenly he withdrew his cock from mom`s ass-hole and took of the condom...To my surprise, this time without saying anything, mom turned around and herself kneeled down on the floor!!! Mr.Lal placed his erect dick in front of mom`s mouth...Mom herself took his dick into her mouth and started sucking it hungrily!!! She was sucking it with lot of hunger and lust...Suddenly, to Mr.Lal`s surprise, mom herself pulled down the palloo of her sari exposing her huge blouse-covered boobs to Mr.Lal and then quickly opened the first two buttons of her blouse...Now mom`s huge boobs and her deep cleavage was clearly visible to Mr.Lal...He was shocked and really liked it...I think it acted as a catalyst and Mr.Lal suddenly said something to mom and took out his hard penis from mom`s mouth!!! Without any warning, suddenly his cock exploded like a volcano with his cum flying all over and hitting mom`s face...Mr.Lal ejaculated a huge amount of sperm!!! Some of the mom hit mom`s face and rest of it fell on her blouse and rolled down into her deep cleavage...Mr.Lal looked tired...Mom somehow took out a napkin from her purse and cleaned her face...

hen she wiped off the sperm from her blouse and boobs!!! After that mom closed the hooks of her blouse and put back the palloo of her sari and got up from the floor...When she started to leave, Mr.Lal suddenly caught mom`s hand and pulled her towards him...Mom was now in his arms and due to the sudden jerk, the palloo of her sari slipped from its position again revealing her huge boobs and deep cleavage!!! This time, mom didn`t care to put back her palloo at its place...Mr.Lal stared at her huge boobs and then suddenly started kissing mom`s lips viciously!!! To my surprise, mom responded to his kisses and then she put her arms around Mr.Lal`s shoulders!!! After kissing mom`s lips for some time, Mr.Lal started kissing and licking mom`s neck!!! Mom now closed her eyes in pleasure...I think she had started to like Mr.Lal!!! While kissing mom, Mr.Lal put his hand on one of mom`s boobs and started to press it softly... Mom opened in pleasure and I think she was moaning...After that Mr.Lal started to open the hooks of mom`s blouse but was struggling...I think the hooks were too tight...Surprisingly, when mom saw this, she smiled and herself opened the hooks of her blouse...Mr.Lal smiled and kissed her...Then he unhooked mom`s bra himself and quickly put his mouth on one of mom`s boobs and started to suck it hungrily!!! Mom put both her hands on his head and slowly started to caress his head!!! After sucking one boob, Mr.Lal moved to another boob and sucked it for sometime...After that, suddenly the school bell rang...The first period had started...So Mr.Lal stopped his sucking and said something to mom...Mom then started to dress up again and wore her blouse and put back the palloo of her sari at its place...After that mom turned around to return...I decided to return but suddenly Mr.Lal grabbed mom from behind and started to squeeze her boobs and lick her neck...mom just closed her eyes!!! Suddenly my eyes fell on mom`s hair, just above her hair...There was something white shining on her hair...I understood it was Mr.Lal`s sperm that had fallen there...but then suddenly I recalled the incident of the LADY ON THE FIRST DAY!!! Now I understood everything...Everything was crystal clear to me now...Now I understood what a bastard HE was!!!

So he made use of every helpless-mother that came to his school!!! After that I ran away and mom also came out...I saw that mom had really trouble in walking due to the heavy fucking she had received in two days!!! Now as I had said that one of our neighbours had returned...So the same evening she came to meet mom to give her some prasaad that she had brought from Vaishno-devi...Now when she saw mom struggling to walk properly she said, Are you ok, Neelam??? You don`t seem to be able to walk properly... Mom was embarrassed and just fumbled and said, No...it`s ok..it`s just some muscular pain... Friends, only I knew how she had got that pain!!! That night after we had dinner, it was 10pm and so I went to sleep...The next day was a holiday due to something...so when I asked mom if she won`t sleep, she just said that she will sleep later as the next day was a holiday...So I just went to sleep but had a strange feeling as mom was usually an early sleeper...So I decided not to sleep till mom slept...After half an hour, that is exactly at 10:30pm, I thought I heard a slight knock on the main door...I quickly went to the keyhole of my room and peeped...I saw that mom quickly went and opened the door...It was Mr.Lal!!! As soon as he entered he said, Is Rohit still awake... Mom said, No...he is sleeping... and as soon as he heard it, he grabbed mom`s face and started kissing her hungrily!!! Mom laughed and pushed him away and said, No...not here...let`s go to my room... and both of them went to mom`s room...After entering the room, mom locked the door.

Mr.Lal immediately hugged her...This time I was really shocked and surprised that mom herself put her arms around Mr.Lal... Mr.Lal kissed her neck and said, let`s have some fun darling... and while saying so he was hugging mom...They went towards the bed and sat down...Mr.Lal was sitting beside mom and they were kissing each other very passionately!!! Mr.Lal while kissing mom, pushed her down on to the bed...Now mom was lying on her back and Mr.Lal was on top of her...After unlocking his lips from mom`s, he started kissing her all over her face...All the kisses were wet kisses...He then proceeded downwards towards her boobs...He removed the palloo of her sari which was covering her big boobs...Now he started kissing all over her blouse...He also licked her cleavage for some time but didn`t open her blouse...He also squeezed her boobs with both his hands and mom was moaning like hhhhhhhhhmmmmmmmmhhhhhhhhhhhhhhh...... Her eyes were closed throughout...She was definitely enjoying this whole heartedly!!! After playing and kissing her boobs for 10 mins, Mr.Lal proceeded downwards towards her belly...Her petticoat was about 3 inches below her navel...He started kissing all over her belly...He then took out his tongue and started licking all over her belly...Mom`s belly was now shining due to his saliva...When he reached mom`s navel, he suddenly inserted his tongue into mom`s deep navel... Due to this mom hissed in pleasure like ssshhhhhhhhhhhhhhhhhhh...................aaaaaaaaaaaaaaaa..................sssssshhhhhhhhhhhhhhhhhhhh..........Mr.Lal licked her navel and belly for another 10 mins...It was around 10:45pm at that time...So when he reached below her navel, he found that mom`s sari was tucked into her petticoat...He pulled out the knot of her sari from her petticoat and mom too helped him in doing so...She got up from the lying position and got rid of her sari and threw it on the floor herself...! I was getting new surprises every second...! I think after everything she had now probably submitted herself completely...Already there was a huge sexual gap of 11 yrs in her life...Now this person had shown her those hidden pleasures of eternity again...So maybe she had accepted Mr.Lal as the owner of her body...! Anyway now mom was only in her blouse which could barely hold her mammoth boobs and a petticoat while Mr.Lal had not taken off a single piece of cloth from his body...! She was looking damn sexy...But she was probably feeling shy too...She herself closed her eyes and lied down on the bed and waited for Mr.Lal...But Mr.Lal had other plans in mind...He spoke after a long time, Neelam...get up and just sit down on the bed... Mom opened her eyes and got up and sat down...Her legs were stretched out in front of her...Mr.Lal now came from the other side of the bed and sat down on the bed...He looked at mom and said, I want to lie on your lap... Mom just smiled at him and blushed in anticipation...

Mr.Lal went close to her and placed a pillow behind mom`s back...Mom rested her back on the pillow and seated herself comfortably...I knew she was liking all this treatment because it was probably the first time Mr.Lal was treating her like a woman/lover...It was probably just the exact treatment every woman on this planet dreams from her lover...! Anyway, mom then seated herself comfortably on the bed and rested her back on the pillow...Mr.Lal then slowly lied down on mom`s lap and rested his head on mom`s thighs...His head was just inches below her mammoth boobs...He placed his left hand behind mom`s head and started pulling down her head towards him...Mom understood his intentions and smiled lovingly at him and she bend down towards him...She had closed her eyes now...Mr.Lal locked his lips with mom`s and started kissing her vigorously...Mom was enjoying the kiss too because she was also equally responding to it...Meanwhile Mr.Lal was caressing mom`s hair with his left hand while his right hand was holding her face...He continued kissing her for 5 mins and then he stopped kissing her...Mom face was shining with both love and lust...I think she wanted the kiss to never end...! Mr.Lal looked into mom`s eyes and said, your hair is so beautiful...so smooth and silky...I want to see them open... and saying so he put his hand behind mom`s head and removed the clip from her hair...Her long hairs fell loose now...She was definitely looking more beautiful now...

Mr.Lal kissed her long hairs for about a min and then brushed them aside...His eyes then fell on the mammoth boobs which were just inches from his mouth...He then said to mom, Mrs.Sharma...your breasts are so huge...They are so beautiful...so smooth and soft... and saying so he lifted his head a little such that his nose was right in between her two breasts...He buried his nose into mom`s deep cleavage and started sucking and licking them...Mom moaned like hhmmmmmm and she arched her head backwards...Her eyes were closed...Mr.Lal continued rubbing his nose in between her boobs...Suddenly he took one of mom`s blouse-covered boob into her mouth and started sucking hungrily...Mom moaned due to this like aaahhhhhhhhhhhhhhhhh..........She laughed at his desperation and said to him, oh... what are you doing...let me open the blouse at least...! But Mr.Lal didn`t pay any attention to her words...He continued sucking her breast over her blouse...After sometime he shifted to the other breast...Due to his sucking and licking, the portion of the blouse just above her breast had become completely wet...Mom`s one hand caressing Mr.Lal`s head...Her fingers were buried into his hair...she moaned like hhhhhmmmmmmmmmmmmmmm... To my surprise she bend down her head a little and kissed on Mr.Lal`s forehead lovingly...! She was definitely in love with him now...! Mr.Lal then started opening the hooks of her blouse...After he opened all the hooks, mom herself pulled off the blouse and threw it on the floor...She herself reached for the bra hook and opened it...Mr.Lal pulled of her bra and threw it on the floor...Then he again started sucking and playing with mom`s mammoth boobs...While he sucked he right boob, he was squeezing her left boob with his right hand...! Mom was continuously moaning like......aaaaaaahhhhhhhhhhhhhhhhh...........hhhhhhhhhmmmmmmmmmm.............. Mr.Lal then took one of her nipple in between his teeth and bit it little...Mom screamed in pain and pleasure like aahhhhhhhhhhhhhhhhhhhhh......She opened her eyes and looked down at him and smiled and said, please don`t bite so hard... Mr.Lal continued sucking her boobs and after 10 mins he stopped...he then got up from her lap...He started opening his shirt and then threw it on the floor...Then he got up from the bed and opened the buckle of his belt and pulled down his pant and left it on the floor...He was only in underwear now...He had a very big hard-on...! Mom looked at it and giggled like a small girl...Mr.Lal then got on the bed and put his hand on the nada of mom`s petticoat and opened it...Mom pulled down the petticoat and left it on the floor...

Mom was now only in her black panty...Mr.Lal reached forward and pulled down her panty too...Then he started fucking her madly...Mom also responded equally...He fucked her for about an hour and finally he came into mom`s mouth...Mom happily drank all of his semen and there was a smile of content on her face...! Mom then went to the bathroom and cleaned herself and after that Mr.Lal went in and cleaned himself...When he returned from the bathroom, mom was lying naked on the bed with her eyes closed...Mr.Lal went to her and lied down beside her and then started kissing her all over her face, neck and her boobs...Mom pulled the bed-sheet and covered themselves...Finally when Mr.Lal was tired, he buried his face into mom`s huge cleavage...He sucked her boobs for 10 mins and then slept off with his face in between mom`s mammoth boobs just like a small kid...! Mom also slept...There was an expression of satisfaction on her face...I couldn`t sleep whole night in anticipation of any further events...But nothing happened the whole night...Mom woke up at 7:30 am...When she woke up, she found that Mr.Lal was still sleeping beside her...He was just sleeping straight on his back with the bed-sheet covering him till his belly...There was a smile on mom`s face...Mom was completely naked too...Her nipples looked very erect...I knew she was up to something...Mom slowly got up and sat on the bed...She caught one end of the bed-sheet and slowly started pulling it off Mr.Lal...! As soon as the bed sheet came off, Mr.Lal`s naked body appeared from underneath...Mom`s eyes immediately fell on his cock...As he was still sleeping, his cock was sleeping too...! It was completely flaccid...It looked very small, about 3-4 inches in the non-erectile state...Mom stared at it for some time and then I saw that she licked her lips in anticipation...! She went closer to his naked body...Her whole body was slightly shivering...I think she was nervous...Slowly she put her right hand on top of his penis...Then she started caressing it carefully as if it was a small baby...! But his penis was still not erect...It was clear that he was still in deep sleep...! After caressing his penis for about a minute, mom suddenly bend down and planted a small kiss on the head of his penis...! She planted about 10 kisses on his flaccid dick...Her mammoth tits were touching Mr.Lal`s thighs...! Mom caught the head of his dick in between the thumb and the first finger of her right hand and slowly squeezed it a couple of times...

Then she slowly stared pulling the foreskin back from the head of his cock...Soon the foreskin was rolled back...As his dick`s head came into view, mom licked her lips again...I knew she wanted to suck on that cock madly and hungrily...! Mom touched the tip of his cock with her thumb and immediately his cock twitched a little...Mr.Lal too shifted his head from one side to the other but he was still asleep...Mom looked at his face and when she was satisfied that he was still asleep, she again looked down at his non-erect dick...Then she suddenly put her head down, opened her mouth and took the head of his dick inside her mouth and started sucking it...Mr.Lal moaned in his sleep like hhmmmmmmmmmmmmmhhhhhh.....and twisted his head again from one side to the other...I knew he was about to wake up soon and I think mom knew it too...! So she started sucking even more hungrily...I saw that slowly his cock started to grow bigger and within seconds his cock grew to its full length...! There was a smile on mom`s face...Mom had taken his cock completely into her mouth and was sucking it hungrily...! She was simultaneously caressing his huge balls with her left hand... Within a minute Mr.Lal woke up from his sleep...First when he opened his eyes I think he didn`t understand what was going on...! But when he came to his senses he understood everything...! Mom looked at him and gave a very sexy smile...! He smiled back and said, oh...what a way to wake up in the morning...! Mom stopped sucking his dick and climbed on top of him...Her legs were on either side of his legs...She bent forward now such that her mammoth boobs hung just above Mr.Lal`s thirsty mouth...Mr.Lal smiled and caught hold of her boobs and gave them a squeeze...! Mom laughed at this...Mr.Lal then took one of mom`s boobs in his mouth and started sucking it hungrily...! Mom closed her eyes and started moaning like oohhhhh-hhhh......hhhmmmmmmmmmmmmmhhhhhh..............yyeeee-eeeaaaaaaahhhhhhhhhhhhhhhh.............Mr.Lal sucked and played with mom`s tits for about 10 mins and then said, oh baby...now come on...sit on my dick...yeah... Mom opened her eyes...She saw the condom lying on the table and put it on his erect dick...Then she positioned herself carefully such that her cunt was just above Mr.Lal`s big erect dick...! Mom caught his dick with her right hand and made it stand absolutely perpendicular...Slowly mom started lowering her body on to his dick...

As soon as the head of his cock disappeared into her wet cunt, she moaned like aaaahhhhhhh...Mr.Lal then said, yeah baby... come on sit on my dick slut... I think mom liked him calling her 'slut' because when she heard that word from his mouth, she just smiled...Then she slowly lowered her body completely into his dick...His dick now completely vanished into mom`s cunt...! When his dick entered her completely, mom moaned like hhmmmmmmmmmmhhhhhhhh......Mr.Lal caught mom`s ass cheeks and started caressing them...He then continued, yeah slut...come on...fuck my dick...yeah jump and bounce on my dick...come on... These words encouraged mom and she slowly started to rise and then fall on his dick...It was a rather very slow movement...Mom`s eyes were closed during this...Suddenly without any warning, Mr.Lal slapped one of mom`s ass cheeks very hard...Mom screamed in pain like aaaaaaaaaaaaaa-aaaaaaahhhhhhhhhhhhhhhhhhhhh.......Mr.Lal moaned, yeah... come on...fuck me faster... Mom slowly increased her speed...Mr.Lal now started slapping mom`s ass cheeks...With every slap mom screamed like aaahhh....aaahhh...aaahhh...aaahhh...aaahhh....aaahhh...I knew mom liked his slaps because she showed no signs of protest...! After about 10 minutes, mom seemed tired and lowered the speed...Mr.Lal understood this and now he started thrusting his dick into mom...Mom started to moan in pleasure like.....yyyeaaaaahhhh......hmmmmmmmmhhhhhhh........yeaaaahhhhhhh.......yyeaaaaahhhhhhhh........yyyeaaaaaahhhhh......During this Mr.Lal sucked mom`s boobs too...! After the previous night ordeal, Mr.Lal`s teeth marks were prominent on mom`s boobs...They were red...Mr.Lal continued to fuck mom for another 15 minutes...His speed kept on increasing...I knew he was about to come...Within a minute, Mr.Lal stopped fucking her and turned her around and took out his dick from mom`s cunt...

He quickly removed the condom and threw it away and then he sat on his knees and went forward over mom such that her dick was right over mom`s face...He started shagging himself and moaned like, oh yeah baby...I`m gonna cum all over your face...you slut...you like your face to be covered with cum huh...oh...yeah... and within 10 seconds hot jets of cum flew from his cock and covered mom`s face completely...Some of the come fell on her hair and her boobs too...! After he stopped cumming, he put his cock inside mom`s mouth...Mom sucked it clean...Mr.Lal was tired and he turned around and lied down next to mom...Mom also didn`t move from her position...Both of them were lying next to each other and breathing heavily...After about 5 mins, mom slowly got up, and grabbed her clothes from the floor and went to the bathroom...She cleaned herself up and came out of the bathroom with full clothes on...Mr.Lal was having a smoke by that time but he was still naked...Mom smiled at him and said, why don`t you get ready, it`s time for Rohit to wake up too...I`ll go and prepare the breakfast in the kitchen and saying so she came out of the room with a smile of content on her face...! Mr.Lal finished the Cigarette and then went to the bathroom, took a shower and came out and wore back all his clothes...I quickly went to my bed and pretended to be asleep...Mom came after a minute and woke me up and asked me to get fresh and she would then prepare breakfast...I washed my face and then went to the drawing room...! Mom was in the kitchen preparing breakfast...I saw that Mr.Lal was sitting on the sofa and reading the newspaper...So I went there and wished him 'Good Morning'...He wished me back and asked me, so did u have good sleep...at least I had a wonderful night... I smiled innocently though I knew what he meant...I switched on the TV and started watching cartoons...After about 15 mins when he completed reading the newspaper, he looked at me...When he saw that I was too busy watching the Cartoons on TV, he quietly got up and proceeded towards the kitchen...On the way he looked back at me to see if I was still busy watching television...Actually I could see him clearly without him even understanding...! You see just beside the TV there was a book case...So I could clearly see his reflection on the glass of the book case...! When he finally took the turn for the kitchen, I increased the volume of the television such that it would be clearly audible even from the kitchen...!

Then I quickly jumped from there and ran towards the kitchen without making any noise...Well, now the kitchen was ...L... shaped...I was at the top end of the L marked by `` while they were at the other end marked by a comma (,) as shown in the figure next ...``L,... Both of them would have to turn So when I reached the kitchen entrance, I saw that Mr.Lal was standing about two feet from mom...Mom didn`t know about his presence and was busy arranging the breakfast...She had made bread-omelette...She had arranged three dishes on the kitchen table with the bread omelette...Beside two plates there were two cups of hot steaming coffee and beside the other, there was a glass of milk with Bournvita...! I figured out that it was for me...The other two plates with the coffee were for mom and Mr.Lal...! Mr.Lal tiptoed towards mom and when he was just behind her, he suddenly grabbed mom from behind...Mom was scared and for a second she almost screamed in fear...Mr.Lal started kissing her neck while each of his hands grabbed each of mom`s mammoth boobs and started squeezing them...Mom giggled and started moaning like...hmmmmhhhhmmmmmhhhhmmmm....But soon she realized the situation and tried to free herself from his clutches...When she saw that her efforts were all in vain, she started pleading to him like, no....please...leave me...not now...please.....Rohit can come in anytime....please not now...later please... Mr.Lal smiled and while squeezing and kissing her neck he said, don`t worry...he is too busy watching cartoons...can`t you hear the noise of the TV...! Mom was quiet...I knew she was satisfied by his answer-...Mr.Lal didn`t care to turn mom around...He kept on squeezing mom`s tits from behind itself while he continued kissing her neck and shoulders...Mom was moaning lightly like ahhhhhh...aaaaaaa....hhhmmmmmm....After squeezing mom`s tits for about 5 mins, Mr.Lal brought his hands behind and started squeezing her ass cheeks...Then with one hand he quickly unzipped his zipper and took out his erect huge dick and started poking it into mom`s ass-crack...! As soon as mom felt it, mom moaned like, no....please...Rohit might come in...no please... But Mr.Lal didn`t listen to her and continued poking his dick into her ass crack from above the sari itself...I knew mom liked it because she brought her right hand behind and caught his dick and started squeezing and stroking it...She kept her other hand on the kitchen slab for support...

So without waiting anymore, Mr.Lal started pulling her sari and petticoat up...Mom weakly protested...He quickly lifted it up to her waist...She was not wearing any panty...Her cunt and ass hole were waiting for his cock...He quickly took out a condom from his pocket and wore it...He then started rubbing his cock up and down her cunt...He then inserted half of his dick into her pussy with a quick thrust...Mom moaned in pleasure like aaaaaaahhhhhhhhhhhhhhhhhhhhhh...He started humping her while squeezing her boobs...He cunt fucked mom for about 15 mins during which mom came twice... After that he withdrew his cock out of her wet pussy...Mom`s pussy was dripping wet...He then placed it at the tip of her ass-hole...! Then with one quick thrust he pushed about two inches inside mom`s small asshole...Mom screamed in pain like ahhhhhhhh.....Then with another thrust he inserted almost his full cock into her...Mom gave another loud scream...Mr.Lal continued fucking her asshole mercilessly for about 20 mins...Then he was close to cumming...He said to mom, oh...slut...you are so good...do you want to drink my cum...Huh... Mom just nodded in affirmation...He quickly withdrew his cock out of her ass and pulled off the condom...! To my and mom`s surprise, he went close to the kitchen slab and placed the tip of his cock at one of the coffee cups and started shagging his dick...Mom was standing surprised beside him...The palloo of her sari had slipped off exposing her mammoth blouse-covered boobs...Mr.Lal bend down and immediately cook one of mom`s boobs into his mouth and started sucking hard...Mom moaned a bit due to this sudden experience but she continued watching him shag his dick into the coffee cup...Within a minute Mr.Lal gave a loud moan and started cumming into the coffee cup...He came in gallons and all his cum formed a white layer on top of the brown coffee...! He lifted his head from mom`s boobs and looked into the coffee cup...Then he said with a smile on his face, you will definitely like this cup of coffee Mrs.Sharma...

This coffee is called Cum-cappuccino...! Saying that he put back his limp cock inside his trouser and zipped it back...Mom was still in a state of shock and was constantly staring at the cup of coffee...Mr.Lal smiled and kissed mom on her lips on which she came out of the state of shock...Mom responded too...Then Mr.Lal said, so it`s time for some breakfast...! Mom took my plate and glass of milk from the slab and started coming out...I ran back to the sofa...I saw that she put the plate and glass and called me to come for breakfast...I went to the dining table and sat...Then she went back and both of them came out from the kitchen with their breakfasts...On the dining table Mr.Lal said to mom, the breakfast is very delicious and so is the coffee...I`m sure your coffee is even more tasteful than mine... Mom just smiled at him sheepishly...! Then she drank the coffee and in the end she just licked her lips...! I`m sure it was the best coffee she had tasted till date...!

26. Swap

After that I have seen a lot of fucking scene of my parents. In the winter nights every conversation between them was audible to me and I enjoyed great act almost every night when I wish to see them in action. My mother loves the position to be on Top and also sitting on the lap of my father facing each each other. In every move the back side BUTT of my mother plays a vital role as it looks superb when she is on top and moves her hips vigorously with the stroke of my father. Up to me I think my father and mother has already been tasted all the fuckiing position in their life. It became a daily routine of mine to see the fucking scene of my parents. Within the course of time recently I have heard strange things from the conversation of my parents while fucking.

One day I have witnessed that both father and mother was sleeping nude side by side with no clothe on body. The right thigh of my mother was on the waist of my father circling his total waist line. Her hand was moving over his pennis. They were discussing some issue among them. Father was telling MOM that there is no harm to taste a change in life once or twice. My mom was serious in her conversation. I was not following their talks. Suddenly MOM told father that Mrs DAS was very much friendly with her and many a times she is telling that Mr DAS wants that we can make a change with us(Mr and Mrs Mohanty). My father said that let us try once to feel the difference. I some how smelled their talks as our immediate neighbor DAS uncle and aunty want a change in partner with my MOM and DAD.

I knew from the beginning that DAS uncle was staring my MOM

always from her back side when she walks out in the corridor. They are having a daughter who is married last year. Das uncle is a very handsome man with a good personality.His height is around 6 ft which adds colour to his personality. Aunty is also a matching woman with a very good height of 5ft 6 inches and figure. She is hardly 39 years of age and no one can tell that her daughter is married. Her vitals are mostly 34-29-36 which is a very good figure. Her waist line is very slim. She is the best friend of my mother. That night when I heard my father and MOM about this plan, I was shocked. I did not believe this instantly. But nothing was within my control, so I remained silent and observed every action of both the families. After that incident I saw many a times my DAD and MOM in action. But one SUNDAY Das Uncle and Aunty were talking with my MOM and DAD at the ground floor.

I was on the first floor in my room. I used to go to the stare case to listen their conversation. Father was making jokes on mother and all were laughing. My mom was on a chair which was adjacent to my DAD. Both Das Uncle and Aunty were sitting close in a different chair. They were planning to go outside but due to busy schedule of my father he was not willing for an outing. Repeatedly he was telling that our house is a better place. In-between MOM was indicating to the up stares to all about my presence. I was noticing everything without their knowledge. On the afternoon of that day all four went in our family car for an outing. I was thinking about what was happening between them. All of them returned at 9 pm at night. I was at the ground floor and MOM asked me when I returned from library.

When I was talking with my MOM, I have noticed that she was in a very cheerful mood. All of us DAD, MOM and I took the dinner along with and I came to my room for rest. It was around 12pm I pretend to be asleep and saw that MOM came to the window of my room. It was dark within. She tried to look within something. I guessed that she was enquiring whether I fell asleep or not. I think she was convinced that I am in my deep sleep. She left that place and switched up the light in the corridor connecting both the rooms. Slowly I got up from my bed and opened my door without making any noise. I saw that mother was with my father going towards the staircase to go to the ground floor. I followed them in the dark. I saw that my DAD was in his trouser and he opened the main door of our house and had some talk with my mother and then moved away. My MOM slowly half close the door and went to the sofa in the drawing room and took rest there. She was a little bit nervous as appeared from her face. I was witnessing everything from the staircase from dark area. MOM was wearing her pink nighty which is slightly down on her neck line.

From top her BOOBS are clearly visible as the cleavage was wide. She was biting her nail. Sometimes latter the main door opened and I was astonished to see Das Uncle entering through. I guessed that my DAD must have gone to the house of DAS Uncle and Das Uncle to our house. I have seen the face of my MOM. She was very much sighing. Das Uncle closed the door and came near my MOM. With a very faint voice he told something to my mother.

She was looking downwards while conversation. I was not able to hear any of their conversations. After a while my MOM looked upward by indicating something. I got scared that whether they were aware about my presence. But after that both of them moved towards the guest room situated on the ground floor. I was very much frustrated that I could not able to see anything at the ground floor. But they switched off the light in the common place in the ground floor to make my move easy. I slowly move to the ground floor to witness the event. The door of the guest room was closed from within by this time and I was searching for a peeping hole. To my fate there was a straight small crack in the door of that room in the wood through which the light source from within was coming. I found a place there and peeped through that. To my luck almost 80% of the room area was visible through that.

I saw within that DAS Uncle was sitting in the bed and MOM was standing nearer the bed by looking at him with slightly nervousness. Das Uncle was telling, Please don't mind bhabi, this is a simple change in life which Mr Mohanty and me discussed earlier. Also Mr Mohanty is very fund of a change and he likes the attire of my wife. My MOM was silent. In between the conversation I have noticed that Das Uncle was adjusting his pennis over his trouser. Suddenly he got up from bed and came closure to MOM. He placed his hand on the shoulder of mother and on another hand tried to lift the face of my mother. My MOM look seductively to him and DAS Uncle gave her a deep kiss on lips. He encircled his hand by embracing MOM and MOM also loosen her body accordingly. After some long kiss my mother spread her both hand around DAS Uncle to hold him tightly. Das Uncle tried to pull mother nearer to the bed and succeeded in that. Both of them came nearer to the bed. Das Uncle moved his hand to the back side of MOM and tried to catch the huge GAAND in both the palm over her nighty. He was massaging her BUTT mercilessly as if he was searching for that since long and got it now. "Bhabi I am a mad fan of your hips. Please don't mind. I used to stare at you from your back and feel very much aroused"Das uncle told to my mother. My position was critical as my pennis got erected up to the maximum level. I could well fantasize the position of my father at the residence of Das Uncle.

My mother was feeling shy when a deep moan came out of Das Uncle. Das Uncle after a deep press to the BUTTS of my mother at once remained separated. My mother was indicating him to switched off the light of the room. Uncle was smiling and told something in her ear. Mom felt very much sigh. Within the process the hair knot of my Mom was loosened and deep long black hair had fallen down to her waist. Then she tried to make a knot by raising her nicely shaped armpit. In the mean time Uncle was undressing himself and he only left with the chhadi. By getting a chance Das Uncle tried to raise the nighty of Mom and she was reluctant as she was tying her hair knot. She made herself slightly backward to avoid the situation. But Das Uncle was not in a mood to obey her.

He followed her and grabs her in the waist to pull her towards him. Now both the hands of Mom were free and she was pressing Uncle to release her with not much force. Now the pressure of Uncle remained unchanged and he tried very hard to pull her to the edge of bed along with him. By this process both of them fell on the bed with mother on top of Das Uncle. She was so sigh that she tried to hide her face on the hairy chest of him. His hand in now trying to lift the nighty and he succeeded in doing that. The night gown of Mom was raised up to her shoulder height and then she lifted her self to make that out of her body. She was still lying on top of him and now I can well see the erotic figure of both. Mom was wearing a DEEP RED COLOUR PANTY and a RED COLOUR BRA. It looked extremely sexy for her body. She has only one fold of flesh in her waist line which is being ploughed my Das Uncle over that area. He lifted the face of her to plant a kiss on her lips. The cheeks of my MOM became red in blush and she is felling herself with the body which is quite masculine in comparison to Dad. My Mom must be feeling the hardness of him as the waist line of her was on the same area of DAS uncle.

Therefore she at times lifts her BUTT to adjust her pubic area so as to make a contact with the hardness of him. Her both the hands were on the hair of him to search something within the head. The whole situation became uncontrollable for me. I almost cummed on my barmuda but waited patiently. Both the hands of Das uncle was within the panty of my Mom in the back side and only the sketch of his palms are visible below her panty as it was seriously engaged in pressing hard to the naked white fresh in the GAAND. He was moving his hands with constant upward and downward movement within the panty and her whole body was moving up and down over his body.

By that way the erected PENNIS part of Uncle was repeatedly being in contact with the Pussy of her. Her expression was out of my imagination. He hold her left hand with his left hand and inserted in between the two bodies where both the private parts are united. Then Das uncle removed his hand leaving only the hand of MOM in between. Nothing in between was visible to me but I could well guess that Mom must be measuring the lengh and size of the rod of Uncle comparing Dad's. The movement of her left hand indicates that she was constantly playing with the pennies of Uncle. In the meanwhile Das Uncle opened up the BRA of her from the back side and tried to lift her to remove that from her body. When she was leaning against the body of him her left hand came out of the junction and rested on his hairy chest. The swinging water melons of Mom was clearly visible to me with a big size dark brown nipple. Das uncle was so excited to see this that he extended his mouth upward to suck her nipple instantly. The sound was so erotic that my hand was on full motion on my dick for my pleasure. Instantly loud moan came out of the mouth of Mom .Uncle was hissing out of ecstacy. The total room was filling with all the erotic sounds. He madly tried to kiss every part of the hanging balls of her .

All of a sudden mother lifted herself from Uncle's body and made herself stand on the bed. Das uncle quickly removed his chadi and his pennis came out of that. The size was good and I think that was same as that of my father. But the thickness is superb. He then started to masturbate with his hand by looking at her actions. In between mother lowered her RED PANTY to show her most vital part to him. She then tried to hide the chhot of her with one of her palm. I can well see the hairs in her pussy even after covering with palm. She lifted her leg to come out of the PANTY and move closure to him. Uncle welcomed her with both his hands and made her sit on the lap facing each other. Thighs of my mother encircled the waist of Uncle like a snake. Out of pleasure Mom was trying to hold him as tightly as possible. Both of his hands are now engaged in real measurement of her BUTT.

In between Uncle inserted his left finger in the ass hole of her and I had noticed that mother virtually jumped over from that and then fell on the lap of him. She was smiling seductively and madly kissing him after that. OOOOOHHHHHH came out of her mouth and her hand came within the joint area of both PENNIS AND HER PUSSY. She tried to hold the Organ and touch the entrance of her PUSSY. Then after a jerk of Uncle probably the Pennis was within her and she started moving her wide BUTT madly. The moan from the mouth of my mother was so loud that probably they forgot that I was in the upstairs. She was looking very sexy. Das uncle started to tell some vulgar words about the BOOBS and BUTT of my mother loudly. That created lot of movement in the mother and she continued to enjoy up to uptimum. After this excersise lasted for about 10 minutes Uncle lied on the bed below and Mom was on her top to **** him mercilessly. I found it very hard to believe the sexuality of my dear mother even after she attained a certain age. After some time everything remained calm after a deep and loud moan from both the side and they slept together encircling each other with their thighs and arms. I found it difficult to resist and came to my room for a jerk off. On my bed I could not believe the scene that I had witnessed some moment back. These old age couples are so experimental in sex activity, I was really amazed to see that. I just looked at the watch and it was 2 AM in the mid of night.

After some time I have heard the opening sound of our main door on the ground floor so I rushed in to the top of stair case to see what has happened. I was Das Uncle opened the door and through that my DAD along with Das Aunty entered to our residence. My father was looking very cheerful and also with the case of Das aunty. She was wearing a blue colour nighty and her short hair and height was matching her to add more maturity to her beautiful face. She came in and entered the room where Das Uncle and Mom was enjoying few moments back. On the other side Dad and Das Uncle was talking something with smile on their face. Both of them sat on sofa on drawing room with ease and Dad took time to smoke a cigarate.

They were chitchatting and after some time I saw from the room my MOM and Das aunty came out to join them in the drawing room. Their voice was very much faint to guess what they were talking among themselves. But from their expression I could well imagine that all of them was very happy for this new experiment. Suddenly I saw that Das uncle stood up and proceeded towards the outside door. I thought the game was over and they are returning, but MOM was following him and went away with uncle at that hour of night. I guessed that probably they were moving to the room of DAS Uncle leaving my father and Das aunty to spend some time together. This left only my father and Das aunty in the drawing room. Das aunty followed my mother and closed the main door after they left the palce. Then she came nearer to father and stood beside the sofa, where father by that time finished his cigarate smoking.

I was witnessing the events with much eagerness. Father was looking towards the erected boobs of aunty which was under her nighty and projected upward. She came more closer to father and sit on the lap of him. He got so excited that he spread both of his hands below her armpit and grabbed both the boobs of her. She was cheering with utmost joy with her head moving upward to give him kiss. She tried to stop the process of heavy massage to her boobs by placing her arms on the hand of father but he was not in a mood to slow down the process. She shouted with pleasure and her moans are easily audible to the top floor. One of the hands of father came below her body and tried to lift her nighty from her thigh zone upwards. Then he inserted his right hand within the lower part of Das aunty and started caressing her Pussy over her panty.

The game was so erotic; I could hardly make myself contained without my hand at pennis. She moved from the lap of father and moves backward and lifted her nighty completely from her boby. WOW! There was no bra within and her boobs hanged immediately from her bare milky white chest. The size of boobs are normal and smaller that of MOM. But the straightness of boobs are intact. She was wearing only a white panty and to her white body that suits her the most. She again came nearer to Dad and sat again on his lap, but this time her face facing his hairy chest. She cuddled up her thigh around the waist of father and holds him tightly. Father moved his hand through her back and inserted his both the hands in her panty at the back side and pumped her ASS. My Dad was only in his trouser.

She held father tightly and moving her hips within to make a contact with the public area of father. In between her hand came within the joint of both the body and did something there. Aunty was taller than my Mom so her figure was looking gorgeous in that scene. After some time I have seen both of them completely nude and father lift her up and took her to the bed of guest room. They forgot to close the door. The lights in the drawing room were on. It was a little bit difficult to see their action in that room for me but I took some risk and went nearer the door of the room. On the side of screen I have seen Dad has started his action on bed. Aunty was holding him tight and father was giving deep push to her . She was souting loudly with pain. Probably that was the second or third time of Dad so the game lasts for 10 minutes and both of them remained like faint in bed. I decided to pack up from this place as the situation was risky. After that incident I have noticed a big change in the relationship of both the families.

My dad remained busy in his work but many a times I saw in the absence of Dad, Das uncle used to sit long in our house and chating with Mom. Also Mom used to visit their place frequently. Also on one occasion I saw them cuddling each other (Das Uncle and Mom) in our drawing room. When at night Uncle was leaving for his house. Uncle was passionately kissing Mom with his hand caressing her BUTT at the time of farewell. Mom also was responding him by a tight embrace.

27. Aruna

I am Aruna. I was newly married and just after our honeymoon it was month of Ashadh when newly married girl does not stay at her in laws. So our in laws started thinking where to stay me and then they concluded to stay me with my grand-father-in-law. He was called Bhagat and then aged around 65. He was practically living in small village around 30 kms from my Sasural. I had seen him only once in marriage. My husband dropped at his place and then bid farewell to me for 4 days. I was not really happy as I was going to live without him for 4 days. Also my departure collided with my monthly periods so it was going to be more than 8 days without sex for girl recently married.

He was typical village background, slim and health well maintained despite age. His wife was around 55 and simple living woman. It was around 7 pm when we were there. She welcomed us decently. I looked at Bhagat and surprised. He was actually looking at my chest. He was ladies tailor I heard about him. I had simple yellow color silk saree with matching blouse. He was looking at my blossom as like he was having magic sight by which he can see through my clothes all my beauty. I was just celebrated my 24th bday. A thought touched my mind "Does he want to enjoy me? Will he fuck me?" I am serious wife by nature but at that moment I wanted to have some fun in anticipation of long wait for me.

We took dinner at 8.30 and then soon we went to bed around 9 pm. I helped Mami to finish earlier. Few minutes she was talking about her past, children etc. They had 3 girls and 2 boys. He was really a MAN. But I was not really listening to her as I wanted to rest. It was small house with one room acting as living cum bedroom and other as kitchen. Rooms were very small. There was only one bed on which he slept and we both ladies slept on ground with mattress. He shut the main light and it was all dark. I also slept after few minutes after waiting for some action.

At midnight I realized something on my chest. As it was dark and i was in sleeping mood, I really did not bother it. After few minutes I realized that my chest is heavying. Also something is moving away from my chest. Soon I started realizing what was happening. Seeing me in fast asleep, he had taken initiative. He had almost opened my front open blouse skillfully without breaking my sleep. He was really a good ladies tailor. And he was working now on me. I was in dilemma what to do? His wife was just few inches away from us and he was trying to enjoy grand-daughter-in-law. We had age difference of 40 years almost two generations! But my body was responding well to his acts. His hands were smooth and gently working on my chest; half covered breasts. My breasts had grown up with touch n excitement and nipples getting harder. I did not object him doing so and he got further encouragement. He started caressing my breasts over bra material. He had parted my saree palloo to my neck side and got good access to my sensitive areas. This continued for more than 20 minutes. His left hand was caressing my left breast and with right hand he took me in his arms. He then started caressing my bare back as blouse was open completely. He shifted little bit so that his lips came to my lips level and without hesitation he put lips on mine. His hands were busy with my both breasts and back. We were kissing intimately for another 20-25 minutes. Then he lowered his hand to my stomach and started caressing it. My left hand was caressing his hairs and right hand around his waist. He started pushing his left hand fingers through my saree from front. I did not get what he was doing and with my right hand started resisting him. I was afraid that my saree will be released completely making me ackward at night. He thought that I am resisting him for further acts and he again pulled me towards me and started kissing me and crushing my erect nipples. I was sighing heavily without caring that his wife was just some distance slept.

After some time he again started caressing my stomach and playing with saree. He "whispered in my ears first time "Where is your belly? I wanna play with ur belly" I replied "Its there only. Some distance down. You may raise saree for same" I had given him green signal to raise my saree and then what! FUCK ME! Soon his hand went on my saree and started pulling it upwards. Then he raised it up to knee level and caressed my bare knees! His right hand was on my right breast, left on my thighs and mouth kissing my soft lips. His hands were working on my thighs feeling me butterflies in stomach. He pulled me nearer and started crushing my buttocks and hips. He had not removed his lips from mine yet. I raised my right leg little and put on his legs crossed. Also my right hand started caressing his hand which was working badly on my gaand. In the heat I took his hand and inserted it in my panties from behind. His hand started crushing my firm gaand(ass). Pressure from my panty waistband was also working on his hand which fuelled heat. I made him caress my ass crack also. This continued for more than half an hour as he used to slow down and again get rhythm. It was not his age but good will power for sex.

Then he made me sleep on back and he ride on me. With both his hands he crushed my soft boobs and firm hips alternately. Then he waited for some time and got up partially. He might have removed baniyan i thought. Instead he opened his pajama and underwear knots (old type undies) Then he started slowly rubbing his tool on my mound / thighs. I started feeling its hardness which was erect totally. Then he pulled my panty to knees and started caressing my mound area with hands. He felt soft bush and my soft yoni arching for sex. I wanted him to touch and caress it. But he simple opened my pussy lips and inserted his giant lund(cock) inside. In few strokes he filled my tiny pussy and started pushing up and down, to and from motions. As I was newly wed, my pussy was really tight and hot with lust and his tool could not withstand much time. He soon exploded in my wet pussy a jet after jets. It was filled with his white juices and dropping on my thighs and partially on my petticoat, saree and bed also. I wanted him to play with me further but then he got up adjusted pajama and went to his bed. I also managed to adjust my fallen saree, closed my boob window and then decided to sleep.

Next day I avoided to see in his eyes ashamed of last night acts. He also kept little distance with me whole day. At night i wore night gown and all other garments except my bra as I did not wore it all the day. Being rainy season my bra could not dry. Just like yesterday, I slept with his wife but keeping some distance between us in anticipation of his acts again. And he did not disappoint me. After just 10-15 Minutes, I realized his hand on my gown. He was touching my abdomen and may be searching something. He then touched my right hand and signals something. I could not understand what he was telling me. So I took his hand in mine and kept for while. Then he bent forward and I realized his mouth was closer to mine. It was totally dark as lights were off. He might be thinking to whisper with me but suddenly his mouth came very close and within fraction his lips met mine. He was not prepared for that and he parted lips and whispered in low voice "Come up on bed"
I replied "No. It will make noise. Let's sleep here only.
He was bit resistant but then decided to follow me.

Soon we were in each other's arms. Our lips met again we started kissing. He kissed my face, cheeks, eyes and neck also. Our kissing continued for more than half an hour. He seemed to be less hurried. We had good sleep at afternoon so we were fressh and relaxed. I also allowed him to take his time considering his age. He was caressing my back with right hand and left hand caressing my boobs over gown. He realized that I had no brassier inside and then his actions started gaining momentum.

He tried to insert his palm inside gown from top. Though gown was loose, it was difficult to do so. However he managed to insert one or two fingers inside and slowly his palm rested totally on my bare right breast. We both had first time touch with total bare breast-palm contact. His hand was soft and he gently started playing with boob. We again resumed our kissing which was little bit disturbed meanwhile.

After some time he exchanged to right breast and started fondling it as like left one. For the same he pushed me backward little bit and resumed kissing. It was difficult than earlier for both of us but he continued. Now I wanted to make him enjoy my bare breasts. I pushed him backward little bit and then unhooked my gown buttons. I opened all four buttons and then parted off it little bit to give him better access to my private property. I took his hand resting on my stomach and placed it on my open chest. He again fondled my both breasts but with higher pressure and gave me further stimulation. Now he started caressing my shoulder from which gown slid down little.

Slowly his hand started working on my back also from behind. His left hand started pulling up my gown as like saree yesterday he did. But I stopped his hand and whispered in his ears "This is gown. You can safely remove my petticoat and under garment without removing gown". He whispered "How to reach you petticoat know. Please guide me. My wife never wore such cloth" I guided his hand on gown and then it reached near my petticoat from down side where my gown was lifted. To add spice into our romance, I held his hand for few time there only and then slowly removed it out slowly. He was bit surprised and resistant to come out. I put my lips on his and then took his hand on my boobs alternately. We continued this position for another 15 minutes or so. Then I parted lips, stretched my shoulder backward and then guided his hand down fromboobs to stomach, then on waist. He reached my petticoat knot, and then he quickly held it and gave it few pulls. It was buried in my panty waistband. It loosedned and finally opened giving him access to my panty and Golden triangle. He kept his hand lingering there for few minutes and then pulled out and then reached same region pulling up my gown. Same time he pulled up my open ghagra and in few seconds he pulled my panty out. I adjusted my legs and both the clothes dropped down. Now it was only gown between him and my bare body. But I did not want to get it down neither he wanted to waste time. I guided his hand to mound and asked him to caress it. He gently caressed the region for 5-10 minutes. He also caressed my waist and hips rigourously. Then he asked me to sleep on back. Then he removed his pyjama and chaddi completely and started rubbing his lund(cock) on my hair bush and pussy. He again kissed me for while and then separated my pussy lips also and started thrusting his tool inside. I could open and widen legs facilitating him enetr deeper. As we hand longer romance, both our tools, his penis and my pussy were wet and the lubrication paid off us. He fucked me more than 10 minutes, longer than yesterday. He took rest once and fucked me another 5 minutes and then cummed inside me. It was only semen and semen and semen in and out me. His jets were still coming out. At last he cummed totally and rested on me. Then he came down. We laid in arms for few minutes. Then we both adjusted our clothes and slept at respective beds.

28. Neeta, Ramya and Jyoti

We are three friends from college days. That will be me Neeta, Ramya and Jyoti. Very soon after passing our college days we got into jobs and within the same year well three got married. Jyoti to her boy friend and we fell for arranged marriages. So we all are very good and close friends. We meet regularly and have fun (now to describe that is a different story altogether.) Anyway once we three were having an afternoon party (it's usually hosted by one of us and we end up on the same bed for intimate talk.) We discuss everything like how our husband are fucking us, how many times in what way and all that. We really enjoy sharing.

Eventually the inevitable happened and we all three got pregnant within a span of 3 to 4 months. We were continuing our weekly afternoon sessions. One went like this. Ramya was fondling my boobs and saying hey Neeta your boobs are really growing in pregnancy and she squeezed my boobs and started fondling them for a long time. Jyoti was complaining that she isn't getting wet enough during pregnancy. Hey listen I am quite dry these days. Should I go and show to a Doctor? We advised her no to and wait for hormonal changes to take effect. I said Ramya how long you intend to feed your baby? May be a year said Ramya. Jyoti was bit not committed but indicated that she would like to feed her baby for at least two years. Nishit (my husband) was looking forward to some nice milk sucking I said Rally said Ramya my husband is not showing any interest in that but I am so keen to feed oh how I would love to Jyoti offered her a solution. Then why don't you feed Nishit also, since he is so keen. He likes your boobs too. The husbands have all played with all three of us in terms of kissing and fondling. Yes, I will love to feed Nishit said Ramya. This talk then continued till we all delivered.

Just one month after settling down from delivery and taking care of babies, we started comparing notes. While Nishit was the most eager one, Jyoti was the most milking. So we arranged that Nishit should suck Jyoti's milk too. She had plenty. Very soon in a weeks time all the husbands were sucking room all three of us. We were enjoying very much. We started having weekly feed sessions. Wherein we all used to meet and group ourselves on a large carpet. We the girls would get comfortable with large pillows. The men would squat and keep interchanging their sucking boobs from wife to wife. The greatest fun used to be when two guys (other than hubby) would squeeze boobs and suck one each making all funny noises. We have no milk now but milking and feeding programmed are continuing. Let me know your experiences and would you like to share your milk with your friends? P.S. Please invite my hubby for the inauguration program

29. Neighbor Aunty

This is my experience of two years with my neighbor aunt she was working as a Teacher in a High School, got a figure of 36-28-36. She was fair in color and very sexy lady. Her husband got a job in U.S. and he went there and she was waiting for her hubby to send her the visa, she was very friendly with everyone and after her hubby left her. She was alone with her three year old son. Her son used to like me very much so I used to go to her house often. She was very friendly with me. One day after my bath I went to her house, she was wearing a blue saree and black bra was visible from it. She asked me to have a chat if I was not busy. As I opted for leave from my work that day, so we chatted for about an hour then her son woke up and started to cry. She asked me to wait and went inside the bed room. I waited for a few minutes and went in for checking on her. I was shocked to see her feeding the baby, she must have changed the side of the breast from one to another and her left breast was completely visible. I stood there and then regained my senses and asked sorry and went into the hall to wait for her. Then she came in after 15 minutes or so and we started to chat but my mind was going crazy. I couldn't forget that scene I started to stare at her breasts she noticed that and adjusted her pallu.

Then slowly she started to talk about sex and she asked me have u had sex before. I said no. then she asked me have u seen any women breasts I said yes. She asked whose. I said yours in a slow voice. She smiled and asked me would you like to touch them. It was like a dream come true I was waiting for this chance all my life. I simply nodded my head. Then she removed her pallu and asked me to touch them on her blouse n bra itself. I touched them it was so soft. Then she showed her right breast. She started to moan slowly Ah. I removed her saree and started to undress myself. I removed my shirt and then pant. In the meantime she also started to undress. She was standing only with her black bra and panties with flowers on them. She was so beautiful I hungrily kissed and sucked her breast on the bra itself then removed it and started to suck her breast. As I sucked milk started to flow from them I drank and drank them. Then she stopped me and said now I want to taste your milk. Saying this she moved towards my dick and planted a kiss on it with my shorts on and then she pulled then down. My dick sprang out like a hot rod. She said you got a big dick and put it in her mouth and started sucking it. It felt so good.

It was like I was in heaven she sucked them for 10 minutes and I cummed directly in her mouth she drank every drop and licked it clean and my cock started to return but my feeling was hot. So I took her into the bedroom and shifted the baby from there to the hall and I pushed her on the bed drank her milk again for a few minutes and then moved to her thighs and kissed them and then pulled her panties down and I looked at her pussy for a min it was so beautiful, hairy and all wet. I drank all her juices and sucked them like a hungry animal and she moaned ooohh ahhhh and I opened her pussy lips and found hr clit and I started to suck it and she started to scream loudly and very loudly and cried stop but she was pushing my head towards her pussy and I continued to suck and with a big scream she released all her juices on my face and I drank some of them even though it was kind of salty I loved it and then I slowly positioned my cock near her pussy and with a big push it went completely inside. Since she had her baby from cesarean, her pussy was still tight I banged her for about 15 minutes and cummed inside her itself and we both lay there for about an hour and I went home after that and then we had sex daily until she went with her husband. Now she is in U.S.

30. Beggar

My wife & I like social services to offer. I'm 30 yrs and she is 28 yrs housewife we decided to do some social service on one night it was winter night 8 pm. we were near railway station we saw one beggar lying on footpath.

He was feeling bit cold as he was not having proper clothing. He was wearing only torn pant and some old blanket over body and nothing inside he must be in his fifties we went to him and asked "feeling cold? Have you eaten something" he was hungry. So we went nearby hotel and fed him good amount of food. He dined feeling his stomach and wishes he was very happy by now. Now he saw us better way.

He asked "why did you did favor on me? Who are you?" we briefed him little bit and asked him what we can do for him further. He was amazed now he told us that he is feeling cold and it will be nice if we can do something for him, we bought new blanket for him when we enquired about his family, he went silent. He told us that his wife died long back due to severe cold and there is nobody caring him he started crying.

My wife came forward and said him "don't worry. We are there. I will take care of you tell me what do you want now?" she patted him with sympathy he felt better. He hugged her and put his head on her shoulder for relaxation. He was touching a woman after years and that too beautiful woman like my wife! She was simple and beautiful. Due to hugging and her warm touch, he felt excited.

His tool started stiffening. We both realized it during gupshup(chats), I asked him "when did you had your last sex?" his eyes shined. He said it must be at least 5 years or so. No sex after my wife death. I asked him directly pointing my wife "will you like to have sex with her?" he was excited by the concept. He readily agreed. We all started moving inside station from backside where no one will catch us or see us on the way I bought pack of condoms and handed over to wife.

We all climbed in one railway sleeper coach. It was all silence there and we were alone there. Lights were coming from yard side and enough to see each other. They went on lower birth and I climbed on upper berth in nearby compartment so that I can see what they do but not disturb them my wife and beggar sat on berth he was looking at her with lot of lust in eyes.

His hands already on her shoulders pulled her and started kissing her lips, neck etc. He was very desperate and looking sex starved he must be hungry for sex also. He didn't want to waste lifetime opportunity he got to fuck my cute wife. He pushed her on seat and climbed on her.

His hands were freely roaming on her body, on breasts, chest, stomach, waist etc. his lips also kissing wherever possible like lips, cheeks, eyes, neckline, boobs etc. Just to control him, she grabbed his head and pulled him towards her. Their lips came closer and in bit of second, they locked the lips. His upper lip was on her upper lip and lower vice versa. They were kissing intimately.

Surprisingly my wife was very passionate to offer him great enjoyment, a lifetime opportunity. Soon their tongues started darting each others. She likes to dominate in this sex act. She was offering him tongue to suck and his was playing with it. He was sucking her tongue with lips and tongue as like sucking candy. Their saliva mixing and falling on her cheeks and neckline. But they were not caring it. They were kissing like long lovers!

After about 10-15 min kissing they separated mouths. She wiped out saliva with her dupatta falling on ground. She had nice red color kamiz which was soft and bit transparent too. Green color salwar was matching it. His hands started caressing and pressing her breasts over the top. He was busy with her lips also in between.

He managed to raise her top up to chest level. He could easily see and feel her big melons. he wanted to rip off them and suck to the fullest. In short time he pulled off her kamiz and swiftly he unhooked her black color bra also. She helped him by sitting n raising hands so that kamiz and bra can be removed. Now she was topless in front of total stranger!

She dominated again, before offering him her big boobs; she raised both hands and asked him to feel the arm armpits. She was enjoying it. Meantime her big melons were free for his hands to crush and drink juice out of them. Her breasts are quite big, yet firm and soft. She has nice tits and small areola around nipples. He kneed both breasts, kissed them, took in mouth even sucked her nipples. He licked every inch of her bare boobs. His rough hands were working on her bare boobs and exciting her further. She offered him to suck and chew her nipples which she likes very much. He readily started sucking them and then started even pinching them. Finally he started pulling her nipples with his lips and make her frenzy. She was pressing own boobs and offering him with ecstasy. They both were definitely hot now and need further action.

They might have forgotten everything, their social and economical status, relations, society etc. Even forgot someone watching them so closely after lot of fondling and kissing, he stood up and asked her to remove his pant. She sat down on sleeper and took condom pack from her purse. When she unbuttoned it & removed completely she saw a miracle. It was rock hard shaft for her fun.

It was surprisingly 10" long and 2" thick. it was hairy lund with may be strange smells and bad odors. By seeing its sheer size, she forgot his and her status and within seconds she took his lund(cock) in her mouth. But still she remembered to apply condom on his long shaft. A beggar was being sucked by beautiful and sexy wife!

I couldn't believe my eyes. But she was more than happy. She started licking it, then applied her saliva on the length and then started hard sucking it. She was gently stroking and shaking his lund(cock) and assisting him to enter fully in her mouth. as it was very long monster, it couldn't enter full but still managed to enter deepest possible. He was very excited by the royal treat to his lund(cock).

He was moaning and assisting her by his waist movements making his lund(cock) in and out her mouth. she scratched his balls by nails which aroused him and he moaned in ecstasy aaahhhh sssshhhhhh oooohhhhhh........ He was in great fun zone. His one hand was fondling her left breast and other hand caught her head and hairs and moving it to and fro to suck his tool hard. In between she signaled him to stop just to get air and small rest.

After few seconds they again resumed but now with controlled speed and rhythm. After plenty of sucking she finally stopped. All the time she was sucking him, he was fondling her bare boobs. She took his hand and placed it on her pubic area over her salwar. she wanted him to rub that area. He started caressing and rubbing over her silk salwar.

She must be wet by now. She offered him her breasts to fondle by one hand and suck other in his mouth. She was feeding him one by other. After that he laid her down on back he pulled off her salwar string and then took it off. Then she pulled down the panty inside and she was totally nude. Just for a unknown beggar!

He was watching my young and beautiful nude wife! She was bit shy far few second but just that moment only. Soon she pulled him and asked him to sit down near her waist. She has very firm and smooth bums and thunder thighs. She don't have any hairs on stomach, legs etc. and other hair near pussy, she regularly clean them.

She took his hand and put on her belly. Other hand she put on her thigh and signaled him to caress her. More and more he cares, she started spreading her legs further. He put his lips on her pubic area and suddenly started licking her pussy. She helped him spreading her pussy lips and allow to suck her deep. His tounge started darting with lower lips now and she started moaning.

His hands also working on her naked body. One hand pressing the boob and other pressing her firm gaand. Soon she reached her orgasm and wanted him to stop sucking her clit. But he was also enjoying and didn't stop at all. She was moaning loudl aaaa....aahhhhh...sssssshaaaaa.....aaa.. She was pushing his head in excitement which was already deeply buried in her pubic area.

Soon her excitement started cooling and he also stopped sucking her. It must be great orgasm she enjoyed lot. He locked lips with her lips and now they started kissing very passionately again. They both were enjoying the sex in true emotions. He said her "You are very sexy and attractive" After some kissing, they separated out.

She raised her leg such that indicating him something. She told him to lick her legs from toe to ass. He again obeyed her and why not! He was getting sex treat like never before! He planted few kisses on her foot and then kissed her foot fingers also. Slowly he was caressing and licking her inner and outer skin of her legs, then thighs and waistline. He licked her waist and folds on her stomach also.

Then she turned such that her back facing him. He was confused. But she was actually giving him more treat. She took his hand and placed on her bums and started gently caress it. He understood now. He further turned her and now she was sleeping on her stomach giving him full view of her gaand. He slowly lingered his fingers on her ass and then started licking it in full. he was pressing it and pinching it also while licking every inch of her tight ass.

He might have licked her ass hole also. She spread her ass crotch and asked him to lick her ass crack. He readily licked it. She whispered "asss..ss....hhhh" He was very excited now and slept on her placing his lund near ass crack and slowly moving it. This started raising his lund(cock) again. He slowly put his hands below her both boobs and started lifting them and start needing them.

He was still pressing his lund(cock) against her ass crack which stiffened it very hard by now. Now both were ignited again. He turned her again and now rides on her. She was just waiting it and spread her legs for him inviting his solid lund(cock) to enter in her tiny juicy pussy. He slowly entered in her wet cunt and started moving his waist to make long thrust in her gili chut.

Soon half and then finally all his shaft was inside her chut. His lund(cock) must be happiest in the world for that moment. He never fucked such a homely lady in life. He was ravaging the sweet cunt and making most of the time. He was catching my wife's boobs and fondling in between. They both had good rhythm by now. Her boobs were shaking with his thrusts. She was moaning like aaaaaa......ssssshhhhh aahhhh....... oooouuc-cch....

He was moaning like oooo....hhh.....ssssss........ Soon he started pumping her with great speed. His monster was deep inside her pussy and enjoying! He was on cloud 9 by now. Soon he reached orgasm and after almost 20 minutes he fired jets. Due to con-dom my wife couldn't experience the wetness, but she felt the warmth of sperm he fired. He was coming for few seconds and then he was finally empty. He collapsed on her naked body ad then rested on her for some time.

She didn't object him for either. They both had great sex and deep relaxation out of it. Soon they got up and sat on seat. He pulled her closer and started kissing her again. She also re-sponded him positive and locked lips. His hands again caressing and fondling her boobs one by one and then pinch her nipples one by one.

He in between kissed her nipples too and then again locked lips. She had now started caressing his lund(cock). She removed his used condom and threw it off. It was drenched with his and her sex juices. She was caressing his bare lund(cock) and balls now. He pulled her further close and they were intimately kiss-ing each other with their hands working on each other bodies. Though he was deeply relaxed and enjoyed lot, he was not yet satisfied and wanted to enjoy again this beauty again.